*To Phil
Best Regd
Hope you enjoy
Love
Brian & Sue.*

The Ballad Of
JESSIE GRAY

and other stories

The Ballad Of
JESSIE GRAY

and other stories

BRIAN CRANE

Copyright © 2017 by brian crane.

ISBN: Softcover   978-1-5245-9737-5
        eBook   978-1-5245-9738-2

All rights reserved. No part of this book may be reproduced or transmitted in any form or by any means, electronic or mechanical, including photocopying, recording, or by any information storage and retrieval system, without permission in writing from the copyright owner.

This is a work of fiction. Names, characters, places and incidents either are the product of the author's imagination or are used fictitiously, and any resemblance to any actual persons, living or dead, events, or locales is entirely coincidental.

Any people depicted in stock imagery provided by Thinkstock are models, and such images are being used for illustrative purposes only.
Certain stock imagery © Thinkstock.

Print information available on the last page.

Cover: Winslow Homer 1836-1910

Rev. date: 01/31/2017

To order additional copies of this book, contact:
Xlibris
800-056-3182
www.Xlibrispublishing.co.uk
Orders@Xlibrispublishing.co.uk
697350

CONTENTS

The Ballad Of Jessie Gray vii

Dedication ix

Playing For Laughs...1

The Last Page..17

From Whence I Came..40

Dust On The Shelf...58

A Minor Deception..94

The Corner Shop 118

The Ballad Of Jessie Gray 172

The Ballad circa 1859..226

THE BALLAD OF JESSIE GRAY

She waits with her lamp on the quay.
Eyes firmly fixed on the sea.
She speaks a silent prayer,
Spills a tear of despair.
For the man her heart yearns to see.

Each night come fair weather or storm.
She keeps her sad vigil alone.
Tight wrapped in widows shawl,
Tattered skirts to the floor.
Bare feet on the cold cobblestone.

She died by her own trembling hand.
Flotsam in the surf and shifting sand.
Her last wish was to join,
The man she loved from a boy.
And carry his seed and be damned.

A few weeping friends gathered round.
As Jessie was laid into the ground.
Like all that sturdy breed,
Being slaves of the savage sea.
Fearing nought but Gods mighty hand.

A stone cross marks her simple grave.
Though time will soon erase the name.
Close by the rolling swell,
And the chiming warning bell.
Cold comfort for the sad Jessie Gray.

Now she waits with a lamp on the quay.
Though no one seems to see her, but me.
So much sorrow in her face,
I feel her grief, I feel her pain.
Will her restless soul ever be free.

1859.

For my wife Sue, for all her support and encouragement. Thank you for just being there

PLAYING FOR LAUGHS

The sound of jaunty organ and drums playing something vaguely familiar filtered through the hissing rain, merely adding to this already dismal Saturday evening. Along the street the yellow glow of the street lamps spilled their light onto shimmering pavements and into pools of rain water. But where the light could not penetrate, the shadows seemed denser and even more melancholy.

Occasionally a car or a van would splash between the lines of parked vehicles, their windscreen wipers fighting a losing battle. Huddled figures would hop scotch their way between the numerous puddles created by the uneven paving stones. Sometimes with umbrellas erect, sometimes with coats tight round the ears or pulled over the heads in desperate attempts to remain dry. All seemed clear on their destinations of either, the Off Licence, the Chippy or the Chinkie.

Suddenly, the music came to an abrupt crescendo then stopped. There was a pause, which was followed by the sporadic clapping of a dozen or so pairs of hands. An amplified, echoed voice trundled out an announcement for bingo as the volume of the chattering audience increased noticeably, belying its size from the previous excuse at applause. For it was not unusual for the Castle Hill Members Only Social Club to have at least a hundred and fifty of its members in place for the Saturday night bingo and live entertainment.

However, the actual venue was nothing to shout about, a converted pub tucked between the Spar and the Superhardware, but which had previously boasted an upstairs function room of sizable proportions with a serviceable arched stage as well. So when the brewery had decided on a change of direction because of falling profits, the 'Castle Hill Members Only Social Club' was born. And with the new millennium just a year away the 'Castle' was enjoying its revival and looking forward to the future.

Now, three broad steps led up from the rain soaked pavement to two wood and glass panelled doors that displayed a hand written poster.

Tonight.
RONNIE LITTLEWOOD
TV Personality.
Plus
BINGO.

In the depths beneath the stage, Ronnie Littlewood closed the door behind him and leant heavily against it.

"Cretins!" he muttered with a sigh as the final bars of the 'Muppets theme' grated in his ears from above.

His eyes wandered aimlessly around this cleaners storage space that doubled as the artists dressing room, complete with a mini sink that only had the cold tap working, and a pretentious cardboard star, pinned on the outside of the door.

The pungent smell from the toilets that were next along the corridor, permeated into his thoughts as his gaze settled on the collection of promo photos that decorated the tobacco smoke stained walls. He cringed internally as he caught sight of the confident, youthful image of himself taken over fifteen years before. He had not been able to afford a more recent batch to be produced, but then he thought he preferred to be remembered as he used to be.

Ronnie moved purposefully across the dimly lit room and sat at the table with the cracked mirror. Pushing the mirror to one side he grabbed at the cigarette packet. He examined it with a sigh before squashing the empty packet in his fist and tossing it over his shoulder. Reaching for the half empty bottle of whisky he took a long drink before forcing the bottle back across the table. The sound of the numbers being called from the bingo session above made him look once again at the young, smiling, cheekily handsome face in the photograph that now seemed to look down on him, mockingly.

The Ballad Of Jessie Gray

In those days he had firmly believed in himself. He was the up and coming new face of comedy going straight to the top, the world would be his. In those days he had those behind him telling him all this. And the ladies, well they had been in abundance.

His mind wandered back, and a grim smile emerged as he thought of the great days of the summer seasons like, Butlins, Pontins and Blackpool, supporting some of the icons of their day. Shaking hands with Morecombe and Wise, being stood a drink by Jim Davidson and now, all those stories were good for was a free pint for their retelling.

But then the smile slowly faded as he thought of the poster on the front door to the club that proclaimed him as a TV personality. That was a laugh! One appearance on New Faces and he had been riding on that for the last twenty years. That was the height of his achievements. From there it was downhill to the pubs and social clubs, and the bruising, unpredictable audiences of the Northern Working Men's Club circuit. Then it was to the level he found himself at now. Where did it all go so wrong he thought, for he had become what he had always despised, a wannabe to a has-been.

So many times over the years he had shared a dressing room with artists he had always respected highly for their craft, singers, comedians, musicians and all the others, talented and just brilliant in their own way. And then years down the line he had seen them scrimping out a living trying to do the best they could at the only thing that they knew how to do, and failing miserably. Embarrassing themselves in front of those same audiences who had seen them at their peak, who had sat enraptured by the talents those same artists had been endowed with. It was sad, so very sad.

Ronnie had always said he would recognise that time, and that he would never let it get to that point. He had vowed internally that he would never allow the audiences to either ridicule or sympathise or say they could remember when he had been good. He had always said that he would know when the time was right. But was it now?

The way he felt at this moment was that he had passed that point years ago and had somehow never taken any notice of the giveaway signs. Those same signs that every performer fears most, the trailing off of repeat bookings, the lame excuses from entertainment secretaries and agents for not offering him more work, and the kind of venue that he was now expected to play. And the worst signs of all, the passive reactions of the audiences to his act.

But he knew no other kind of life. How many times had he heard that being said! How many others had sat in front of a cracked mirror in dumps like this and had seen the whole of their life through the bottom of a whisky bottle. He picked the bottle up and again drank deeply.

"Stupid fool!" he thought. "How are you going to get home? And if you lose your licence, well you can't afford a driver, that's for sure."

Again he thrust the emptying bottle down, but this time he had the sense to push it beyond temptation.

He suddenly remembered Crazy Jimmy Dixon from years before. He had worked with Jimmy in his heyday. Jimmy had been of the old school of vintage comics who could hold an audience in the palm of his hand with his quick fire patter. There was nothing smutty or offensive like they are nowadays, just good honest comedy. Even he had reached that point when the laughter had gone from his ears.

And that last time when Jimmy had gone on stage at some dive of a club up North. His opening line had been "This is the end!" and he had collapsed and died of a heart attack, there on the stage in front of all those he had pleased on so many occasions, who now sat laughing and applauding thinking this was Jimmy's new act. The morons! Was that his time! Or had Jimmy gone past that time and had simply not recognised the signs until it was too late.

Ronnie suddenly thought, was the way he was feeling now how it had been for Jimmy, in not accepting the inevitable.

He reached for the whisky bottle, but stopped himself from picking it up.

"What's it all about?" he mumbled to himself as he contemplated his damaging lifestyle.

His morose thoughts settled on the seemingly incessant travelling from one end of the country to the other just to make ends meet. And the constant need to always be the professional the bookers and the bookings demanded. You might have a star on your dressing room door, and you might succumb to the patronizing plaudits that invariably come your way by those who wish to ingratiate themselves by association with celebrity. But in reality it was all so very fragile and transitory, and could melt away as quickly as snow on a hot stove. Then there was the fact that there was no anchor in his life, no stability. His short marriage had been testament to that.

Now it was all taking its toll on his health and stamina. And the dream, forever just chasing that elusive dream and all the time not realising how it was turning into a nightmare. He bowed his head into his hands and the semblance of a sob emerged from between his fingers.

What had he become, just a shadow of all his expectations. Like so many before him he had reached the bottom and was treading water in the hope of someone throwing him a lifeline. But in this business you are only as good as your last gig.

And 'gig', what did that mean? He suddenly remembered, 'God Is Good' as the black jazz musicians used to say when they were actually paid for playing, back in America's deep south in the twenty's. And if that was all this life had to offer then the road was always going to be downhill.

There was a gentle knock on the door and instantly Ronnie had flushed his gloomy thoughts completely out of sight as a face appeared around the jamb.

"Ted...Come in mate," Ronnie said as cheerfully as possible.

Ted Stallard was the entertainment secretary for the club, and the man who booked and paid the acts. He entered and stood counting the money he had in his hand.

"Another good night, hey Ted?" Ronnie enthused, though at the same time thinking it had been forty five minutes of torture for the audience as well as himself, and which had culminated in the keyboard and drums rendition of the "Muppets" theme as a parting, ignominious gesture to accompany his 'get off'.

"Those keyboard and drums of yours are great....Note perfect every time," Ronnie praised sarcastically.

"Yes Ronnie, worth their weight in gold, good backing!" Ted mumbled, counting the notes for the third time.

"And the audience, always a good crowd here Ted," Ronnie commented, trying to speak with as much fervour as he could muster for he had detected a certain reticence in Ted's usually friendly manner.

"Yes," he continued. "I always look forward to playing here Ted, always a good night."

"I've got your money Ronnie," Ted stated as he moved over to the table. "Count it and sign the receipt please. Eighty five....that's right isn't it?"

"Yes.... that's it," Ronnie said, hesitantly taking the money and scribbling out his signature.

Ted retrieved the receipt form and turned towards the door.

"What did you think of the night, hey Ted," Ronnie added seeking confirmation, but his voice lacked conviction.

Ted halted at the door and slowly turned to face the comedian.

"Well Ronnie, you haven't changed your routine much!" he declared.

"Like hell I haven't!" Ronnie pounced. "That's a well run routine Ted. I know where I am with it you see. No sense in changing something that you know works. It's the weather that's dampened the audience tonight. There's nothing like a good downpour to put the mockers on things."

"Yes...well!" Ted muttered looking at the floor.

"I remember when I did those TV warm ups for Granada, this routine went down a storm," Ronnie said thoughtfully. "The old jokes are the best Ted. I've got no time for filth and smut like the young bloods rely on nowadays. Just good clean fun I say."

"Yes.....well!.... I'd better get back upstairs for the last card of bingo, and I want to get home early tonight," Ted said, almost apologetically as he placed his hand on the door handle.

"So when do you want me again Ted. Three months?" Ronnie stammered, yet fearing the answer.

Slowly Ted lifted his head so that his face was in full view and his expression was serious. It took a moment for him to compose himself for what he had been putting off saying.

"Well you see Ronnie, it's like this," Ted sheepishly replied. "We're having a shake up here. The committee is changing and I'm stepping down as entertainment sec. So from next month Bill Ryder will be doing the job and he prefers to go through agents. So he'll be contacting Charlie Baxter for all the entertainment. You do know Charlie?"

"Yes I know Charlie, Charlie Baxter, CB Entertainments," Ronnie said sitting back in his chair. "I've known him for years. A good lad, I've done quite a bit through his books. But Ted we've always gone private."

"I realise that Ronnie. But it's not my call now."

Ted was becoming a little anxious at this conversation knowing what the inevitable outcome was for Ronnie. Now, he wanted to get this business over and done with. He had known the comic for many years, and it genuinely saddened him to see him as he was now. But he had been approached by some of the audience complaining about Ronnie, and that saddened him as well. And when the backing duo had chosen to humiliate the comedian by playing him off to the 'Muppets Theme' he had actually lost his temper and had threatened to sack them. But now he was, in effect sacking someone who, at one time he had respected as a top line act. He wanted to let Ronnie down as easily as possible, but he also knew that Bill Ryder would not book Ronnie again. Not even through an agent.

"I'm sorry but that's the way it is Ronnie," Ted continued. "I've done this job for 11 years now and I've had enough. Too much hassle. I want to be able to come here and have a quiet pint without all the aggravation. So Bill will be taking over next month, and Charlie Baxter will have the sole agency here."

"But it means commission Ted. It means I'll have to pay commission of 20%. I'll have to ask for more to cover it," Ronnie responded as his voice petered away thoughtfully. "I don't think Charlie will come through with that."

"Well...that's how it is," Ted remarked with a lightness of tone that contradicted how he really felt now that his unsavoury job was done.

He hovered by the door for a few seconds longer, fingering the handle in agitation.

"Yes... well.....I'd better get off. Betty's waiting for me so I'll see you around Ronnie." he said with a hint of embarrassment creeping into the tone of the words.

"All the best," he added as he scurried through the door, closing it quickly behind him.

"Yes...Bye Ted!"

Ronnie was now speaking to an empty room, a room that in an instant had lost any kind of warmth that it may have possessed. He leant back in the rickety chair with his eyes staring at the yellowy ceiling. He found himself examining the various patterns left by the decades of smoking singers, comedians and the rest who had frequented this 'Stars' dressing room. And now were only remembered by their stained images pinned or sellotaped on the wall.

Ronnie sighed, not at his surroundings, but at himself. At that moment in time he felt emotionless, devoid of any feelings for he was fully aware of the desperation of his situation and that it was slowly enveloping him. But all he could feel was an emptiness that seemed to stretch to the farthest reaches of his own being. The door closing seemed to symbolise his whole life being terminated in a flash. Like a judgement on his talents, and now the jury had returned with their verdict and it was as if he was tacitly accepting his fate.

He swore fervently in his buzzing mind before blurting out to the void he now found himself in.

"Damn! Damn! Damn! all committees and all entertainment secretaries. Jumped up petty little mobsters the lot of em! Only in it for what they can siphon off for themselves. And damn all agents, parasites all of em, living off the talents of others. And damn the whole bloody business to hell!"

Snatching the mirror round to face him he stared intently at the middle aged face that stared back. The bloodshot eyes that seemed to be supported by an increasing amount of bags, the sallow skin and the tightening of the lips with the corners beginning to drop. Then as he pushed his hand through his hair, he groaned audibly as he scanned the thinning pate and temples. All this seemed exaggerated by the dim glow of the single 40watt bulb that dangled ominously, directly above his head in the centre of the ceiling. Even so it was all a jolting realisation of the blatant truth.

Ronnie breathed out in a deep, thought invoked sigh before he slowly stood and unclipped his red bowtie, slipped out of his light beige suit jacket, and began to unbutton the white shirt with the thin red pinstripes. His uniform, unchanged in colour and design for over twenty years, but looking so much better on the impressive young man in the promo photo.

Suddenly he was aware that the door had opened again and spun round to be confronted by a tall man of his own age. He stood framed in the doorway, smartly suited beneath a camel hair coat, buff coloured fedora hat and carrying a slim, brown leather portfolio case, the epitome of the public's conception of the prosperous, agent promoter.

"Charlie!" Ronnie stammered, recognising Charlie Baxter.

"Hello Ronnie. It's good to see you again. How are you?"

The enquiry seemed genuine.

"Oh not so bad Charlie, not so bad," Ronnie said once again trying to pull himself together. "How's tricks with you now? How's the agency?"

"Doing very nicely I'm pleased to say. And it's management and agency now Ronnie. CB International Entertainments," he answered proudly as he walked across to the table. "You're not on this stuff are you?" he questioned, picking up the nearly empty whisky bottle. "Every entertainer's nemesis you know, Ronnie!"

"It's not a problem Charlie. The one thing I've learnt from experience is, that stuff works in moderation only."

He spoke earnestly because he actually believed it.

"That's good," Charlie commented while he surreptitiously examined Ronnie's features for some sign of effects. But he seemed convinced that Ronnie's words had a ring of truth in them.

"Yes Ronnie it's International now," he continued. "I've just landed an important Cruise Company contract. It's full steam ahead you might say," he said smiling briefly at his own joke.

"That's probably why I can never get through to you on the phone," Ronnie declared with a touch of bitterness coming into his voice. "I'm always being told you're in a meeting or out of the office."

"And we're into the continent with some really big deals," Charlie continued trying to avoid the issue of not wanting to speak to Ronnie, until he was ready to. "Summer seasons and TV, and now we're into management. Young Brian Morris, new age stand up comic. You've met him I think?"

"Yes..yes...I supported him in Sheffield three months ago," was the terse reply that spoke volumes.

"Well that guy's on the way up. He's been offered a spot on a new comedy showcase with Channel 4. He'll be very big. I've also got Sonia Giffard, she's been offered a recording contract with Sony Records."

Charlie stopped himself and looked sternly at Ronnie.

"And how are things with you?"

"What is all this Charlie. Have some respect, we've known each other far too long for you to beat about the bush like this," Ronnie said looking the agent fully in the eye. "You know how things are. That's why I can never get hold of you for work."

This was said with something of an accusation in the tone.

"You're right Ronnie," Charlie admitted. "The fact is I caught your spot tonight. I was in the back bar. I didn't want to embarrass you by coming out front. However, I did want to speak to you face to face, that's why I've avoided speaking to you on the phone. Well you see Ronnie we have a good bank of comedians now."

"There's one word you've left out Charlie!" Ronnie interrupted.

"And what's that?"

"Young!"

"Yes....yes...Well, you're probably right," Charlie conceded reluctantly. "Anyway, I wanted to tell you to your face Ronnie, and not for you to find out from other sources. I felt I owed you that at least. Well....the fact is, I won't be using you again."

If a bolt of lightning had suddenly burst through the building and only aimed at Ronnie's heart he could not have been more shocked or taken aback. His world suddenly condensed into what he could see and hear solely at this moment in time. His ears hummed loudly with those devastating words and all he could utter in response was.

"Right.......I see!"

"I'm sorry Ronnie," Charlie continued. "But you're right, it is a young man's show now. It's all changing. I've had to change, and quite frankly Ronnie from what I saw tonight only tells me that you haven't and I can't afford to take a risk with you."

Charlie watched as his words struck home like a series of daggers at the very soul of the comics pride and self esteem.

"You know the score Ronnie," he added trying to make what he needed to say as painless as possible. "You know what it's all about. You've been around long enough to know that tonight was no one's fault but your own."

"My fault!" Ronnie spluttered, seemingly accepting the criticism without any thought of arguing the point. "Yes....Yes. You are probably right, perhaps it was my fault. Perhaps I have been around too long."

He sighed, digesting the whole significance of what had been said to him, and what he was confirming with his own words. But most of all it had been made so pitifully obvious to him by someone he knew and respected. He was stale bread, out of date and he had been kidding himself that the blame lay with everybody else, the audiences, the committees, the venues and even down to blaming the weather. But

The Ballad Of Jessie Gray

in that one denouncing statement of "No one's fault but your own," a window had opened and he was able to see the full truth in the words.

Even so it was the ramifications of Charlie's decision not to book Ronnie that would resound around the business and other agents and bookers would take the same view. Then questions would be asked, resulting in doors being closed to him or he would be simply be told....

"He's in a meeting!" or "He's out of the office!"

It would in affect be a total shutdown.

"Ronnie, I'm sorry it's come to this," Charlie said, almost to himself as he considered Ronnie's acceptance of what had been said to him. He watched as the truth seemed to dawn in Ronnie's eyes altering the pallor on his cheeks. For Charlie could only guess at what it must have cost this once, proud comedian to actually admit to where the blame should rest, and the fact that perhaps he had been around too long.

It was then, at that moment that Charlie Baxter realised just how fortunate he had been when he had made his defining moves to alter his own attitudes to the entertainment business in general and to have had the vision to see where the future was taking him. To seeing what was demanded by the business and the audiences, and also to having the aptitude and insight to provide it.

Entertainment was a constantly changing world, and you had to be at the front as a leader and not as a follower. He was a business man with a logical and adept approach to life, and of how to make it all work for him. Unlike those with the artistic temperaments that he had to deal with on a day to day basis, the dreamers, very talented dreamers for the most part, but none of them it seemed with a firm grip on reality. The Ronnie's of this cruel industry.

But he was not as hard as people liked to paint him.

"I hope you appreciate that I wanted to be honest with you," he continued. "I've known you a long time now, and I hate myself for being like this. But that's the business Ronnie. That's the business."

"But I don't know anything else," Ronnie disclosed with his head lowered in subdued acceptance.

He had battled all his working life to try and reach the top, but always, always sliding back down to this inevitable pit. Like so many before, and like so many would do in the future. It was a mugs game he thought, grasping hopelessly at that dream of stardom and then having to face the crippling knowledge that he was a failure and all the ensuing consequences of that failure. All in all it was such a very bitter pill for him to swallow.

"I'm sorry Ronnie. Truly I am," Charlie said holding out his hand in as friendly a gesture as he could muster. He liked Ronnie and it hurt him to have to bring him to his knees like this. But like he had just admitted, business was business and emotion and conscience could not be allowed to interfere with that.

Ronnie took the hand almost in a daze and shook it limply, as all his strength had seemed to have dissolved with the full realisation that his future was like some fathomless void. No matter how hard he tried, no matter how hard he reasoned, he could not see any distinguishable form or shape on which to focus to give him some semblance of comfort or reassurance.

Charlie stared at the forlorn figure of the broken comedian and suddenly felt embarrassed at having to share this moment of his humbling defeat. He had realised that the task he had set himself, of confronting Ronnie face to face, was never going to be easy. But equally, he was shocked at how it was now affecting him. He was a business man and what he had just done was all part of that business. And, he decided very quickly that it was a side he despised.

Charlie turned towards the door and opened it.

"I'm sorry Ronnie!"

And with that he slowly closed it behind him.

Ronnie now stood looking down at the floor, wishing it would open up just like some black hole and swallow him up to leave no trace of him actually ever having been here. He felt breathless, unable to move, his mind whirling in a kind of vacuum where nothing seemed to make sense. He was struggling with all that he had feared and with all that he had now been presented with, and the conundrum merely left him confused and without a solution. There was no light to be seen at the end of this tunnel he finally concluded.

He sought out the small table to support his weight as it felt like the stability in his legs had momentarily deserted him. From deep within him emanated a long soulful groan as he recalled the words Charlie had left him with and which now seemed to be echoing around inside his head.

"I'm sorry Ronnie!" the voice crooned.

"What the hell does that mean!" Ronnie thought angrily to himself. "Sorry, as the axe falls! Sorry, as the noose is placed round your neck!"

Dropping his head forward with a long sigh of exasperation he could feel an engulfing sense of hopelessness begin to sweep over him.

"Sorry," he mumbled under his breath. "It means nothing! Nothing! It's just a bloody get out clause for not saying....Sod you mate I'm alright!"

But this maudlin frame of mind was now becoming all imposing, all consuming sucking him down into a quagmire of despair as his thoughts dwelt heavily on his collapsing world. Even as he considered the inevitability of his situation he was still able to direct his aggravation towards those who found it so easy to employ a selection of meaningless, glib clichés to placate or deceive, purely to disguise and cover up their true thoughts and motives. And this business he decided bitterly, is full of those with not just one but two, even three faces of duplicity and each of the three very capable of accompanying their devious machinations with a smile.

"I'm sorry Ronnie!" the words once again exploded inside his skull.

"And with that," Ronnie told himself angrily. "Charlie can walk away and dismiss from his mind the consequences he leaves in his wake."

"I'm sorry Ronnie!" he muttered to himself. "That's all I'm left with......I'm sorry!"

And in those few syllables now lay damnation, the end, and so tritely put.

But that did not answer the question.

"What happens now?"

Ronnie continued to stare blankly down at the table unable to move, unable to generate a sequence of rational thoughts into his mind, when he became conscious of footsteps on the corridor floor. The footsteps stopped, and the door to the 'Stars' dressing room was given a sharp tap and a voice announced.

"Can you come now Ronnie, the steward wants to lock up."

****

The rain had stopped, leaving the night with a sense of relief. There was a keen dampness in the air that ironically felt refreshing after the clamminess of the club. For a few moments Ronnie stood on the top step to the doorway of The Castle Hill Members Only Social Club and gazed first one way and then the other, looking up and down the silent glistening street. Not a soul was about, nothing moved at this late hour, apart from a scurrying cat that disappeared down a side alley next to the Chinese Takeaway.

Even the absence of the rows of parked cars only seemed to add to the sense of desolation for Ronnie, leaving him with a growing feeling of being alone, even isolated. For Ronnie was a people's man, only happy when he was the centre of attention, cracking jokes, always the funny man playing for laughs. That had been his life and now this fear of solitude, of being on his own with the nagging prospect of never doing what deep down he felt he was born to do, left him with a shiver of apprehension to ripple like a chill through his body. The whole of the damp, rain soaked bleakness that filled his eyes merely seemed to epitomise completely where his life now stood. And such a sense of dejection filled him as he had never felt before.

A key turned and bolts were hammered into place in the double doors behind him, and he realised that it was the cue for him to move away.

Taking a deep breath, and with suit bag and holdall in his hands he stepped down the three steps to the pavement and walked slowly towards his car, and his uncertain future. The shock of the truth being so mercilessly thrust into his face, a truth he had fought so hard not to accept was now forming all manner of conflicting images in his tormented mind. Vivid images of the great days, the bad days, but most depressingly of all was the fact that he had a blind spot as to where he was to go from here. Although he always knew that the inevitable would be just round the corner he had now turned that corner, and what lay before him was a cross roads with a distinct absence of signposts.

He reached his aging Ford Escort Estate and fumbled for his keys. Unlocking the car he disposed of his bags onto the rear seat and slammed the door shut. He leant with two arms outstretched against the roof and lowered his head, suddenly realising that even though he had drank, against his better judgment the best part of half a bottle of whisky the keen fresh air had something of a sobering affect on him.

That, and the rising dampness from the street was leaving a mistiness on his face and clothes, and he pushed his hands through his moist hair and then round his neck. It felt good and refreshing for the moment that it lasted. But then his thoughts strayed back to the present and he was once again confronted with the awful truth that had descended upon him like an avalanche, and he did not think he had the grit left to dig himself out.

Wiping his hands along the roof of his car, he buried his face into the cold wetness of his palms, and then stood and slowly massaged the chilly moisture into his eyes and brow and felt the exhilarating tingle that it produced.

He was so engrossed in his despondency that he was unaware of a BMW that had silently cruised up the empty street and had pulled alongside his own car.

A voice he recognised thrust him out of his despondent musings.

"Ronnie!"

Ronnie looked up and over the roof of his car and into the face of the driver.

"Charlie!" he said with a look of surprise.

"Ronnie," Charlie continued. "Listen!... I shall be looking for someone to take over the club circuit. You know, showcases, visiting the clubs we already have and bringing new ones in, sorting out new acts as well. I don't have time for that side of the business now, and I don't want to lose it either. And Ronnie no one knows the club circuit business better than you do....And I respect that!"

"What are you saying Charlie?" Ronnie queried whilst being quite mystified at what he really thought the agent was trying to imply.

"Ronnie what I'm saying is, call me Monday morning and we'll meet to talk about it. And Ronnie I will be there to answer the phone. See you Ronnie, and don't forget!"

And with that the BMW accelerated up the street as Ronnie stood back and watched the tail lights disappear round a distant bend and out of sight.

Suddenly a smile of realisation broke across Ronnie's face.

"Yes Charlie...I will phone... Yes!..Yes!" he shouted as the penny finally dropped. "And thanks!"

Suddenly a glimmer of light had appeared at the end of the tunnel and Ronnie's world seemed that little bit better place to be in.

****

THE LAST PAGE

The thunder rumbled ominously. It seemed to rumble in a 180% arc, like tumbling boulders echoing and growling menacingly down distant mountain slopes. Starting over the far side of the town centre and sweeping across the heavy brooding horizon of the dark, shadowy shapes of houses, high buildings and church spires that stood out in stark relief against the dismally grey, opaque sky. A sky that appeared sinister and morose and in a constant churning, swirling motion like some evil wizard's concoction.

Every so often, a louder explosive clap of thunder and a streak of curving lightening would intersperse with the grumbling, unsettled background of noise.

For many days now the humidity had been gradually increasing in pressure. To the point that made it inevitable that sooner or later it would peak and then break with a storm and lift the heavy, oppressive, breathless strangle hold that had been the consequence of the atmospheric changes.

However, to accompany all this was the monsoon like downpours that always struck so suddenly and unexpectedly that they always seemed to catch you unawares. Such as when you were crossing a street with an absence of obliging doorways, or confronted by an open space and a dash with your shopping, or with your umbrella safely folded away in the hall cupboard at home. And so it was for Norma Stanley, soaked and miserable, and cowering in the bus shelter that for the moment had been a haven from a recent deluge.

She scoured the prematurely darkened sky for the merest indication that the rain would soon abate. But she could not find any.

In fact the rain seemed to pound even harder on the perspex roof of the shelter and bounce off the road and pavement in a creaming silvery spray that resembled, through her somewhat blurred vision, the white water of an angry river.

Again the grumbling thunder seemed to encircle her, and vibrate the metal framework that she leant against for moral and physical support. She brushed the tendrils of wet hair from her face, and sighed deeply as she listened to the orchestrations of the various sounds the ensuing torrent were composing.

For the first time in many days she felt a chill run through her. A chill that was instantly welcome, until she realised it was a false impression for it was caused by the droplets of rain infiltrating the weaknesses of her transparent, pacamac raincoat and seeping down like miniature streams between her shoulder blades.

But this was now in sharp contrast to the clammy sweatiness caused by the plastic of the coat, and the sultry humidity of the atmosphere. She also realised that this was only part of the reason. Guiltily she pressed a trembling hand against the hard shape of a bottle in her shoulder strap handbag, one of a succession of bottles of vodka that had become her constant companion by being secreted there over the last few months.

The instant her hand caressed that so familiar shape, she felt those simmering regrets about the path she had been treading. It was a path that had been underpinned by a growing dependence on the contents of that bottle, and the countless others like it. And midst this pool of self analysis she reluctantly accepted that the fuzziness in her head was not so much caused by the heavy, humid weather, but more as a consequence of her own stupidity, her moral weakness and self pity.

It also combined with the liquid lunch that had been taken in the lounge of a nearby hotel bar, away from the prying eyes of her work colleagues.

Again she pressed at the hardness of the bottle and ironically, this time she felt an inner calm and reassurance seep through her. Then clutching the bag closer to her breast she sighed so deeply in remorse that a tear trickled down her cheek to be lost as it merged with the rivulets of rain water from her hair. To Norma that one, lonely escaping tear from that sad bloodshot eye, was a symbol of the contradictions that had come to haunt her life.

The Ballad Of Jessie Gray

The thunder continued to rumble angrily though it seemed much further away this time. And the rain now was no more than a spiteful shower, even though the gutters struggled desperately to cope with the floods that overflowed over the pavements. Norma peered round the side of the shelter and decided it was time to try and make a sprint to her house. It was only two streets away, but she now felt she needed to be there, to feel the encompassing warmth and security that it offered. So tucking the collar of her pacamac firmly around her neck, and with her head bent low against the drizzling rain she scurried out of the shelter and splashed her way homeward.

****

The front door of 34 Chester Road slammed shut, and Norma stood gasping after her exertions. Leaning against the door she unbuttoned her pacamac, seemingly oblivious to the widening pool of water around her feet. Discarding the dripping rain coat onto the hall cabinet, she briefly caught sight of her bedraggled image in the mirror. For a few moments she gasped at the tired, pale face that stared back. The face seemed like a stranger to her, someone she did not know anymore and a deep, weary sadness crept over her as she peered searchingly at the red, mascara stained eyes above the groins of brown lines that overstated her 43 years.

Pulling herself away from the disturbing image in the mirror, she bent down to retrieve the various envelopes of the morning post. Then slowly and unsteadily she walked towards the kitchen and pushing the door open with her foot she stood staring at the debris of the last three days. At the pile of unwashed crockery and pots on the draining board, at the accumulated remnants of breakfasts and evening meals.

And then her sweeping glance settled on the gathered heap of clothes and sheets that had not quite made it into the washing machine. All this chaos seemed in contrast to the cheerful country and western music emanating from the radio that was permanently on, supposedly to deter burglars.

Suddenly the music stopped for the three o clock time check and news headlines. The spritely male voice of the news reader was saying something about an IRA bomb, and then something about William Hague and a bi-election.

But Norma was not paying any attention to the news or anything else as she stumbled into the kitchen table and sank down on a chair with her head in her hands. The dampness of her clothes left her feeling clammy and uncomfortable, but even this did not make her feel that she wanted to get out of them. No, all she wanted to do was to sit and indulge in her misery.

She fumbled in her handbag and brought out the bottle of vodka. Scattering the various items of crockery on the table she scooped up a glass, and pouring the clear liquid into it she drank it back in one attempt.

Straight away she resented the action. In fact every time she took a drink there was always some sense of remorse. But refusing to be intimidated by her conscience she lifted the bottle and momentarily examined it, so fighting and delaying what she knew she should not be doing. Even so she pressed the top of the bottle against her pouting lips and caressed it upwards into giving her a long, long pull of the fiery spirit.

Angrily she slammed the bottle down as a flare of pain burst at the back of her throat and permeated up into her nasal passage making her cough and splutter with the sheer, burning hurt it caused. Then with her eyes and face throbbing, she sat back in her chair reeling from its blinding, sobering effect. But this sense of reality did not last long and her head once more dropped onto her breast with a deep sigh of self condemnation.

What had she come too, she would never have lowered herself as far as this when her Graham had been alive. Norma found herself wistfully turning the gold wedding ring on the third finger of her left hand. The same ring that had been placed there by Graham on their wedding day, the wedding ring that had never been off that finger before he died or even now twelve months later.

Suddenly, all the recriminations of her life over the last year settled like a dark, heavy cloud. The 24th February 1988 was the day her life had ceased to have any meaning whatsoever. The day her Graham, her beloved husband and soul mate had suddenly died at the hands of a hit and run driver. Someone the police had failed to arrest. In that one instance everything that she had held dear and lived for had been switched off like a light. She had never known any other love than her Graham. It had always been Graham and Norma. Always! That was until the 24th February 1988.

Her mind was racing now, like that speeding hit and run vehicle, and it was totally out of control as her vision began to blur and distort causing her to sway from side to side as she sought to stabilize her jumbled thoughts and impressions. But at the same time nothing was making any sense to her, until it all stopped abruptly and once again she was confronted by the stark, irate features of Mr Williams, her office manager.

At first the apparition that was now so deeply implanted in her mind merely mouthed silently at her, but suddenly she could hear the words that had terminated her employment at Saunders and Sons. A job she had held down since she was eighteen. Again she could hear Mr Williams' voice ringing like a death knell in her ears.

"It's happened too many times Norma. We can't tolerate it anymore. Collect your cards!"

He had been waiting for her as she had crept back from her liquid lunch. He had not needed to smell her breath, her lurching gait and dishevelled appearance had been evidence of her intoxicated state. His condemning speech had included his disgust of all those who indulged themselves of the demon drink and had concluded with references to the tardiness of her work and time keeping before sending her on her way.

But instead of the embarrassment of facing her friends in the general office, she had walked straight out of the fire door she had been using to sneak in. Then, not even the heavy downpours of rain and the rolling thunder had helped to soften, or cool her fevered sense of disgrace. She had stumbled away from Saunders and Sons, away from her past and from what should have been her future. And the bitter knowledge that the contents of her shoulder handbag had been the sole contributor to her own downfall and humiliation did nothing to diminish this heavy shroud of shame.

She gave a sigh, an intense thoughtful sigh and leant back in her chair with her head facing the ceiling. Closing her eyes she took in several deep breaths that helped to steady and clear the numbness that had started to encroach on her mind. She had been able to detect the ominous signs of drunken oblivion setting in, and her experience on the subject had now come to her aid.

Pushing herself forward she snatched up a handful of the morning post and began to examine the envelopes in an effort to identify from whence they had come. In that moment the thoughts of Graham sifted through. The little things he always took care of just to relieve the pressure on his wife. She thought back and realised that she had rarely seen a brown envelope let alone the demands that lay within them. The bills had always been paid on time and in many ways that had been detrimental to Norma, who had now been thrust into a responsible world without any guidance. So now the red letters were a common occurrence on the mat inside the front door

"Oh Graham!.....Why!...Why did you have to leave me!" she mumbled in a haze of self pity.

Again she reached for the vodka bottle and tipped the last few drops into her glass. She clasped the glass in her hand and peered disdainfully at it before taking the contents down in one go. She pushed the empty glass away so that it clattered into the pile of crockery and stale food. With an air of resignation she began to open the small collection of envelopes.

"The rates!" she exclaimed, and discarded the envelope and its contents over her shoulder with an increasing sense of aggravation.

"Washing machine payment final demand....Well they can whistle for that one as well!" she muttered and that went the same way.

"TV licence! How can they charge for the crap that's on the damn thing!" she angrily stammered.

This one received a more aggressive demise by being furiously torn into small pieces that were thrown into the air like confetti.

Norma confronted the envelope which had her banks logo emblazoned in the bottom right hand corner. She was already aware of what the letter would be saying. It would be informing her that she owed two payments on the loan she had taken out to pay for her Graham's funeral. This envelope was tossed with even more aggression and was accompanied by a wild scream of despair

To think that she was even defaulting on her Graham's memory, by owing the bank money she had borrowed for his funeral. And this was after humiliating herself to the bank manager to get it. Norma had been at her very lowest, and he had drawn every ounce of satisfaction from her pitiful state before he had finally agreed to the loan. The memories still pounded at the door of what little pride she still retained.

Now the effort of trying to focus and to concentrate at the same time was tiring her, and again she leant back in her chair with her eyes closed fending off the muzziness that seemed adamant and perverse in its attempt to confuse any tangible thoughts that might appear.

However, almost by force of will she was able to slow her breathing and by degrees her thoughts began to queue up, almost for scrutiny. Some good, some bad or indifferent but all had a purpose to push forward for consideration. But one thought seemed to take precedence and brought a glimmer of a smile to her lips. It was the mere fact that the house was paid for, and it gave her a brief moment of comfort. And that had all been due to her Graham's conscientious approach to the family finances. But that fleetingly pleasant thought was short lived and passed on into the mire of her despondency and she opened her eyes once more on reality.

Peering through the alcohol induced haze the last envelope instantly held her attention, cream in colour with the red, white and blue edging and 'Par Avion' airmail logo, with her name and address written in those easily recognisable flowing italics.

"Bob," she breathed.

It was the name of her younger brother, and it was spoken with the first hint of sensitive emotion she had felt all day.

"Bob," she said again.

Eagerly she flipped the envelope around in her fingers trying to absorb the perfect symmetry of each letter that made up her name and address. Again she flipped the envelope round, again and again. And each time she did so an image would swiftly appear and then disappear, indistinct at first until she was able to focus through the blurry mist that was hampering her vision. Round and round the envelope went as her thoughts became entangled with the hypnotising motion. Round and round it turned, and like a drowning person, memories began to skip before her eyes like the clips of a film of her past, but now at an increasing speed, until the pace seemed as if it was in the fast forward mode of her video player.

Clearer images became recognisable of her childhood, with her younger brothers face ageing into the man she remembered from the last time she had seen him. Then she was imagining the family holidays by the sea and birthday parties, and school. Just meagre glimpses of happy times and happy places, now all rushing by at such a speed it was making her mind stagger to keep up.

Suddenly the faces of her parents manifested themselves, smiling with that ever present glint of love that they always seemed to share with each other, and with their children. But then their expressions changed, and she could feel that they seemed to scrutinize her from beyond the grave as their smiles evaporated into those of fiery rebuke.

Then there was her Graham, her husband and steadfast friend, standing next to them with such a pained look of hurt in his eyes that she could actually feel the disapproval that was being aimed at her.

The rotating envelope suddenly spun away from her fingers, and went twisting in the air as the array of scornful looks instantly disappeared, but not before she was abruptly brought out of her trance like state with a start.

Her trembling hands instinctively covered her eyes as she sought to cut out the impressions that had been left by the swirling, reproachful apparitions. She tried to fight off the fact of the shameful realisation that it was the alcohol that had induced this melee of self pity. A series of sobs gurgled in her throat as she attempted forlornly, to steady her chaos of thoughts.

What would any of them think, let alone say if they could really stand in front of her and see the pathetic mess her life had become.

She squinted up at the ceiling and felt the room spinning almost uncontrollably. In her mind she wanted it to cease, knowing full well what was causing it, but physically she was unable to stop it. She could feel herself swaying with each rotation, but in fact her limp body was glued to the chair.

Closing her eyes behind her hands again she tried desperately to regulate her breathing. Time itself had seemed to stop beyond the clawing fingers that held her face so tightly, as if she was in fear of falling. But gradually a more stable feeling began to take hold, and she was able to remove her hands and penetrate the glare of the room, and in stages it ceased to spin.

There was a pot of cold coffee left over from breakfast sitting central on the table. Emptying a half filled cup of dregs into the sugar bowl she poured herself a cup and drank the cold, black, tasteless liquid in one long gulp. She followed this with another as she tried to quell her agitated senses. As this second cup flowed over her tonsils she was able to feel her efforts were beginning to pay dividends and she sat allowing herself time to draw back a little, to take stock and finally to gaze around the kitchen without the feeling of falling from her chair.

Once again she picked up the cream coloured, air mail envelope from where it had fallen under the table and ripping it open she slowly focused on the large sweeping writing, and began to read.

Hi Sis.

> *How are things with you my big sister. I haven't heard from you for a while. I do realise that this last twelve months would have been difficult for you. Did you get my last letter and the Christmas cards. I think yours to us must have been lost in the post. I did try to phone you on Christmas day. Sometime around about 3 in the afternoon your time, but perhaps you were having dinner out somewhere.*
> *You do still have our number don't you?*
> *You said in your last letter that Sharon might be getting engaged to that Alan. From what you've said he seems like a decent guy. What's on that front, are we going to be invited to a wedding?*
> *How is Saunders and Sons, as you said some time ago that they had made a few people redundant. Are things any better, as I get the impression that you are not happy there anymore. A shame, as you have given them twenty five years service. It is twenty five isn't it?*
> *I expect you're still in the grips of the British winter, wet and cold. I certainly don't miss that. Things couldn't be better over here. It doesn't seem like seven years since we came to Canada, but it is. It was the best decision we evermade when I accepted that offer to come over with the company.*
> *We spent the New Year up in Calgary skiing. Simon and Lily loved it, and Gina is a natural. Me, I prefer to go hunting. Well hunting for the nearest bar, and then to watch from a safe distance.*
> *We've made a great circle of friends and soon we will be in the barbecue season.*

I've taken up golf and I like to get a few rounds in during the week. The company encourage this kind of activity as they believe it helps to bond a good working team spirit. It's all so different over here from the UK.

Anyway Norma, I've got some really great news. I've been promoted. As you know we've been in Vancouver since we came over. I've worked hard and it's paid off. My promotion has brought me to Toronto and my own department. It means a massive pay rise and a house. Gina and the kids are still in Vancouver, but will be joining me in May when everything is settled here. Isn't that just great Norma. I hope you are pleased for us.

Which brings me to the other news which I hope...

"I can't stand anymore of this!" Norma stammered.

Scrunching the letter into a ball she tossed it angrily towards the pile of dishes on the draining board. Immediately she regretted the action, and with a sigh she stood and stumbled over to the sink. Retrieving the crumpled letter she tried desperately to straighten and smooth the misshapen pages before discarding them onto the table.

She stood for a moment frantically trying in vain to understand the reason why she had recovered her brother's missive. Anger, envy, drunken fury perhaps had instigated her initial reaction of tossing it aside, even though she realised through the haze, which was now clearing that she was pleased for him. He had made something of his life, and deep down she was pleased. What she could not take was having it thrust in her face with this 'Oh how wonderful life is!' drivel. It was almost stomach wrenching to Norma.

She let out an exhausted sigh, for even though her thought processing was making little sense in her befuddled mind, the sheer effort of standing to unravel her brothers letter had made her feel tired. Once again she moved shakily around the table and slumped back into her chair.

"What have I become," she thought. "Am I a drunkard! Yes!...Am I alcoholic! God forbid!...Have I slipped to the level of those disgusting creatures I've had seen on the benches in the Memorial park, drinking from bottles disguised in plastic bags."

In her mind's eye she could see those disgusting creatures, dirty, ragged, debauched and continuously being moved on. This was something she despised in others, and now she could see it in herself and she despised that even more. Her dignity, her self esteem all were in jeopardy of being flushed away as easily as the three day old washing up water in the sink. All she needed to do was to pull the plug and the stale water would be gone. So easy, it could all be gone in an instant.

But the thought of it being gone in an instant, at first frightened her, then intrigued her, and finally seemed to make a kind of sense. All gone in a moment, flushed away as easy as that. And what would she leave behind. Sharon was on the verge of a new life with Alan and he seemed steady enough. Bob and his family were all set on their future in Canada. As far as relatives were concerned there were none to speak of and friends she could count them on one hand. And now with no future at Saunders and Sons she was left with the terrifying thought of having to find another job.

So, what would she leave behind, nothing! Absolutely nothing! And that thought seemed to frighten her the most. With her parents now dead, and Graham dying so cruelly young and leaving her on her own, there was no one to blame for the situation she was in, and no one to truly miss her or to mourn for her if she went the same way. No one! Life would stop for a moment, and then move on without a second thought. Norma struggled to understand this disturbing brew of notions that seemed to clutter and confuse. But she also realised with a sigh that her reasoning was beginning to return and she became aware of a heavy weight of oppression as she began to ponder on her situation more closely.

****

The front door of 34 Chester Road opened and banged shut and a voice called out.

"Hello Mum. You home?"

Norma remained silent in her own thoughts. Sharon, her daughter, would already know the answer to that question from the discarded coat and the puddles of water. Norma had hoped that Sharon would still be with her boyfriend Alan, for she had been away for three days at his parents outside of town and had said she might stay until the weekend. That is what Norma had wanted, but no! Sharon had obviously changed her arrangements and would walk in to witness the shambles she was sitting in.

She turned her head towards the ceiling and could now hear footfalls cross floor above her. Sharon must be in her bedroom and would be down soon and then the inquisition would begin.

Norma sank her face into her hands in dread of the inevitable. She listened to the movements above her head in desperate anticipation, almost visualising exactly what her daughter was doing, moving about with the buoyant enthusiasm of youth as she occasionally picked out a few bars of some song that she now had playing on her radio. Some trite, meaningless words, sung in a squeaky tuneless voice that grated on Norma's ears as well as her nerves, as they fought for dominance over Connie Francis on the kitchen radio.

And it all meant so little to her. She just sat at the table head bowed forward, waiting for the axe to fall.

It was the same with everything. Even her own daughter's apparent happiness meant nothing to her. All she could feel now was the grim knowledge that in a few moments the kitchen door would fly open with a rush and the arguments would start all over again.

The kitchen door did fly open with a rush, for this was how Sharon always made her entrance.

"Oh here you are. Alan dropped me off and...."

She stopped directly behind her mother gazing around in despair at the mess and disarray and then down at the hunched figure.

"What the hell have you been doing," Sharon cried in exasperation. "I can't let Alan come in here. He's picking me up later..... What's been going on Mum?"

When there was no response she walked around to the opposite side of the table and with hands defiantly on her hips she glared down at the pitiful scene before her.

"What's been going on Mum?.....It's happening again isn't it? You're drinking again!" she said as she snatched up the empty vodka bottle. "Mum!........Answer me!"

"Is it still raining?" her mother mumbled still with her head bowed

"Mum!" her daughter exclaimed.

"Just leave me alone Sharon...Just leave me alone," Norma growled into her hands.

"No Mum...I'm not going to leave you alone! This has got to stop. You're not only ruining your own life. It's ruining mine as well. I can't go on coming home to this. It's not fair Mum. It's not fair!"

She strutted over to the pedal bin and dropped the offending bottle into the empty recess. With great affectation she strode slowly back to face the sorrowful shape of her mother. Folding her arms tightly she struck the pose of the prosecutor.

"So come on Mum.....I want the truth!" she demanded. "What the hell has brought this on? It's pretty obvious that something has happened or is it like this because you thought I wasn't coming home till the weekend. That's it isn't it. You thought you had a couple of days to get completely smashed, and time to sober up and clear the place. That's it isn't it Mum. When I do have a few days away I normally come back when I say I will. Until today! Well I've caught you out haven't I. So what have you got to say Mum?"

"Just leave it will you. Just leave it," Norma said sighing heavily into her hands, the defiance had now drained away to almost a whimper. "I don't need this Sharon! I really don't need this!"

Norma was now finding it increasingly difficult to keep her mind focused on the reality of the moment, and yet still unable to meet her daughter's scathing stare she proceeded to hang her head inches from the kitchen table.

"You can cut out the self pity Mum!" Sharon said in attacking mode. "It doesn't work anymore. I've got no sympathy for anyone who will allow themselves to sink as low as this. You should see yourself Mum. It's sickening to see a grown woman getting like this. What are you trying to prove? And what about Saunders, what the hell do they think of all this?"

For the first time since Sharon had entered the kitchen Norma leant slowly back in her chair and glared at her daughter.

"Well Sharon that is not a problem I have to face anymore," Norma stated obstinately.

Sharon allowed her hands to gradually drop to her side as she stared down, mouth wide open as realisation and disbelief took the frown from her face.

"Oh my God!" she said in exasperation. "You've had the sack!"

"In a nutshell Sharon. Yes I've had the sack."

"Mum! Twenty years service down the drain!"

"No Sharon. It's twenty five years service!" Norma snapped. "But yes you are correct, down the drain."

"You bloody fool!" Sharon cried throwing her hands into the air in anger.

"Very well put Sharon. A bloody, bloody fool!" came the reply now with something of defeat in the tone.

Ironically the tension between the two women seemed to evaporate in an instant. A kind of mutual depth of feeling had imperceptibly filtered into the almost claustrophobic ambiance of the kitchen.

Norma wiped the back of her hand across her forehead as a miasma of alcohol induced sweat appeared on her brow. There was such a stillness in the air as Sharon waited for an explanation and Norma hesitated to provide one.

After a few seconds Norma took a deep breath, leant forward onto her elbows and spoke very deliberately whilst staring at the chaos of crockery before her.

"I'd been in the Park Hotel during the lunch hour," she admitted with a deep regretful sigh.

"Drinking I take it!" Sharon said once again folding her arms.

"I had a drink yes. And....I was late back to work."

"How late?"

"Forty five minutes."

"And?"

"Old man Williams caught me sneaking in the fire door to the stairs to my office....Well... he saw the state I was in and guessed what had caused it, and it was instant dismissal."

"Oh Mum!" Sharon said as she released her arms to her side in dismay.

"It's my own fault Sharon. I had a warning two weeks ago about my time keeping."

"Oh Mum!" Sharon's voice had now dropped to a sympathetic tone.

"Well it will save them making me redundant I suppose," her mother answered sardonically.

"That's not the point Mum. Redundancy would have meant a reference and a good payout."

"Well that's it Sharon. In a nutshell," Norma slurred with a wry smile on her lips.

The confession had somehow brought a brightness to her cheeks, but that was short lived when the realisation dawned on her that finding another job with a sacking hanging over her would certainly limit her employment chances, that and her age.

Her guilty disclosure and its consequences were at least providing her with some very sobering thoughts. She could now feel some semblance of normality with the numbness lifting from her damp body and her eyes beginning to focus properly again. And that feeling of unsteadiness, even when sitting down was now just a bad memory, although the onset of a pounding headache was just infiltrating like a tightening band across her brow.

"You won't find another job that easy mum. Not in accounts like that one at Saunders," Sharon said with a degree of sympathy edging into her voice.

"No........ you are probably right," admitted Norma with a resounding sigh.

Norma felt that pang of desperation she had experienced when, just a few hours earlier, standing in a sudden downpour she had looked up at the sign Saunders And Sons. With the merciless rain soaking her and splashing all around her, she had found it hard to accept that she would never be allowed to enter that building, that office, that other world that she had known for the last twenty five years ever again.

Twenty five years of her life that she had foolishly let slip away. Where she had met Graham on her very first day there, and where the police had come to inform her that he had been killed after being hit by a car when crossing the road to his van after making a delivery. Even there, with her face upturned to the stinging downpour, staring at that sign with the rain seeping through her clothes, so many more vivid memories had entered her head and had been dashed to smithereens so abruptly by her overwhelming sense of stupidity.

She was brought out of her despondency by Sharon's voice asking.

"So what happens now? I can't keep us both Mum."

"I won't ask you to Sharon. That I promise," Norma replied. "But all I can see is my past getting longer and my future getting shorter, and the present...well...nothing whatsoever. That's what comes with aging, Sharon. That's life!" she added thoughtfully, almost to herself.

There was a silence that crept in as both mother and daughter considered the consequences to each on their own lives.

Norma peered intently at her good looking daughter, and reflectively visualized how she used to maintain her own appearance until twelve months ago. She marvelled at Sharon's make up so perfectly applied, the fashionable perm of shoulder length hair and the slim, shapely figure, at the moment slightly hidden by the jacket and shoulder pads that were so much in vogue. It all gave the impression of an attractive, vibrant young woman ready to take on the world and to enjoy every minute of the experience.

And here she sat sinking further into her despair at the thought of her own future being so cruelly curtailed.

Sharon peered down at her mother, and a deep regret burned in her breast at the way she had been so dismissive about her mother's torture over the last year and also that she had not recognised the cry for help that the drinking had signified. She suddenly felt a heavy pang of guilt at realising this was simply because of her own selfish rejection of any problems that did not concern her personally. And she could not shake off the grinding feeling that partial blame for her mother's situation should be laid squarely at her feet.

Now as she continued her sad study of the dishevelled, tired woman sitting in crumpled defeat before her, she felt as if she was staring at the inevitable direction her own destiny might take, for she could almost see herself in twenty years time. And with that image so vividly clear in her mind she reconciled herself, there and then to always be aware of the signs and inwardly vowed never to be so foolish and succumb to the weaknesses that seemed to be destroying her mother.

She gave an almost imperceptible shiver and consciously brushed all her brooding notions aside for they were beginning to unsettle her. Straightening her posture with a conscious flick of her hair, she attempted to lighten the aura of despondency that had descended on the two occupants of the kitchen.

"So what was in the post," Sharon said as lightly as possible whilst trying to break the stilted silence.

"Bills! Unpaid bills...Oh........And one from your Uncle Bob," her mother replied.

"What did he have to say?" Sharon enquired.

"Oh just how bloody wonderful life is for him in Canada," Norma said disparagingly. "It's there read it for yourself. I could only stomach the first couple of pages."

Sharon sought out the scattered, crumpled sheets of paper that constituted her Uncles letter. She made an effort to straighten the creases and then placing them in order she pulled out a chair opposite to her mother. Sitting down she began to read, occasionally quoting a line or an interesting phrase or passage or voicing an opinion.

"No photo's!....Uncle Bob usually sends some snaps of the kids.........Oh mum why didn't you reply to his letter before Christmas?..........And he even tried to phone Christmas day!..........Yes!..He's got it right about Alan. He is a nice guy!........It is twenty five years you've been at Saunders!....What a waste!....Calgary...Wow!......He really has landed on his feet......Good for him...Golf!...Ah well he has gone up in the world. I remember what his views were when golf came on the telly....He's been promoted....They're moving to Toronto......He's got some more news"

There was a long pause in the commentary as Sharon continued in silent reading. Then she stopped and looked at her mother with a hard searching stare. Norma caught the look and fidgeted uneasily.

"Have you read this letter mum?" Sharon questioned accusingly. "I mean all of it including the last page."

"No I couldn't stand anymore of him patting himself on the back," Norma grumbled.

"Well you should've done!....Listen to this."

And she continued to read aloud.

> *"Which brings me to the other news, which I hope you will find interesting. My new job will allow me to do my own hiring and firing and I've cleared this with my direct superiors.*
>
> *Sis, there's a job waiting for you here doing basically what you were doing at Saunders before they downgraded you. That was the first step to redundancy you know. Well the jobs here, and also a small annex to our new place in Toronto. That's*

for as long as you like or until we find you a place of your own. The company are committed to assisting financially in that direction.

It's all here Sis, a new and fresh start. I've organised it for the first week in May. That gives you about two months. I'll take care of all the paperwork, permits and the like, just make sure your passport is up to date. The company will pay your fare and I'm not taking no for an answer. If necessary I'll come and fetch you.

Seriously though Sis, this is a chance of a lifetime, a complete new start. Sharon looks like she's moving on, so there's nothing there for you now, you've hinted as much in your letters.

Take a long hard look sis, it's all here waiting for you.
I'll ring you soon so please answer the phone.
All our love to you and Sharon.

Bob.
PS. Make the right decision."

There was a throbbing silence between the two women as the full extent of the implications contained in the words of the letter, settled in their minds.

"Wow!……Mum!" Sharon exclaimed with disbelief in her tone.

"Who the hell does he think he is!" Norma snarled with a mixture of anger and amazement, not only at the offer her brother was making, but also at the profound ramifications which now seemed to appear so formidable in her alcohol tainted state of reasoning.

"Who the hell, what!" Sharon stammered as she pushed herself to her feet in a display of frustration and anger. "What a wonderful chance mum. Talk about him landing on his feet...Wow!"

"There is no way I'd go," Norma said slurring her words. "Drop everything on a whim. He always did have his head in the clouds. What would I do by going to Canada?"

"You'd start living again Mum," Sharon said leaning over her mother. "You've got to move on. Dad wouldn't want you being like this. You're at the bottom Mum. You can't go on like this. There's nothing here for you now."

Norma stood, thrusting the chair back across the kitchen floor.

"I'm not listening to this. I'm not going and that is final. I don't want to hear anymore."

Unsteadily she staggered to the door. Turning she gave Sharon a penetrating look along a jabbing finger.

"So Sharon, you keep your nose out it!" she threatened.

And the door slammed shut behind her.

Sharon stood and listened to the stomping footfalls on the stairs and landing, and then the door to her mother's bedroom being slammed shut.

"Oh Mum!" she said to herself and the empty room. "As stubborn as ever!"

Norma thrust her way into her bedroom and tried desperately to hang onto consciousness while allowing her damp clothes to fall to the floor in a heap. Struggling into her dressing gown she stumbled to her lonely bed and flung herself face down, sobbing deeply into the pillow. The pillow she had not washed since her Graham had died. It still seemed to retain an essence of his smell, so much of a comfort to her. It also covered the pyjamas, neatly folded and waiting for him, as Norma waited.

She lay there sobbing with her mind in a dizzying whirl, not only with the remnants of the vodkas influence but with the agonising thoughts of her situation. Mentally she cursed Bob and his letter with his demands that she should make the right decision, which now simply aggravated her. Inwardly she was damning any thought about going. What would she do in Canada, she wasn't a charity case, she did not need anybody's sympathy least of all those of her own brother. The sobbing got deeper as her mind fought the creeping feeling of nausea that was beginning to churn in her stomach.

Turning onto her back the room seemed to fill with leaping images and memories. Haunting faces and places from her past crowded her head, unstoppable like a rising tide as they rushed up the beaches of her muddled mind. Faces and places that leapt from one to the other with no apparent sequence or purpose. Her eyes circled the room trying to capture and retain each fleeting glimpse of something that was so precious from her memory.

Sharon's voice called out from downstairs.

"Alan's here Mum...I won't be late!"

And the front door closed with a bang that vibrated through the house.

The strident voice and the banging door seemed to jolt Norma back to reality. She became aware that her mind was wondering again, and that it was all due to the latent effects the Vodka was having on her reasoning. There was a stillness that was encompassing her even though she could just hear the radio in the kitchen permeating up into her room. But even that seemed so distant, so far removed from where she was. She turned to face the window and the almost black sky beyond, and the action seemed to quell the growing uncertainty in her stomach, but did nothing to halt the disturbing thoughts that circled in mesmerizing patterns in her head.

"What was the purpose of all this," her bleary thoughts were saying. "There really is nothing here for me. I really do have nothing to live for."

When a person reaches this low, and there is no helping hand or way out that can be found then the despair can become crushing. Norma knew that everything Sharon had said was the truth, but she did not have the strength or the will to accept it. A person can drown in their own self pity, it can become all consuming. Once again the ghosts in her mind began to take shape, tormenting the logical thoughts she sought so hard to come to terms with. But it was a losing battle and again she buried her head into the pillow seeking comfort. She tried hard to forget, to fight against all those confusing images, but to no avail.

"STOP!" she cried. "STOP!!!"

But she could not find any relief.

Then a thought did creep through the melee and stood like a large hoarding that blocked out all other impressions. She could only see that one, dominant thought that appeared like printed words before her eyes, words that she had read somewhere quite recently but she could not think where. She was fighting hard to remember and the frustration brought on more sobbing with tears rolling down her face like the downpours of rain she had endured earlier.

Then she remembered, it had been the dinner time only two days before. She had passed a little bookshop on her way to the Park Hotel for her liquid lunch, and a new book was being featured in the window. At the time the title had intrigued her, fascinated her to the point that it had held her attention for almost five minutes. She now found she was holding her breath and reading the words again so that they seemed to take over the whole of her reeling senses. Over and over she repeated the words, and they became louder each time she spoke them. And as she spoke them she realised that the words were the most sensible thing she had ever read.

"Only Death Has No Memory."

****

The door to 34 Chester Road opened with a rush, and Sharon stood in the doorway vigorously shaking the residue of the rain from her umbrella. Stepping inside she pushed the door closed with a bang. She propped the umbrella against the wall and placed her handbag onto the hallstand exactly where her mother had always used to put hers. Slowly, methodically, she unbuttoned her coat and hung it on the hook that her mother's coat had always occupied. Stooping she retrieved the various envelopes of the morning post from the floor and then stood before the hall mirror, examining closely her makeup and her hair. She decided with a slight grimace that both would need some remedial work before Alan came to pick her up.

For a few more moments she just stood absorbing the resounding silence in the house. It had been silent like this for the last eight months, every time she had come home. Even when Alan had stopped over, the silence had been tangible. The radio that had always seemed to have been on was silent. For eight months it had been silent, but tonight as the silence dwelt so heavily on her eardrums, Sharon actually wished that the radio was on. And in that instant she would have admitted that she actually missed it, no matter what programme it would be tuned to she would have given anything just to hear it as she had walked through the door.

For the house was not only silent it was still, unmoving, immobile with a distinct sombre edge to it.

And there was no smell of cooking, something else she would give anything to come home to, or even the washing machine at full throttle for that matter. Simple things that made a house a home, but not missed until they no longer existed. Even in the darkest hours of the night time, when for one reason or other she had lay awake thinking her dreams, the house had always seemed to breathe and pulsate with life, but not anymore. Not for the last eight months.

She moved slowly but with deliberate purpose towards the kitchen door and opened it. The kitchen was neat with everything in its place, almost as if it was never used, which in fact was very near the truth. Sharon very rarely cooked for herself nowadays. The most she would do was coffee and toast in the mornings, and possibly a pot of tea at night. Alan liked to eat out, either a bar meal or pizza and that suited Sharon.

The fact was, since she had opened the Sharalan Hair and Beauty Salon with Alan there had been little time for the menial everyday activities and if truth were known, that suited her also. Even so, as she dropped the mail onto the table and sat down, it was with a certain heaviness of heart, actually wishing that the house was not so silent and so still and that it could be filled with all the reminiscent aromas of the Sunday roast.

For a few precious moments her imagination took hold and deposited her back to those transient days of sublime childhood. But the instant was only a fragment of time, and she shook herself free of nostalgia. She leant back, and with a sigh she picked up the scattered envelopes, scanning them she recognised gas, electricity, a bank statement and then one that stood out from the rest with the airmail emblem from Canada.

Ripping it open she began to read.

Hi Sharon.

> *This will only be a short letter to tell you that I've sent all the papers back to the solicitors in England. When that's completed the house will be yours. It's what I want Sharon, and I know it would be what your dad would want as well. It's our wedding present to you.*
>
> *Uncle Bob has agreed to give you away and the family will be over there for the wedding. And of course I will be there. We're all looking forward to it so much. Just think it's only six weeks to the big day. My only regret is I won't be with*

you when you choose your dress. But I know you will look beautiful, and I can't wait to see you.

How is the salon doing. I like the name, it sounds really Professional, Sharalan Hair and Beauty Salon, really posh. Some more news. I've got my own apartment here in Toronto. It's only fifteen minutes from your Uncle Bob's so I see them anytime I want. Or when they need a sitter!

Work is just great just what I really wanted Sharon. I've got my own office, and three young girls working under me. Also Sharon I've been seeing someone from another office.

His name is Walter Shultz. He's four years older than me, and he lost his wife five years ago. It's nothing serious, we are both agreed on that for the time being at least. But we've been out a number of times for a meal or the theatre and he really is good company for me.

Sharon, thank you again for convincing me to make the decision to take your Uncle Bobs offer to come over here. I truly believe it saved my life. I didn't know where I was going back there in England. It just seemed all doors that had been open to me had been slammed in my face.

Anyway love, I'll close for now. We all send our love and look forward to seeing you, and please give our love to Alan.

I'll write soon.

Love Mum.

Sharon leant back in her chair, and smiled to herself as she carefully refolded the letter back into the envelope.

"Good for you Mum," she whispered to herself. "Good for you!"

She listened intently to the silence, and as she did, she did not feel quite so alone.

FROM WHENCE I CAME

There are certain occasions in life that have a tendency to remain secreted and hidden in your mind like some musty old photograph that you thought was lost but you come across in the bottom of a drawer. Moments or events that at the time seemed insignificant and unimportant, but as the years roll by they can take on a completely new relevance and understanding when they are rediscovered. And like opening that drawer and coming across that photograph, memories once considered ordinary and mundane when dusted off, can immediately transport you back to the time and the place of their formation.

Then you are able to question those recollections by thinking.....

"I wonder what happened to so and so?" or. "That view across the valley was really beautiful!"

For a memory can easily be jolted by something as simple as a word, a phrase or a song. Or even a smell, a feeling, a colour or the texture of something you may touch that switches on the light of a flashback in time and ignites those long lost images that have been lying dormant and gathering dust in the darkest depths of your mind.

It is then that you can stretch those tangled impressions to form a composite, like a jigsaw puzzle piecing each piece together to complete the full picture. And when you have each piece in place you can examine the memory in its entirety, just as you would do with that long lost photograph in the bottom of the drawer.

So now, the glowing embers of sentiment and emotion that accompanied the memories when they were first being shaped in your mind are allowed to be rekindled. And through the distance created by the passage of time, you can then view that memory from your own ensuing life's experiences. You may see and feel how that moment or event has altered or affected you. How it may have changed you by forming, or reforming your opinions or attitudes, outlooks and even your ambitions. It is possible to perceive that memory as a window, a time capsule to your past and actually see yourself as you once were.

And yet, while the revelations you uncover of yourself can be enlightening, they can also be frightening and disconcerting. But either way they can be a useful tool to bring you back to earth for a brief instance of soul searching, or at the very least to just make you stop and to consider where life has taken you.

For it was by sifting through the distant shadowy images of my former self that I have been able to pick out and reassemble those precious moments that had been lying hidden away and in danger of being forgotten.

Now almost forty years on, I can see that my work, my life style and the vagaries of what I wanted and what was forthcoming to me had kept me away from the town of my birth. The place where I had grown up, the place of my infant, junior and senior schools and the place of my first steps on the employment ladder by way of apprentice machinist in a local factory. But hating that with a passion, I had very quickly found myself a sales assistant job at a local supermarket.

Having said that, even after all the passing years and all that I have experienced passing through them, it is still the place where I was born and brought up and ultimately where I had considered my roots to be truly embedded.

Looking back, I had been one of the lads enjoying those transient, character shaping years like everyone else of my age, a product of the sixties taking advantage of opportunities with the opposite sex and sometimes drinking myself stupid with my mates. All those things that made life un-boring, and this included my position of outside right on Sunday afternoons for the North End Football Club. Nothing unusual in any of that for I took life as it came and enjoyed myself in the process. I believe I had been a good son to my parents and in retrospect I had been able to give them much to be proud of.

Although, with each of these memories as they appear being greeted with a certain fondness, I can revisit them, see them and relive them. And it is only when you reach a certain point in your life that memories really find their full value.

For instance, as I am thinking this, I can see my mother's face with tears in her eyes and almost feel my father's horny handshake as I got into my Mini Cooper at the age of twenty three, to drive nearly ninety miles to my new job as an assistant manager in a branch of the supermarket chain I had joined as a teenager. Thus, taking me away from all that I knew to what I had to learn all over again. Now why should that memory crop up out of the blue, just like that! But memories have a habit of doing that.

And, as my thoughts seemed to be pursuing this particular route, I am suddenly visualising my parent's faces as they filled with pride when I was able to tell them that I had climbed even further up the ladder of promotion, when I became the youngest manager of a large, prestigious branch in the chain. This was a progression my parents had really been able to speak proudly about to friends and neighbours, even though the job was to take me and keep me over two hundred miles from my home and my roots.

That was me, like millions of others from rather frivolous beginnings in their teens to charting out a path for themselves in the best way that they could. Some would fall by the wayside, some would never reach above the level that they had started at. But as my mind pondered thoughtfully back over the years, I felt that I had been one of the luckier percentage and had grabbed the chances offered to me in both of my grateful hands.

However, it is one particular series of dusty old memories that had been so firmly concealed and locked away in my mind that have caused me to really take a long in depth search into myself, and to question why they should affect me so profoundly. It is also very strange and puzzling for me to admit that over the years I cannot really say that I have ever given much thought to what I am about to relate to you. In reality the memories only seemed to have materialised fully into my consciousness since I have returned to my old stamping ground.

Hence, I can now recall the whole episode, and I will tell it as it happened.

And so, after forty years with the same company I had taken a generous early retirement package, which ironically coincided with my recent divorce. Our three grown up children had each flown the nest in various directions and I was more than happy with the directions they had chosen for themselves.

My wife, who had been younger than me by a few years, had taken the direction she had been moving towards for some time and had disappeared with our neighbour, settling somewhere in Cheshire. I cannot say I was sorry, the marriage had been teetering on the edge for many years and it had only been waiting for our youngest daughter to go to University to tip the balance.

As a result, the course that had opened up for me, had been to sell the house in Newcastle on Tyne, split the proceeds with my ex wife and head in the direction of the town of my roots. Once there to purchase a smaller place that fitted me better and so to settle down to the few quiet years left to me.

Over the years, my infrequent visits back home had been merely fleeting, to see my parents or for a wedding or a funeral or such like. The outcome being, that now I had lost contact with all my old friends and I was a stranger to the remaining relatives who had once known me. Both my parents had died some years ago, and so in reality I was alone. And to say that it disturbed me would be a lie.

Apart from the short hiatus when I worked in a factory, all my working life I had been surrounded by the hustle and bustle of a large supermarket, and then all the pressures that went with promotion to the manager's job. Many times being a family man interfered with that job, with the hours being long and demanding, and all this went to push the participants in the marriage further and further apart. However, we had both sat down sensibly to carve out an amicable conclusion and each got what they wanted with little or no fuss. So the children were never subjected to the undercurrent of animosity these break ups could invoke.

Now after nearly a month in my new two bedroom bungalow, I had revisited all the old haunts that I had frequented in my misspent youth, and even as I did not once did I find regret in any of the memories that seemed to float through my mind. The only feelings of remorse came where there was change. For example the area where my grandparent's house had stood for almost a century, had been pulled down and replaced by a new housing estate. And the football fields where I had tried to emulate my hero Georgie Best was now an industrial trading complex.

But, the one change that really seemed to bite at me and to epitomise the sadness of time elapsing into infinity was the pub I had spent many a night falling out of with the bunch of mates I had belonged to. Now it was an up market steak house with restricted entrance on those without jackets and ties. I tried to relive the past by sitting down for a meal, but had made my excuses to leave before I had even read the menu.

Change hurts, and really does make you sit back and wonder where you have come from when your roots are not necessarily pulled up, but very seriously disturbed.

And so my journey around my past life finally found me sitting on a bench in the park that was adjacent to the supermarket that I had first worked in so many years before. Progress had seen it greatly extended, with the chain name and logo of the company I had so recently retired from displayed in large letters. In those early days of my employment there, my lunch hour had been between one and two o clock, and even back then I was always keen to seek out that little bit of solitude that an hour in the park with a pasty and a cola could offer me.

Now, on this late Spring afternoon I was able to sit and ruminate over the multitude of thoughts and memories that had been tripping their way down the years to settle in my mind's eye. For the park was the one constant that had not felt the heavy hand of change and I could almost swear the trees bore the same leaves as when I had last seen them so many years ago.

I was smiling openly to myself as I gazed across the expanses of sweeping, well manicured lawns to the lime tree lined pathways that led all through and round the park and its twenty or so acres.

On the far side to the north, just inside the main gates was the war memorial depicting a WW1 Tommie in full kit resting on his upturned rifle. It had been erected in 1921 by public sponsorship to commemorate the local fallen and each year since, on November 11th it was the focal point of the Remembrance Day services.

To the west was the ornate Victorian bandstand which was always well supported, and still seemed to be. A few hundred yards over to my left was the same Little Tudor Tea Rooms with the wrought iron tables and chairs under umbrellas.

The central feature of the park, fondly referred to as the 'Gorge,' was the large, horticulturist's dream, a water feature garden landscaped with alpine borders of colourful bedding plants, shrubberies and a number of ornate rock pools. From the outside it could be viewed as an extensive bush and tree enclosure, but once you stepped through one of the numerous arched portals you were treated to the colour and splendour of a really magical place. Benches were placed at many points to optimise the view of the rock pools with the placid ducks and moorhens and the gamut of flowers, fauna, bushes and trees. Even I, in those far distant days, had appreciated the beauty and tranquillity of the place.

Slowly and methodical I was now allowing my mind the freedom to wistfully peruse while a collection of memories shook of the layers of dust and cobwebs and began to take shape and substance. Memories that, until that moment in time had lay so inconspicuously in my subconscious that I had almost forgotten that they had ever been formed. And so I now allowed my conscious mind to openly invite them to re-emerge for me to remember.

My thoughts wondered back gathering pace and intensity and began to shuffle and reorganise the increasing surge of images and impressions into a semblance of a chronological order. Carefully selecting each piece of the puzzle and to fit them into their rightful place so as to form a complete picture that would correspond to the infiltrating emotions I was beginning to feel.

I was now tip toeing back through the years recalling to mind a time when I had only recently and very reluctantly left my teens behind. It was not by accident that the bench I was seated on was the same bench from all those years ago, it being convenient for my place of work at the supermarket and also with the vantage point of taking in the whole of the panorama of the park.

And now once again I could see it all so clearly in my mind's eye, as it had been so many years before.

It had been a Tuesday lunchtime just after one o clock I remember, and I had been particularly busy at work. I had just finished the last of my pasty and cola when I had caught sight of an elderly couple strolling arm in arm along the path towards me, and all the time for some inexplicable reason I became fascinated by them.

I can still recall how I had sat there nonchalantly watching the elderly couple in their slow approach. It had been a game I had often played, just sitting and watching people and using my imagination to try and construct their personalities, their lives and backgrounds. Trying to discover through my observations who my subjects might be and to try and build a picture of them in my mind. Even to visualizing what thoughts might be dictating the expressions that were displayed on their faces.

So many questions that may have led me to many erroneous conclusions, but an innocent diversion that I felt certain did no one any harm. In fact it was a useful practice I had found myself utilizing on a day to day basis later in my manager's role, sorting out those who I felt warranted my trust or for possible promotion.

And so the memories continued to flow and I felt myself beginning to relive them.

Almost casually I quickly decided the elderly gentleman had a military bearing, not an officer but serving in the ranks. He had a pride in his gait that spoke volumes as did the grey suit and hat worn almost like a uniform. And as he got closer I noticed the tie which was familiar to me, as it was the same as my father and grandfather had worn on Remembrance Sunday. It was the local Infantry Regimental tie, as was the bugle horn lapel badge that I could now just distinguish displayed on his coat.

The couples pace was slow yet purposeful, and I suspected it was adapted to accommodate the elderly lady who clung tightly to the gentleman's sturdy arm. She was dressed in a lilac, floral dress with a multicoloured crocheted shawl over her shoulders and a small straw hat covering her pure white curls. Round the bowl of the hat was a red ribbon sash which finished in a tiny bow, and under her free arm she clutched a small red handbag.

All this information had been collected and absorbed in a matter of seconds, and now the couple were directly in front of me. The elderly lady turned her face towards me and smiled, as the elderly gentleman simply touched the brim of his hat. And then they had past me, complete in their own company and once again oblivious to everything but each other.

I continued to gaze, almost mesmerized as they slowly took the path that led to the Little Tudor Tea Rooms where they stopped. For perhaps a minute, they stood watching the people at the outside tables eating and drinking. They looked on as if they were trying to decide whether to find a table, until the man slowly shook his head and they moved away, slightly dejected I thought. Still I watched them in a kind of fascination as they strolled on and out of sight.

If you had asked me then and even now for a plausible reason for my continued interest in them I could not have provided you with one.

Now as I sit here on the same bench forty or so years later, I felt the memories were becoming so very clear in my mind as they pressed on regardless to conjure up more for me to ponder and to reminisce on.

The next day had been a Wednesday, and I made sure I was sitting on the same bench at the same time. I had finished my Spartans lunch of a pasty and cola and so I waited with a certain amount of trepidation in my manner. I felt a strange kind of anticipation in the hope that the elderly couple would make an appearance and quell the overriding sense of disappointment I thought I would feel in the event if they did not.

In some respects I also felt an unusual nervousness about the impending encounter that I really could not explain. All the previous evening and through the morning at work I had been totally distracted by the events of the previous lunch time to the point that it had been noticed by my mother at breakfast and my colleagues at work.

Even so, in my admitting to all this I could not give myself a satisfactory explanation for the strange effect it was having on me.

As it was, at a approximately a quarter past one I saw the elderly couple enter the park by the ornate side entrance and begin their walk down the curving path towards me. Slowly and in step they approached, and like the day before as they drew near the elderly lady looked in my direction and smiled and the elderly gentleman touched the brim of his hat, and then they were past me. This time, however, I had been able to respond with a smile and a rather nervous slight bow of my head. I watched them as they moved on towards the Little Tudor Tearooms, where again they stopped to look rather wistfully at the diners, before continuing on their way and out of sight.

For many minutes afterwards I sat bewildered at the questions that were buzzing round my head. What was this fascination I had for this elderly couple. I did not know them and until the day before I had never set eyes on them. I did not know their names or where they came from, I would even have been guessing if you had asked me how old they were. All I really knew were the gathered, precarious assumptions that I had constructed in my imagination from my own character observations during the very brief encounters over the two days. But I also felt a strange kind of kinship towards them that made me want to know more.

The Thursday, Friday and then the Saturday I managed to arrange my lunch to be in my usual seat. Each time, right on cue the elderly couple appeared as usual, with the elderly gentleman in the same suit, hat and military tie, and the ever present bugle horn lapel badge proudly defining his military allegiance.

And like the previous days the elderly lady was dressed in the style which she seemed to favour. That of pale floral dresses with matching sashes round the bowl of her straw hat, also the multicoloured, crocheted shawl and clutching her red handbag.

Again, as they passed me it was with a smile from the elderly lady and a touch of the brim of the hat from the elderly gentleman before moving slowly on. And as always they stopped at the little cafe where they briefly watched the people eating and chatting over their lunches, before reluctantly turning and strolling away.

And so the Sunday was no different. Only this time because I was playing football at three o clock I still made it my business to be on the bench at one. It now seemed as if it was becoming something of an obsession for me to be on that bench at the same time, even on my days off.

I also found myself consciously thinking about the elderly couple at really odd times. Something, even the most insignificant things would set my mind racing at the most inopportune moments to easily confound me. But still I was totally unable to explain why.

The ritual never varied, I would sit on the bench, the elderly couple would slowly approach and in passing the elderly lady would give a smile and the elderly gentleman would touch the brim of his hat.

And as it happened, on this Sunday I was not disappointed, even to the point of the elderly couple standing and watching the customers in the little cafe and then turning away almost disappointedly. And like the previous days I watched completely enthralled and not for one moment could I admit to understanding any of it. They seemed to dominate all aspects of my day.

In retrospect I feel I was lucky that it did not interfere with my work.

And so this procedure continued through the following week and varied only in the minor details of the pastel shades of the outfits that the elderly lady wore. It was as if you could set your watch to the second by the whole ritual and I could only sit and wonder what the elderly couple thought of my part in all of this. They must be as curious of the young man in the dark suit who was always seated on the same bench at the same time every day including weekends, as I was as curious about them. Perhaps they were analysing me. Perhaps I was perplexing them as much as they perplexed me.

Even so, it continued through the week end until the following Tuesday.

Now exactly two weeks to the day from the first appearance of the elderly couple, I sat waiting for them and right to the second they appeared. The elderly gentleman dressed exactly as usual, with the elderly lady in a pale blue dress and shawl, and the straw hat and matching ribbon. And as usual she smiled and the elderly gentleman touched the brim of his hat, and as usual they moved slowly on towards the little cafe. Here they stood for perhaps a minute.

But this time instead of passing on, they moved between the tables and selected one on the edge away from the others and took their places.

I was astounded, yet why should I be astounded. It was quite a normal thing to do. But it had now broken the spell of the routine of what I was expecting. So I got up from my bench and strolled as inconspicuously as possible and stood with a tree between myself and any sight line from the elderly couple. They both had menus and were chatting as to what they would order. So engrossed were they that they did not see me walk to the far side and sit down at a table. From where I was placed I could see the elderly couple, but they would have found it difficult to notice me.

I had coffee and a teacake, and I saw that the elderly couple were enjoying what looked like a salad lunch. But I remember distinctly, as I sat there watching them a great sadness came over me, to the point that I felt a lump climb into my throat as I held back my embarrassment with a determined effort. I was a man and men did not cry, I thought. Well only when Manchester United lost, so I could not understand this blatant show of emotion over an elderly couple who, I did not know anything about, not even their names.

Again the question rose up in my mind, what was I doing here stalking this kindly couple while they innocently had a quiet lunch on a pleasant afternoon in such convivial and peaceful surroundings. Guilt started to replace my feelings of interest and intrigue, and now instead of peering inquisitively I averted my gaze for fear of being seen.

And that was another point that registered with me, in all our encounters over the last two weeks not once had they appeared perturbed or worried or in the slightest way concerned. They seemed to have regarded me as another stranger who they simply acknowledged in their well mannered way, with a courteous smile and a touch of the brim of a hat, and nothing more.

An impulse took over my actions and I left my table still carefully trying to look unobtrusive and went to the small counter that accommodated the till. I paid for my coffee and teacake and then asked the young girl assistant to take for the elderly couple's lunch. I told her they were relatives and I wanted to surprise them. I also asked her not to say who had paid, just that it had. And with a knowing smile she agreed. I left the little cafe with something of a sense of relief at my actions and without looking round I followed my route back to work.

The following day was a Wednesday and as was my habit I arrived at the bench a few minutes after one o clock and sat eating my pasty and sipping my cola and waited in anticipation.

The day before I had played my hand, for I had stepped beyond the casual observer going about his business innocently watching the world go by. However, just by chance each dinner time, sitting on the park bench had coincided with the appearance of the elderly couple. That is all it had been, a mere coincidence. No one could ever see any malice in that.

But in my mind I had now become a stalker. By following the elderly couple to the cafe, because I had observed that they had broken their habit of not going in, I had become a stalker and no amount of excuses could cure me of what I now thought I was guilty of. Not even the fact that I had slyly paid for their lunch to appease my conscience and the lingering doubts about my actions.

There was no one I could confide in to convince me otherwise. My mates would have died laughing and my colleagues at work would have found some way of using it against me, of that I was certain. And my parents, well they would never have understood and I would only have given my mother something else to worry about.

All through the previous night and this morning at work I had considered confronting the elderly couple to apologise and explain. But what could I have said without looking like a moron.

And so I waited.

Quarter past one came and went and so did the half hour, but there was no sign of the elderly couple. The hands on my watch crept ominously towards ten to two and I should be making my way back to work even though I felt I wanted to wait, no matter how long it would take. I waited till four minutes to two, and then I ran with all the speed of my football training, just arriving back at work at one minute past two.

All that afternoon I worked in a trance. It was delivery day, and I had a great deal to occupy me and I did it in a kind of automated, robotic manner. The kind of manner, that because you are familiar with a job or a routine, it allows your mind to be in a different place entirely. And for me, that was on the park bench waiting, just waiting for the elderly couple to make their way slowly towards me along the path.

However my thoughts and apprehensions remained with me all through that evening and into a restless night, and to be fully awake and dressed ready for work by six thirty. It had been a real shock for my mother to find me sitting at the kitchen table drinking tea. But being the ever tactful person that she was, she could only comment by saying.

"You're up early?"

I cruised through work that Thursday morning and went for my lunch break at one o clock only to be disappointed once more when the elderly couple failed to appear. This disappointment was now turning to deep concern, when the Friday, Saturday and Sunday came and went and again with their non appearance. Each day as it now passed left me agitated and fretful, yet with the contradictory question in my mind of, why should I let all this bother me so much and cause me to react like this. The whole situation was inwardly upsetting me by this point and I could not find a sensible answer to any of my brooding questions.

And so Monday came, and I started to feel a kind of resignation that my actions of paying for the elderly couples lunch the previous Tuesday had been found out and somehow unnerved them, and now they felt awkward about seeing me each day. Perhaps they were now timing their daily walks not to coincide with the times they had seen me. Perhaps they were taking a different path, because the park was large enough to be able to avoid me. Now, all I wanted to do was to apologise, and to seek some way of showing my good intentions.

And as each lunch time during that whole week and into the weekend came and went, the desire became more and more profound.

So another new week began, but that Monday lunchtime I had other things on my mind. The day before, my team had lost five goals to two, which meant that we would be the butt of all the jokes in all the local pubs. But at least my mind was able to dwell elsewhere than worrying about the elderly couple. And the welcome feeling of abstraction that it produced came with a relaxation in my thoughts at work and through that Monday evening and night.

It was with an easier mind than I had felt in quite a while, that I left work on the Tuesday lunchtime and strolled the short distance to the park. It was with such an air of nonchalance that I must admit that it never occurred to me that it was now two weeks to the day since the incident at the cafe and the last time I had seen the elderly couple. It could have been a hundred years in the past for all it was coming to mean to me.

That is the way things can be, time can slip by so quickly with other things demanding your attention, that when you try to recall something that was said or something that may have happened, then time brings in its ally of the distance between the present and the past. It is then that you find it difficult to immediately reassemble the details.

On this occasion I was a few minutes later than normal in reaching the park.

However, as I approached the bench where I had been conducting my lunch time vigil, I noticed a small solitary figure seated there.

Instantly my heart sank as I recognised the lilac, floral dress with the multicoloured, crocheted shawl over the shoulders and the small straw hat with a red sash and tiny bow covering the white hair. I stood for a few moments in disbelief trying to take in the full connotation of what I was seeing, which was being brought about by the obvious absence of the elderly gentleman.

Slowly I approached the bench as the elderly lady looked up and smiled. As I returned the smile I was unsure of what to do next, should I speak or just walk on by. I was so undecided, and it must have been apparent to the elderly lady. She must have sensed my indecision and tried to move, whereby her small handbag fell from her lap spilling some of the contents onto the grass.

Without thinking I was on my knees retrieving the scattered items, a hairbrush, a silver compact, a packet of tissues, a small bottle of tablets and some coins from her open purse. Then I caught sight of something gold by the leg of the bench and as I picked it up I jerked back as if I had been kicked. It was a ring, a gold wedding ring and too large to be worn by a woman. My heart genuinely sank as the full significance of that ring became apparent to me.

"Yes," said the elderly lady in a sweet, gentle tone. And then obviously reading the unspoken question in my expression she added. "It was my husband's,"

My face must have gone crimson as I stammered for the right words to say. In the end I could say nothing and I just knelt there unable to either speak or to move.

A soft hand came down and gently took mine between her fingers.

"He passed away nearly two weeks ago," she declared gazing a little absently into my eyes. "He hadn't been well for quite a while."

Still clasping my hand in hers she gently took the ring and replaced it with the bugle horn lapel badge I had noticed the elderly gentleman wearing on his jacket, that first day and each day after.

"He wanted you to have this," she said with a sadness that seemed to be catching up on her.

I looked down at the ancient bugle horn emblem, the traditional symbol of the Light Infantry Regiments, and all I could mutter in my stunned frame of mind was.

"Why?"

"For your kindness," she said. "And for paying for our lunch!"

So my little ruse had been foiled and I smiled to myself as she continued to hold my hand and to peer deeply into my eyes.

"And for being here on this bench those last few days of his life," she said in a voice that was now beginning to tremble with emotion.

She paused for a long moment before she continued in subdued tones.

"I don't want to know your name," she declared. "But I do want to explain."

She took a deep breath as if steeling herself for what she was about to say.

"That first day we saw you it was like seeing our son Richard. He would be about your age when he died. He was killed in Korea in April 1951 at a place called Imjin River. A great battle had been fought there and our son had been one of those who did not return. My husband and I went to the library and the kind girl there managed to find it on a map, such a small, insignificant place for our son to die. He was our only child you see, our treasure, and it was National Service that took him from us. And seeing you sitting here, was like seeing our son sitting here. For it was on this very bench that we last said goodbye to him on his last leave before he was sent to Korea."

Her eyes were beginning to fill with tears and all I could do was kneel before her, entranced by every word she was speaking. She took a tissue from her handbag, dabbed her nose and eyes and continued.

"My husband had been badly wounded at the battle for Caen in France in 1944, six days after D Day. After that we found it very hard to even think that we would see our own son die before us, before he had even started to live. He was only nineteen when he was killed. I'm afraid we never got over it. And that first day we saw you sitting here, on this bench, we thought you were our son, here waiting for us on this bench. So many times over the years when we have taken a walk through the park, we always managed a few minutes to sit here and remember you see!"

Once again, with her eyes filling with tears she straightened her back and dabbed the moisture away with her tissue.

"He had been a good son to us," she said in a soft, wistful tone. "Our only child…I..I..I am so sorry."

At last her resolve seemed to abandon her as her free hand came up to touch my face. And even with her eyes awash with so much sadness, they never faltered from their study of my own.

"But the resemblance is truly astonishing," she said with an essence of wonder creeping into her voice. "And that day we saw you sitting here, I can't tell you how we both felt. Then each day we came at the same time just to catch a glimpse of you sitting here. Just to remember."

Slowly with a deep heartfelt sigh she let her hand slip from my face and into her lap.

"Even to stopping by the Tudor Tea Rooms, as if we were watching the people eating when in fact we could quickly sneak a look back at you," she said with a smile appearing on her lips as she held my scrutinizing gaze with her own.

But then the moment was gone and she continued apologetically.

"Please forgive a silly old woman."

Suddenly, an overwhelming sense of deep empathy for this elderly lady, shuddered through me. It was a sensation that I had never experienced before. I could actually feel and hear my heart as it seemed to pound in my chest and head. I had an impulse to put my arms around her, to comfort her in some way, but I did not know how. I looked far into those sad eyes. Eyes that had seen the world change beyond recognition, even in her own lifetime. And now at the end of that lifetime she was left with nothing. Not even a son to show comfort in her remaining time.

"No please I assure you there's no apology necessary," I said feebly not knowing what else to say.

I felt she sensed my uneasiness and she gently released my hand leaving the bugle horn lapel badge in the palm.

"I am so sorry about your husband," I said. "He seemed like a true gentleman."

"That he was!" she replied with a sniff as she again dabbed her nose with a tissue. "That he was!"

Looking a little unstable, she slowly got to her feet.

I stood up quickly and was able to steady her. She reached onto the bench and picked up a walking stick that had been hidden behind her.

"I didn't need this when I was with him," she said with a rather pensive smile. "He was always my support."

She looked up and once more stared straight into my eyes. And with a smile that seemed to illuminate her whole face in one glowing beam, yet still trying desperately to disguise the hurt and the pain she must be feeling, she spoke in a voice that had now steadied but still rang so sweetly.

"You will never know how much pleasure and peace of mind our little encounters have given my husband and myself," she said. "For that I am so deeply grateful to you. And I sincerely thank you, for the both of us."

Again she stretched her free hand up to my cheek and softly stroked it.

"Have a good life," she said and slowly turning she walked away.

"Thank you!.......God bless you!" I said to the receding figure, but my words sounded so trite and insincere, though in all truth they were certainly not meant to.

My mind seemed to be in turmoil. I could still feel the gentle touch of her hand on my cheek. I could still hear the soft voice with the slight tremor in the words as she spoke of her dead son. And securely held in my clenched fist was the bugle horn lapel badge that the elderly gentleman had so proudly displayed on his coat. But then in a sharp moment of realisation it suddenly occurred to me that the lapel badge would, and most certainly should have gone to his son, if only he had lived.

For once I was totally lost for words, or at least at a loss for the right words to even try to describe how I truly felt.

Then in a sudden spark of insight, as if a curtain had been drawn from my eyes I also realised that instead of me stalking the elderly couple it had been them that had, in a way stalked me. In the elderly ladies own words they had seen me sitting on the bench and had thought they were seeing their long dead son and had come to this place at the same time just to catch a glimpse of him, in me. Even to stopping at the Little Tudor Tearooms on the pretext of watching the diners but in reality to merely catch another glimpse of their son. She had also sounded so certain when she had remarked at the astonishing resemblance they had seen between their son and myself.

A sudden, tangible shudder of humility embraced all my senses as my eyes continued to follow the slow progress of the elderly lady. Was it by chance that my lunch hour had coincided with the elderly couple's daily walk through the park. And what were the chances that I had resembled their dead son so closely to make them take the same route at the same time each day. And why should I have made such an effort to be here on this bench in the park anticipating them, and allow them to dominate all my thinking, every moment of every day since I had first seen them. What was the connection and by what possible finger of destiny had pointed to the direction by which our paths should cross.

Lost in my musings and with these questions probing my reasoning senses, I gazed absently at the frail frame of the elderly lady as she slowly negotiated the path to the ornate East Gate. And without once turning to look back she was gone, leaving me to stare down very thoughtfully indeed at the bugle horn lapel badge sitting in the palm of my hand.

As I am doing now, staring down at the bugle horn lapel badge sitting in the palm of my hand, that had been given to me over forty years ago.

And so, as I sit pondering on the flood of memories that have just been released to me and that I have just related to you, I also wonder at the fact that it has taken me to revisit this park and this bench to really appreciate exactly what this simple token means to me.

"Forty years," I whisper to myself. "Forty years...Almost a lifetime ago!"

So many times over those years since the elderly lady gave me the lapel badge I have taken it from my wallet, and it has always been that the memories have seemed jumbled and vague. But today, here on this bench in the park it has all been so vividly relived for me, and for that I am truly thankful.

And as I look out over the expanse of the park, it being such a vital feature of the town from whence I came, I think to myself where have all those years gone. So much has changed, and not all of it for the best.

Thank goodness for memories.

****

DUST ON THE SHELF

Angela Reed preferred to walk home from her work. It was that brief hiatus between the enjoyable demands of her job at the bank and the not so enjoyable demands on her when she crossed the threshold of her home. The distance took no more than twenty minutes and it led her out of the town centre, past the park with its rock pool feature and winding tree lined pathways, to the residential side where she had lived for all of her forty two years. For Angela was at that point in her life when womanhood is dangerously close to becoming spinsterhood. And when she was in one of her more pensive moods she would ask herself sharply....

"What have I done with my womanhood?"

She was passing the end of the park now, where it gave way to the Edwardian Terraces that lined either side of the road. It was an abrupt transition from the wonderfully random colours of the park to the austere formality of the brick and slate. She looked round as a bus trundled obediently on its route. The number 29, the bus that would have carried her three stops further on to drop her directly outside her house. But she would only ever use it to transport her home when the weather dictated, although she was always grateful to it first thing in a morning to whisk her away from that dark pile of misery, and to her other world at the bank.

However, at the bank she was considered by the other members of staff to be something of an oddity. Saying that, she was still liked and respected by everyone though socially she was at a distinct loss, for it had come to a point that any event like an after work drink or celebration of a birthday or Christmas, everyone knew Angela would always bow gracefully out. Equally, she was never offended when she was not invited or involved, though she would always be the first to give a present or contribute to a collection and be content to leaving it at that.

And it was not that she was unattractive. Although, there was a mature plainness about her appearance which belied her forty two years, and yet her youthful features merely seemed to contradict the modest conservatism about her dress sense. On the occasions that she had been the subject of her colleague's conversations it had been agreed that if someone had taken the time to help Angela then she could easily have found a man.

But Angela was aware of all this, and had somewhat reluctantly accepted her lot in life. Her work at the bank occupied her during the day, and the cloying domination of her widowed mother at breakfast, evenings and weekends.

Now as she walked on past the houses, each one so familiar after so many years, she could feel the tension as it built up inside her. It was a tension that was always absent during the day. At the bank she was that ever pleasant face behind the counter window. A quality recognised by management and colleagues alike. Even so, on the occasions of advancement being offered she had always declined saying she was happy dealing with the daily business of the customers.

This was always done with a genuine smile, a kindly word and an efficient manner that customers recognised. There were those who would even give up their turn in the queue just for the pleasure of a few minutes having their business dealt with in an uncomplicated passing of the time of day.

However, it was such a customer that quite by accident had contrived to step beyond that self imposed boundary that Angela had constructed as a defence line against the showing of any frailties in her public image.

His name was Nigel Ernest Smout.

At first, Angela had estimated his age at around forty five, though she attempted to do this with many of her customers. It formed part of a discrete character reading that at least made the brief encounters interesting. The innocuous conclusions that she would come to always remained firmly inside her head, for she would never think of gossiping. Her thoughts were always her own, and she made sure they remained so.

All she had seen in Nigel Smout was another customer, who was tall, slender built with thinning hair and a rather austere manner, but with a firm brightness of the eyes behind his brown rimmed glasses. And like so many he would give up his turn in the queue so as to have his few minutes.

He had told her that he worked at a solicitor's in the town as an accounts clerk, and that it was only when his employers had changed banks that he had started to come into Angela's branch.

On one occasion he had volunteered the fact that since his parents had died he had rented a small flat above a grocers shop on the edge of town, and which seemed to suit his situation. But it was these exchanges with Angela that were just like so many others. For in fact she could recall so many details from so many of the customers, all merely conversation and all being recounted innocently through the window of her counter.

That was until the day Nigel Smout had chosen to stroll through the park after a particularly busy morning, just to clear his head.

The Municipal Park was a modest affair by any standards. In fact one of Angela's colleagues had referred to it as being no more than a pedestrian lay by. Though in reality, it had an intimacy of pathways between numerous ornamental, floral features of rhododendrons and hibiscus, flowering bushes and large shady trees in a generous four acres.

Central to the park was a small, ornate rock pool and bushy island, were the collection of breeding ducks and mallards could nest. This area had a path that ran round its perimeter with its original protective Victorian fence still in place, low enough to allow the inhabitants of the rock pools to be fed, and just high enough to discourage being climbed over. And throughout the park numerous benches were strategically situated to accommodate those who would sit and rest and be thankful for the peace the park could offer.

All in all, it was a place of sanctuary for the stroller, the sitter, the morning jogger, the pushchair pusher or the ponderer on life in general.

Nigel had come across Angela eating her lunch and reading her Peoples Friend, sitting at her favourite spot where she had a good view of the water fowl and their antics. It was a place her father would bring her to as a child, and she now found it offered her a little respite from the two worlds she seemed to exist in. After an embarrassingly formal greeting, Angela and Nigel had exchanged pleasantries, followed by a stilted conversation about the weather and the attractiveness of the surroundings before wishing each other a rather regretful "Good Afternoon."

But after that brief encounter Nigel had contrived to take his lunch hour in the park at the same time in the hope that they coincided.

And so they had.

Soon it was clear that they both enjoyed the diversion that each provided, so that they began to arrange their lunch times together. However, it was also very clear that the relationship that was blossoming was borne more out of a need for companionship, rather than for any other kind of attraction. It was merely a unity of two lonely, kindred spirits that seemed to come to life in each other's company.

Those first meetings were casual affairs, always in the park, always on the same bench, always between 12 and 1 pm and never lasting more than 40 minutes. They would sit and chat innocently about everything and yet nothing in particular, sometimes just enjoying the warm silences that crept in as they munched their sandwiches. A harmless and wholesome meeting of two people enjoying the respite offered to them by a few minutes in each other's company, in what they both agreed were delightful surroundings.

The spring had matured into a warm balmy summer and most lunch times saw the couple in what could only be described as convivial conversation. At a few minutes to one they would both stand, bid each other a good afternoon and return to their places of employment. That little bit richer by the encounter. But as the summer moved inexorably towards the autumn it was becoming very apparent to both that the little meetings were in fact developing far more significance than either knew why, or for what. Both it seemed had a very well defined line that neither sought to cross, and which excluded any expression or show of any depth of feeling, or emotion.

Even so, when on the odd occasion that a meeting could not be kept by either for reasons of weather or work, then unaccustomed strange thoughts and feelings would seem to bother them, a slight emptiness, regret or even a sense of remorse. In fact, for Angela, the weekends began to drag with a wistfulness for Monday lunch time to arrive. But when she had tried to analyse this phenomenon she had been unable to actually identify a reason. She had merely wondered if it was the same for Nigel.

Then just today, Friday, Nigel had ironically remarked to Angela as they had parted from their lunch time sojourn that.......

"Monday always seems such a long time away."

"Yes," Angela had coyly agreed.

A brief moment of anticipated silence had dwelt between them before Angela had spoken again.

"Perhaps!...Perhaps!," she had added trying to summon up the courage to utter the sentence she had been mulling over for so many weeks.

"Perhaps?....Perhaps what Angela?" Nigel had enquired.

"Perhaps you might like to come to my house for tea on Sunday?" Angela had blurted out.

She had not even considered the consequences of such a brash invitation. But in an instant, regret had been dashed aside and in her bravado she had given such a welcoming smile that had suddenly quelled any doubts.

"Well...yes," Nigel had stammered. "That...would be very nice."

Quickly Jessica had scribbled her address on to a piece of paper found in Nigel's pocket, and 3 o clock had been agreed before they had each gone their separate ways.

Angela had now turned out of Stapleton Road and into Laburnum Avenue with its 30s style semis set back behind lines of hedges and trees to shield them away from curious gazes. Her pace now began to slow decidedly as she approached Rose Cottage. A name totally inappropriate since no roses had grown in or around that house since her father had died nearly twenty five years previously. Angela did a little to the gardens back and front, but not inheriting her father's naturally green fingers she was somewhat hampered. The fact was, she would only find things to do outside when it became too traumatic to endure her mother's continual bickering or biting remarks.

Ever since her beloved father had died her mother had purposely become a chair bound critic of everything in general. Angela was the breadwinner and household skivvy all rolled into one. She was expected to run the house, cook the meals, clean, polish, and even put her own mother to bed at exactly 9pm every night. And then to be on call through the dark hours for any whim that may take her mother's fancy.

All this in the full knowledge that no medical condition or disability affected her mother, merely the constant need to be cosseted, fed, bathed and patiently endured in every passing impulse that were designed to control and manipulate her daughter. This was always accompanied by an incessant barrage of snide comments and derisory remarks aimed totally to maintain the upper hand and dissolve any show of self confidence that her daughter might display.

In fact the rot for Angela had been set in place at the moment of her birth. She had always been fully aware of her mother's disappointment at being presented with a daughter, and not a son. This had been made abundantly clear to Angela in the countless bitter taunts she had been forced to endure from her mother's mouth.

Though now it seemed to Angela that her mother had only ever existed with the sole purpose in mind of providing a ceaseless torrent of sneering, spiteful, antagonistic actions and observations which were all contrived to eat and devour her daughter's inner person.

However, the inner person, albeit severely subdued and bruised over her forty two years, had survived, purely through Angela's own determined, silent defiance. And yet, that inner person had still remained a stranger to Angela, thwarting any attempts to be known or understood. As a consequence she was now endowed with an innate innocence of worldly knowledge and experience, which all added to the confusions in Angela's mind.

Even before his daughter had been born, Angela's father had been subjected to his wife's controlling whip of a tongue and had taken it on himself to try to constantly appease his devil kept situation by fawning to his wife's every need and fretting over every vagary of her tempestuous nature. It had forced him into the position of housekeeper and provider with absolutely no input from his wife. The result was she had become the domineering force of every moment, of every day for Angela's father. And with all of this he had also had to work hard at his job in insurance, often trying to keep up with the demands by bringing work home, and toiling at it well after his wife had gone to bed.

Many times Angela had sat by his side at the dining room table with her jigsaw puzzle or colouring book while he had toiled well into the small hours. It was this bond between them that had strengthened over the years. And all the time Angela's mother had developed her wanton selfishness whilst decrying the fact that she had never been given the mothers right to cradle a son, and constantly accepting her father's slavish ministrations without a single word of gratitude.

As far back as Angela could remember, she had also been subjected to the position of unpaid lackey, for she possessed no childhood memories of games, or playing with friends. Her father had, out of necessity had to arrange to take Jessica to school early because he could not be late for work. And then as soon as school was over Angela had to walk home with a kindly neighbour who had volunteered, knowing her father's situation. Then Angela was expected to prepare a meal for her mother whilst cleaning and all the other household chores, and all this from a very early age.

These were her only memories, bitter memories that were all Angela now had to dwell on.

Then at the age of seventeen her beloved father had suffered a stroke. It had taken him three days to die, and throughout that time all her mother could do was to bemoan the fact of what would become of her without a husband, or a son to look after her in her declining years.

Many times since then, in moments of deep soul searching Angela would remember the words her father had often said to her when out of his wife's hearing.

"Angela...my angel. You know that I love you my daughter. From the moment I first held you I have loved you. No matter what your mother says I have always...always been grateful to God for giving you to me."

Angela had sobbed so painfully into her father's hands that even now, as she stood before the gate to her house she was able to feel a stinging blurriness filter into her eyes to hamper her vision. It was a strange sensation, for she very rarely cried. In fact she had always endeavoured to curb any show of emotion for fear of it being misinterpreted as a decided weakness, especially in her mother eyes. So it bewildered her to accept that conversely, she felt exhilarated just thinking of the wild invitation she had made to Nigel.

But then a steadying sensation swept over her as she recalled her father's last words. He had managed to summon up the strength to take her hand in that so familiar grip of his and to whisper.

"I know you have never agreed to the way your mother has treated us, but that is the way she is, and I do love your mother, if only for giving you to me. Now, I cannot look after her anymore. Angela, please promise to do this. Promise me... Angela!"

And so the burden of her father's life had been passed on to his daughter. Between her tears she had made her promise, never ever realising the consequences on her own life. A few short hours later her father, her one constant in a world that had never begun to open up for her, and from that moment never would, had passed quietly away.

From that moment her life had become totally and irrevocably constricted like a prisoner who was never again able to stretch or to express herself, and her memories were so tainted that she could not remember a time when it had been any different. Her existence, for that is how she viewed it, rested firmly within the two worlds of the light provided at the bank and the darkness within Rose Cottage, and each being such a dominant feature of all her wakeful hours. And even through the night time hours Angela had also been subservient to her mother's nocturnal whims and demands and had accepted this in her well practiced, phlegmatic manner.

However, recently she had also begun to be subjected to her own prolonged and troubled sleepless nights. To the point of quietly sneaking into the kitchen to sit until daylight, drinking her hot chocolate whilst pursuing her lonely mission to try and unravel the strange contradictions of her disturbing, predatory feelings. In her innocence she had attributed it to her passage into spinsterhood, a vast step into the unknown that she was so desperately trying to come to terms with. She had thought about Nigel, and had searchingly asked herself if he could be the answer.

But even there a cloud of doubts had entered into the equation. What was the real reason for moving their relationship forward by the invitation to come to Sunday afternoon tea and to actually place what little remained of stability in her home life at such a risk. In the whole of her forty two years she had never even had the opportunity of offering an invitation such as this. She had always been so aware of what her mother's reaction would be.

However, now as she stood with her hand on the latch of the gate that opened onto the short path that led to the front door of her house, she gave a shudder as she realised that she must have been standing there for many minutes. What was it she was allowing herself to be drawn into, she wondered.

She felt the cold hand of apprehension tighten on her shoulder as she flicked the latch and pushed the gate open while dipping into her handbag for her key. It took three attempts of her trembling hand to fit the key into the Yale lock and finally to turn it, and no sooner had she stepped over the threshold before a terse voice had spat out.

"Where have you been? Its five past six, you're ten minutes late. You know that means my tea will be late as well!"

Angela did not answer. She knew better than to provoke an argument this early in the evening by offering an excuse. Instead she replied with.

"Hello mother. I'll get it now."

Throwing her coat and bag onto the hall table she went straight into the kitchen and busied herself while giving unspoken thanks to Mrs Wilson. She was the daily help who Angela paid to come in for two hours every weekday to give her mother the lunch that Angela had prepared before leaving for work, and to make the beds and generally tidy up. And if time allowed she would also prepare the salad for her mother's tea.

Now Angela mouthed another thank you to the kindly Mrs Wilson as she lifted the plate of salad from the fridge and peeled back the clingfilm covering. Even the tomato soup was in the pan ready to warm up.

Within minutes she was placing the tray on the side table next to her mother, amidst its debris of newspapers and periodicals, library books, jug and glass of orange squash, spectacles, tablets and medicines, sweet wrappers and more.

Angela stood back for a moment and stared down at her mother as she fidgeted herself into a more comfortable position. The grey curls, the solid heavy brow over the pebble like eyes to the streamlined nose over the slash of mean lips. All encrusted in a maze of sallow lines, with every aspect of the old woman's countenance just oozing bitterness and resentment.

"Get me my tissues, and put the radio on!" her mother demanded as she picked up the heavy poker and agitatedly thrust it into the already glowing coals.

Summer or winter and the fire would be burning, producing an even more oppressive atmosphere that Angela could only tolerate in short spells.

Angela moved silently to obey, lifting the lid of the radiogram and switching on the radio to the inevitable classical station. It was always tuned to the classical station, and it was the sweet sounds of the Four Seasons that endeavoured in a vain attempt to lighten the sombre, heaviness of the room.

Without another word being spoken Angela placed the box of tissues onto the side table before escaping back into the kitchen. Now she could waste an hour or so by getting her own meal and then cleaning and washing up.

Later, as she stood over the sink and washed the gravy from her plate, she once again found herself pondering wistfully on the twisting thoughts that had been plaguing her mind so much over the last few months. Thoughts that attempted to feed her imagination and to lift her from the confines of her prison like existence. But every time she seemed to always be thwarted from ever conjuring up a realistic theory on how to achieve a release.

For she felt bound, not just by the promise she had made to her father, but by a total lack of maturity in dealing with the wider world. She could not see beyond the four walls of the existence that had been imposed on her. Her thoughts twisted and turned in her mind as she sought out a solution, but inevitably all they ever seemed to do was confirm she should solely concern herself to accepting the continuance of her situation. But she also realised deep down that this could not go on, that there had to be an end to it, but how.

The clock showed the time to be 7.49 as the next order came ringing through the closed kitchen door.

"I want my cocoa! Angela! Can you hear me skulking in there. What are you doing?"

"Nothing mother, just clearing up. I'll make your cocoa now," Jessica calmly replied.

"Just like your father, he was useless as well, always skulking somewhere or other, never of any use!"

The grumbling tones were deliberately provocative in their manner and content. But Angela once again did not rise to the bait as she had learnt to do over so many years of the same tactic. She simply poured the already made cocoa into her mother's coronation cup and saucer, and pushing the kitchen door open she delivered it.

Now was the time, she thought. Now was the time to tell her mother of the invitation for Nigel to come to tea on Sunday. She placed the steaming cocoa onto the table and picked up the tray of used tea things. She walked towards the kitchen and taking a deep breath she turned, courageously controlling the shaking crockery on the tray.

"I have a man friend coming here on Sunday for tea," she stammered.

The cup of cocoa was half way to her mother's lips. It hovered there in mid-air, and for the first time that evening she slowly turned her head to look directly at her daughter. Seconds passed as she digested this seemingly ultra profound statement.

"What did you say!" she snarled. "A man...coming here! A man...A friend! What kind of a man would be a friend to the likes of you! The wrong kind of man!...I tell you now!" she said hissing and spitting the words threateningly as a snake ejects its venom. "No man will cross the threshold of this house......You!.....You slut!"

Every ounce of Angela's restraint came cascading to her aide as she reeled from this ominous, if typical outburst. An outburst she had expected and planned for, but when it was actually fired in her direction with all the bitter poison that lay curdling within that evil breast, it still came as a shock. But Angela stood firm and tried to equal the glare from her mother. But in this she failed miserably, though when she spoke her voice did not falter.

"I said.... I have a man friend coming here on Sunday for tea," Angela announced in firm but direct tones as she moved forward gaining strength from the words she had just uttered. "A man I have met nearly every lunch time for the past five months. A man I have come to be fond of."

This statement surprised her, even though she could not commit herself to any deeper feeling.

"And I am telling you now mother," she said in an uncharacteristic show of defiance as she bent low into her mother's face. "That this will not be the only time he will be coming here because I intend to see more of him. And if you don't like it mother you don't have to see him........You can stay in your room."

The suddenness of her mother's reaction surprised even Angela as the cup, full of cocoa and followed by the saucer went crashing against the opposite wall in a spray of the brown fluid.

"You hussy!..You slut!..Ohhh!" she wailed. "If only I had a son to protect me instead of this witch who only seeks to torment me!"

The words were delivered in such a theatrical flurry, yet so well rehearsed over the years and totally intended to merely intimidate.

"I tell you now Angela," she said pursuing her assault with a pointed finger thrashing like some imaginary whip. "If that man comes here then you will go! You can get out! I will not have you living under my roof!"

It was such an empty threat simply because it contained so little self belief in its contents. Threats delivered in the heat of emotion seldom have real substance, and as soon as the words had left the lips of Angela's mother she had felt a regret at speaking them. Simply because she knew she had contrived, through her own selfishness to be totally reliant on Angela. A selfishness she had developed through the weaknesses in the fibre of her late husband and then later to be nurtured in the refined sense of duty of her daughter. The daughter who now stood before her devoid of the reactions she would normally have anticipated. In fact, there was no reaction at all, just an out of character, condescending smile and a slow, contemptuous shaking of the head.

Angela stepped back as she continued to look down at her mother, considering the profound meanings that lay within this latest, unguarded outburst. She smiled again, and the smile developed into laughter. For perhaps the only time since her father had died Angela laughed and she continued to laugh until the laughter bordered on the hysterical, for she had momentarily glimpsed into her future.

Like a caged animal seeing a gap in the fence of their confinement, just waiting for the time to escape. She had seen the one flaw that had been there all these years, the one chink in the fabric of her mother's armour. In that one sentence she knew the way to go. She stood back catching her breath as her mother, no more in total control, scowled with all the vile toxin in her expression that she could muster.

"That's it mother!" Angela stammered in triumph. "That's it....All these years I've been ground down under your heel so much I've never been able to see the light. But it's been there all the time. What a fool

I've been. You needing me so much because all you wanted was an extension of my father. He admitted to me that his love was blind and he had buckled under your controlling ways."

"How dare you speak to me like that! Get to your room. And!.. And!.. Just think of how you have hurt me...you're mother! Just think of how you are pushing me closer to my grave," she whimpered, her voice muffled by the tissues dabbed feverishly at her tearless eyes.

"It's like a curtain opening," Angela continued in a much calmer wistful voice.

For in that one bile ridden last statement from her mother, the full realisation that had been eluding her for all these years, had in that one moment of glaring truth allowed Angela to assume the controlling factor.

"But the one difference is though mother," she said, now pursuing her attack with just a hint of menace. "Is that my father loved you. You knew that, and you thrived on it. My father would, and did die for you. His last breath was all about you. But thankfully that will not be for me mother. Where my father loved you, it is only duty to his memory that has kept me within these walls."

She moved towards the kitchen door and turned.

"So....on Sunday afternoon" Angela said in soft contrived tones. "Nigel...for that's his name, is coming here for tea. You can meet him or not. I don't care which. But mother things are to change. I've realised that the hold you had over father was that he loved you. I certainly don't have that failing. You can get yourself to bed. I know you are more than capable of looking after yourself when Mrs Wilson or I'm not about. But until this moment I've been too blind and too stupid to see it, or even to admit it."

Angela glanced round the room but this time with fresh un-blinkered eyes and breathed deeply with a sense of relief. It would be later that the regrets would infiltrate into her conscience. When she would think that she had betrayed her father's last wishes.

"Good night mother," she said in a tone of icy syllables as she closed the kitchen door behind her.

****

Saturday passed in total silence. Not a word was uttered by either Angela, or her mother. Apart from Angela's weekly visit to the local

Co-op, the whole day was uneventful with Angela's mother sitting stony faced eating the meals she had placed in front of her with a few chosen grumbles, or reading her Catherine Cookson or listening to the classical station on the radio. All of which was interspersed by the angry, strident poking of the fire.

It was this particular action that irritated Angela more than anything, the poking of the fire. Every time she entered the room her mother would stop what she was doing, eating, drinking, reading or even napping and pick up the heavy poker to aggressively vent her turbulent wrath and frustrations within the flaming coals. In Angela's mind, she felt that her mother was merely using the poker on the coals as she would poke and goad her daughter in that insidious, callous way that she constantly employed with her words and actions.

But even this, Angela was now able to assign with a little effort to its correct place, as being trifling and petty. For apart from the dutiful attendance on her mother, Angela actually enjoyed herself imposed seclusion while she pottered about doing the necessary chores like the washing, the ironing, cutting the small front lawn and all the accumulated tasks from the week before.

This also included cleaning up the consequences of the angrily discarded drinking chocolate from the night before. However, even in this menial task there was a mixture of satisfaction and annoyance for Angela. For while she felt that her guided ultimatums had been able to stab beneath her mother's inflexible shield of perpetual contempt for her daughter, she also felt aggrieved at succumbing to her mother's devious control by actually doing what was expected. And that was to continually adopt the servile position of having to clean up her mother's mess.

Even so she was still able to shrug this off completely as she went about her day, quietly questioning the lightness in her step, the ease in her mind, the smile that for once illuminated her face, but which brought a deep scowl of disdain from her mother each time their glances happened to coincide.

Angela knew she was looking forward to three o clock the next day, but she also knew that it was not the whole reason for this change, because for once, the world seemed like a different place to be in. It felt light and airy, a joy to be a part of and not that pit of drudgery and despair that had seemed to be her lot in life. And it all seemed to have come from that brief confrontation the night before. There had been arguments in the past, too many and too often, but last night had been different. With each syllable she had spoken in those quiet purposeful tones she had felt the shackles that bound her slowly loosen and an overwhelming sense of freedom descending upon her.

Now as this day of enlightenment drew to a close, and as Angela lay in her lonely bed staring at the moon light that flooded her room she breathed a sigh that bordered as near as possible to contentment. And for once her eye lids dropped and Angela succumbed to a dreamless sleep.

So, Sunday came and at exactly three o clock a tentative knocking was heard on the front door. Angela hesitated for a moment in something of disbelief, was this actually happening, was she actually going to open the door to someone she had invited to her home. Her smile broadened noticeably as her mind teased with the thought.....

"There's a first time for everything."

The smile was still in place as she opened the door to an equally smiling Nigel and she ushered him through into the small dark hallway.

And still smiling, she pushed open the door into the living room, and for once in her reserved, austere existence she felt an intense sense of embarrassment at what she would be presenting to someone who basically was still a stranger.

Even so it was only a momentary realisation as she looked on the room as if she was entering it for the first time in her life. The furnishings, the dowdy wall paper and carpet, to the pictures, the ornaments and even the large mahogany radiogram and black bakelite telephone that all seemed to resemble an image from the Picture Post and other 1940s wartime magazines of her mothers, than a living room from the late 1990s.

And then there was the constant fire in the fireplace illuminating her mother in her usual armchair which she had more or less occupied for most of her married life. In fact Angela could not remember a time when her mother had not occupied that chair during daylight hours. Even now the fire glowed brightly as her mother leant forward to fervently poke it into submission.

Angela tentatively guided Nigel towards the glowering countenance of her mother, as she thought to herself how fortunate it had been that she had alluded to her mother's bizarre ways during their lunchtime conversations in the park. So at least Nigel was forewarned as to what might await him. It was hard for Angela to try and read anything into her friend's face and manner as they stood side by side waiting for some reaction from her mother. When it came she was even more taken aback.

For Angela's mother slowly replaced the poker back against the fire place, raised herself from her chair, exchanged her well honed scowl to something of a long forgotten smile and offered an outstretched hand, beckoning to be shaken by Nigel as Angela nervously made the introductions.

"Nigel this is my mother…Mother this is my friend Nigel…Nigel Smout"

"I'm pleased to meet you Mrs Reed," Nigel said, taking the proffered hand and politely dropping his head in a slight bow.

There seemed to be a tangible buzzing in the tension being created and Angela instantly thought the fault lay with her, simply because of the suppressed anticipation she had felt since the invitation to tea had been given. But this feeling was only momentary before her mother spoke.

"Oh please Nigel…… call me Margaret….. Now Angela dear, you go and make the tea while Nigel and I get to know each other better," she said with something of a guarded sneer that only Angela would have recognised.

Taken completely aback, Angela stood for a moment utterly confused by her mother's totally contradictory attitude before the old automaton mode clicked in and she obediently retired into the kitchen. There she took her time as she made the tea. All the while she was aware of the animated conversation that emanated from the living room as she puzzled over the mother she had left chatting to Nigel. This was not the mother she had come to know and fervently detest for over forty two years.

Now a flare had been fired in Angela's brain. A warning flare! Bright, and demanding her attention, but there was such an innocence about her that she could only surmise what the warning flare was trying to tell her.

She swiftly replaced her thoughtful frown with a smile and re-entered the living room with the tea things and the plate of cakes she had bought especially. Cakes that normally would have been forbidden in this house, but which Angela had purchased as another point to her sense of rebellion. But she could not dismiss the feeling that this rebellion was now tending to flounder badly.

"Oh...my favourite.... éclairs!," her mother announced.

And so the conversation dwelt on the trivia as the tea was drank and the plate of cakes disappeared and all the time Angela desperately tried to analyse this phenomenon. She was not practiced in the art of casual conversation, so it was that the interaction lodged firmly with Nigel and her mother, though surprisingly her mother seemed to be very adept in the art form.

Angela sat looking from one to the other, occasionally offering a view or a specific point, but more often being ignored as merely a spectator. It was so obvious to her that her mother was desperately attempting to ingratiate herself on Angela's guest. And it was equally obvious that this contrived demeanour was totally lost on Nigel who seemed to be warming to the old woman.

Now conflicting emotions started to gather in Angela's mind amidst suspicions as to her mother's motives, because this was quite simply out of character. Where was this all leading to? Had she made a mistake in bringing Nigel here? What would be the questions he would inevitably ask considering the rather dark picture she had already painted of her mother. And it was while she was lost in these thoughts that her mother's voice cut through.

"Angela!....Nigel is speaking to you!"

The words were spoken with just a hint of the underlying bile that was only apparent to Angela.

"Oh... I'm sorry!" she said apologetically.

"I was just saying it's nearly five, so I had best be going," Nigel said placing his cup and saucer onto the tray.

"Well it's been very nice meeting you Mrs Reed," he added with a confident smile creasing his face.

"Margaret.. please!" came the cloying, overly polite correction.

"Yes, of course..Margaret!" he declared raising himself out of his chair.

And as Angela stood to escort Nigel to the door, so did her mother, once again with her hand outstretched to be shaken.

"And you must come again Nigel....and soon!" she insisted, gripping his hand in both of hers and smiling.

"Yes I will. Thank you," he stuttered with a quick glance at Angela.

So, as Nigel closed the gate and waved his goodbyes and walked off down Laburnum Avenue, Angela and her mother watched from the doorway, so oddly side by side. They remained there for a long moment, until their visitor was out of sight. Then Angela turned to her mother who stared back with that so smugly, knowing expression that Angela had come to despise so much.

"I don't know what your game is mother," she said gritting her teeth, and with her face just inches from her mother's. "But even Nigel will get to see exactly what you are really like!"

The insidious look of her mother's did not alter as Angela watched her turn and shuffle back to her chair, where she picked up the inevitable poker to continue her habitual poking of the fire once again. Angela stood in the doorway seething over the events of the last few hours. She could hardly remember her mother ever acting like that before and her mind changed from anger to very serious thought.

Closing the front door she stood and watched her mother from the hallway as she used the poker to meticulously turn each piece of coal over, one after the other. And as each coal was turned it produced a brief flurry of sparks that crackled like distant pistol shots.

Angela's mind hummed with unanswered questions as she continued to watch the huddled figure in the glow from the fire, resembling some odious sorceress at work on her spells. What was her mother thinking? Angela knew quite well that her mother was aware that she was being observed, and she also knew quite well that her mother would be revelling in that knowledge.

This behaviour was all so strange, and at the same time so very typical. Angela's mind stretched back to the last time they had stood together in that front doorway. It had been to say goodbye to the few colleagues of her father who had respected him enough to attend his funeral. And even then it had been necessary for Angela to make the point to her mother that it was only courteous to the gathered mourners for them to look like a united family for once, if only for her father and for the sake of appearances.

It also reminded Angela that there had been no relatives from either side of the family who had felt obliged enough to have attended. This deepened her feelings of isolation and that saddened her even more. Because of her mother's intractable and dominant nature Angela had never known any of her uncles, aunties or cousins, or even had the means to be able to contact any of them. She was the only child of a mother who had never wanted a daughter, who had never shown the merest inkling of maternal love, just deep rooted resentment and contempt.

For Angela firmly believed her mother to be totally devoid of any human, let alone normal, maternal emotions and feelings, and her thoughts and resentments began to stretch back to the day after her father's funeral.

She had returned home from work at the bank to discover all material reference to her father had been removed and disposed of, his photographs, clothes, books, and even his prized record collection. Everything had gone without trace or mention. It was as if he had never existed, or even lived at Rose Cottage.

But now Angela gave a little smile to herself as she thought about the snapshot of her father with his six year old daughter feeding the ducks in the park, a snapshot that she had secreted in the bottom of her wardrobe.

Slowly she closed the door of the living room and shut out the disturbing image of her mother, obviously in deep thought on some new connivance, and sought the sanctuary of her room.

Later as she stood before her mirror in her long, virgin white, flannelette nightdress she wondered what she had been born for. What was the purpose of existing like this, for it to continue unabated to whatever final conclusion awaited her. And what had her father gained from his servile existence at the hands of a wife with such evil, manipulating designs.

And was the image that now stood before her in the long mirror, the image of Angela Louise Reed in the neatly laundered night attire, merely the image of herself in her funereal shroud, already dead and just waiting to be laid into her coffin. She stared hard and long at the image and a deep, penetrating sadness seemed to engulf her in complete contrast to the inner elation she had felt the night before when contemplating her invitation to Nigel for Sunday tea.

She turned away to her virgin's bed, to spend yet again another lonely night of sleepless sleep.

****

When change occurs it can be a subtle, gradual transformation, and in Angela's case, to all her colleagues and customers the changes at first were almost imperceptible. But not for Angela's mother, every subtle amendment to her daughter's appearance and behaviour were observed, analysed and filed for further research and action.

For never before had Angela used make-up, but now there was an increasing suspicion of lipstick and blusher. Never before had she taken the advice of the fashion pages with regards to her wardrobe, but the frumpiness was gradually being discarded. Even Angela's day to day contact with her mother was now being discharged with even more indifference to the old woman's moods and eccentricities.

But now, although nothing extravagant these indulgences were certainly a deviation from what was expected of the rather dowdy Angela. There was an air of self confidence and an outgoing approach that was rewarded by a growing acceptance by all those who she had contact with. And she was particularly pleased by the effect her self confidence and appearance was tending to have on the opposite sex. Nothing untoward or intrusive, but Angela came to notice the odd passing glance and smile.

And this included Nigel, who took quite a number of weeks and several Sunday teas before he had summoned up the nerve to approach the subject, stammering out the words on a late autumn lunch time in the park.

"You......you're different Angela!" he said.

"You've noticed!" she had replied dryly, as she continued to look away with a guarded smile. "I'm glad."

And the conversation had then continued to trundle down along its normal, mundane pathways.

Now, even though the old regime at Rose Cottage never faltered with her mother's grindingly demanding ways, the changes in Angela continued to become more and more apparent and not only in her outward appearance. A difference was now being felt in her mind as well, for it seemed to hum with this newly released freedom of thought. Out of sight of her mother her step had become lighter and there was something in her whole manner that tingled with expectancy.

Christmas came and went, but not as in the past with no recognition of the welcome frivolities of the festive season. Since her father had died it had become accepted for the inhabitants of Rose Cottage to never celebrate either Christmas or birthdays. Each would pass without a single reference being made.

And yet, this year Angela after a brief, out of character festive eve visit to the pub with her colleagues, had strode into the living room of Rose Cottage with a small, but highly illuminated artificial Christmas tree. This she had placed on a doily on the mahogany radiogram with great ceremony, accompanied by a fierce torrent of abuse from her mother.

But Angela had simply ignored the blustering, and with a jovial "Merry Christmas mother," had left the foaming woman to her own ranting misery.

However, as she leant against the closed kitchen door with her mother's almost deranged blusterings piercing every minuscule recess in her brain, she had simply tilted her head to the ceiling, and beating her temples with her fists, had whispered with so much pent up emotion......

"Merry Christmas father... Oh I do miss you....I do love you."

And for once, just once in a very, very long time she had allowed herself the luxury of spilling a well deserved tear of self pity.

Even so, the one blip in Angela's metamorphosis was her mother's almost pantomime dame performances on the occasions of Nigel's Sunday teas. There was such a comical aspect about her now, for she would completely contradict her normal cantankerous conduct and instead utilize overly polite conversation accompanied with such disarming grace, which did not go unnoticed on Nigel.

And it became a point of specific reference on numerous occasions during the lunch time chats. Whereby Nigel openly commented on the endearing and amiable nature of Angela's mother, which was in complete and annoying conflict to Angela's own bitter viewpoint. This resulted in brief but stilted silences from Angela as she fought to contain her boiling aggravation at Nigel's blind and absurdly erroneous observations.

Angela chose not to make any reply to his comments. She felt she did not want to get into any in-depth debate about her mother, and this came to trouble her more deeply as time went by. Not because it focused on her mother, but because it was now obvious to her of her inability to confide her innermost feelings and fears to Nigel. She had come to realise that everything about her relationship with him was simply placed firmly on the surface of each other's lives. Also that there was no physical attraction towards Nigel, in fact she had never been prone to any normal female instincts in that direction, and until now it had simply never seemed to concern her.

This new Angela was asking the questions she had always deprived herself of under the constant shadow of her mother. Questions that now delved deep into her inner self, but now answers were beginning to surface which only added to the confusion in her mind. And she was also recognising a definite reticence in Nigel to ever offer any real insight into himself as well, which meant she could only guess at what he really thought or even what he saw in her.

Time and time again she would walk back to work from their lunch times in the park realising she knew less and less about him, and that he probably felt the same way about her. After almost a year they were still just friends, just acquaintances. It was going nowhere and it was becoming abundantly clear to Angela, that it was all she wanted from the relationship, just friendship and nothing more. She would admit that she had a fondness for Nigel, but that was as far as it went. What she was becoming ever more aware of was the fact that she wanted more from life.

Thus, with the latter weeks of winter passing with the frequency of their meetings being dictated more and more often by the weather, and then with Spring tipping its hat to warmer days, it still came as quite a shock to Angela when Nigel announced that he would only be able to meet, weather permitting, on Tuesday and Thursday lunch times. Apparently, this had been caused by a change in the office routine.

In the quieter moments of her long nights alone, Angela would admit to herself that she was disappointed, but she would also say that she realised this decision only seemed to reflect her own cloying doubts on their relationship. Equally, she also considered that it might allow them time to re examine what they actually meant to each other.

However, the Sunday teas every second week remained, to the apparent pleasure of Angela's mother and to the growing annoyance of her daughter as a distinct pattern had now emerged. This had been set on the very first occasion, whereby Angela had become the waitress spectator to the animated dialogue between Nigel and her mother. And this never varied with Angela's mother in full, voluble form and Nigel almost entranced by the exchanges. With Angela fussing between the pair with the tea and cakes, and the odd interjections that were becoming less and less noticed within the conversation.

She had even tried to put an end to these tea parties, but in this one area she had lacked the required strength of conviction, and had failed.

Even so, this one bad apple in her barrel of ripening ambitions would inevitably need to be plucked out and disposed of.

****

From the early weeks of the new year and into the summer something defining was happening to Angela. Her whole physical appearance altered, to the disquiet and dismay of the bank and customers, the astonishment of Nigel and the total apoplectic annoyance of Angela's mother. For the jaundiced old woman was now being given even more excuse to furnish her own particular brand of embittered comments about her daughter's flaunty attitude to her appearance. She had found new heights of sarcasm and ridicule at Angela's increasing use of stark makeup, but she had been beside herself with anger when, for the first time in her life Angela had taken to visiting the hairdressers, not just once, but on a weekly basis.

But when her daughter began to dress twenty years younger than her forty three years, the fury had escalated to fits of temper that were nothing less than demented seizures of anger from her mother. For now, lying beneath this outward display of her seething wrath, it was becoming abundantly clear to Angela's mother that the days of her control and manipulation over her daughter were now well and truly numbered.

Angela had also become the topic of concerned, subliminal conversations for the bank staff and customers alike. To the point, that Mr Edwards the manager had found it necessary to have a 'quiet word,' and had asked Angela to 'tone it down a bit,' for she was becoming something of an embarrassment to the bank.

Mr Edwards had liked the methodical, reliable old Angela and had inwardly worried about the distinct changes that were happening to her. He realised he had been allowing her to go beyond the normal acceptance levels of behaviour and appearance that the bank rules demanded.

However, he now viewed her newly found familiar attitude towards the male customers very disconcerting, for it had been noticed that they did not hang back as they had done before so as to take advantage of those few precious minutes at her window. Now they chose to queue at other windows to avoid either some awkward innuendo or flirty glance.

But it all seemed that Angela was enjoying the notoriety which was so far removed from the Angela of even twelve months previous. She seemed to be revelling in the attention and problems her appearance and her attitude were causing, and this was epitomised in her time keeping as well. For even that was also becoming erratic and unacceptable.

There had been a villainous rebel stalking inside this once, mild mannered, respectable woman. But, like a disease it had eaten through the purity and fundamental integrity of a woman who had simply craved from something more from her life. And it was the innocence of the woman that had not been able to detect the destruction this inner insurgency had been imposing on her.

And so it was that this rebel took the final step and goaded Angela, after one sunny, Wednesday lunch time of window shopping, to simply decide she was not going back to the bank.

It was not an instant decision on her part, but a decision that had been fermenting in her disturbed reasoning for many months. Like a smouldering ember it had burnt its way into her rational thought patterns causing the irrational to surface in her persona. So instead of turning into the staff entrance of the bank, she blatantly walked past it to the bus stop and as carefree as a school girl truant, jumped onto the number 29 bus and within ten minutes she was standing outside Rose Cottage.

A fever pitch of thoughts and emotions seethed in Angela's head. There was forty three years of bitterness like a bubbling geyser just waiting to finally boil over. She was now ready to confront her mother once and for all, not only with all the hatred and latent passion that lay seething just waiting to be vented, but with a decision, an ultimatum that would define the rest of her life.

She had finally decided her mother was going into a home. Rose Cottage was going to be sold along with all the bleak and traumatic memories it contained, and then this reborn Angela was going to face the world afresh with her own flat. From there her life would begin again, to create new and meaningful memories by rediscovering her lost youth.

The answer to all those brooding questions that had confounded and confused, that had tormented and teased, now seemed so simply resolved. So much time had been wasted and she was blaming every second of that wasted time on her mother.

Now, almost a year to the very day that she had stood at this same gate summoning up all her inner strength and resolve before daring to enter with the declaration that Nigel was coming to tea, she paused and felt an excited tremor course down her spine. It could also be said that the excited tremor resembled the one from twelve months before, because it had signified a change in her life, a metamorphosis that was an irrevocable progression to a different Angela. Twelve months ago she had begun the move away from her mother's control, and today she was about to complete that process to its final conclusion.

Angela laid her hand on the latch of the gate and realised that she had been standing there for some minutes.

Gently she opened the latch, and equally gently she pushed the gate open and closed it behind her. In her mind she was visualising the reaction that her mother would give to what she was about to declare. Angela was not prepared to waste her life anymore on someone who, who had not an ounce of gratitude in her body, but outwardly voiced her utter distaste for her daughter.

Almost from the time of her father's death the regular visits of the doctor had only confirmed that there was nothing fundamentally wrong with her mother, apart from her aversion to any form of activity. In fact for years the doctor would casually state to Angela that as long as she was prepared to tirelessly wait on her mother, then her mother would simply take advantage of the situation. But now that was about to change.

Angela placed the key in the lock and quietly turned it, and standing in the hallway she braced herself to enter the living room. But as she was about to open the door, laughter emanated from the other side. She stood back in utter shock trying to piece together her jangling thoughts, for she had planned this moment so carefully that now she was completely stunned as she listened to the light hearted conversation and intermittent laughter. Her breast heaved with a pulsating anger at the realisation that she recognised not only her mother's voice, but the other participant.

And with this firmly fixed in her mind she pushed the living room door open and stood gazing in disbelief at the snug, intimate scene before her.

The room beat in an ominous silence as Angela moved steadfastly forward. Never before had she felt this deep sense of humiliation and anger, even though her mother had attempted to constantly undermine any essence of self esteem she may posses with her evil machinations. But now, as she glared at the cosy pair either side of the ever glowing fire, her head throbbed with a blinding rage.

Her mother at first looked shocked at Angela's unexpected entrance, but that was soon replaced by that so familiar hideous smirk. But it was Nigel's expression of a mixture of surprise and embarrassment, accompanied by a complete draining of colour from his cheeks that convinced Angela that the conversation had been all about her.

"Ah there you are!" Nigel mumbled. "Yes…Hello Angela…I..I," he said pushing himself stiffly to his feet.

But this action was interrupted by Angela's mother who leant forward and grabbed at his coat sleeve forcing him back into his chair.

"You're home early dear?" she said in a suppressed, patronising manner that Angela knew from past experience disguised a frothing anger deep inside her.

"So it would seem!" Angela stated glaring at the sickening intimacy of the scene. "And how long has this little arrangement been going on?"

"Surely you've no objection to Nigel visiting me Angela. Surely you don't begrudge your mother a little company. The days are so long!" her mother bleated as she picked up the heavy poker to prod at the glowing coals in the grate.

Angela felt the sweep of added warmth the action created and also the increase in the oppressive atmosphere in the room.

"Nigel. I'll ask you!" Angela said switching her attack as her controlled fury began to brim over menacingly. "Well! How long have these little heart to hearts been going on, these private little audiences with this God Almighty Bitch. And remember Nigel you told me that our lunch times would be forfeit because of your work..... Well!" she fired taking a step closer to the now cowering heap in the fireside chair.

"Well...it's...it's...Well it's only been a couple of times Angela!"

"Don't be intimidated by her Nigel," Angela's mother said interrupting the cringing Nigel. "The truth is, Nigel has been kind enough to keep me company twice a week for the past two months," she said waving the poker in the direction of her daughter as she tried to regain the momentum of the encounter. "And that arrangement is to continue without any interference from you my girl!" she snapped, gritting her teeth in an attempt to regain the dominant position. "I'm not having you dictating who I invite here to give me a little comfort. Someone to break up the long hours I have to tolerate on my own."

She spoke in a voice that petered away into an effected tremor.

"Don't give me all that, mother!" Angela said throwing her hands in the air in mock astonishment. "No one ever comes here because you've frightened everybody away with your cantankerous, nasty, evil ways."

"You see what she's like Nigel!" her mother said with a whimper in her voice, and a sneak look at the grovelling form in the opposite chair, hoping for a reaction. "I told you what she's like!"

"I....I don't think you should speak to your mother like that Angela," Nigel nervously squeaked as his voice rose to almost an octave above its normal pitch.

"You keep out of this. What on earth did I see in you! You're nothing but a spineless creep. You two deserve each other. Look at you," she said laughing uncontrollably. "The witch and her cavorting toadie!"

"I think I'd better go," Nigel stammered, raising himself from his chair. But again a hand stretched across and gripped his coat sleeve, and he sank back anticipating the next onslaught.

"No...you stay there!" Angela shouted. "I always felt there was something totally distasteful about you, and now I've had it confirmed. You come sneaking round here when I'm at work. When were you going to tell me about these snug little meetings Nigel. There's something rather sick about this little set-up of cups of tea, knee to knee round the cauldron, whipping up the intrigues."

She began to pace agitatedly.

"Yes," she continued. "I should've guessed as much from the instant I invited you here. Yes it's all here isn't it"

Angela ceased her pacing and stood hovering over the pair. Her mother stopped poking the fire, and sat glaring sheer hatred at her daughter while Nigel simply withered even further into his chair.

"Whispers," Angela continued. "Whispers and more whispers. I can hear them now."

She stood looking round for this statement surprised even her. But it seemed to answer so many questions in her mind.

"What are you blathering on about!" her mother hissed almost spitting each word out as if they were a poisoned dart aimed directly at her daughter. "You're not talking sense you pathetic creature."

Angela lunged forward and pushed her mother back into her chair as Nigel sank further into his, eyes bulging with the terror that he was now sensing.

"I'm talking about whispers behind my back," Angela shouted, staring deep into her mother's eyes. "Whispering behind my back, and more whispers! You would do anything to undermine me. Anything to blight any crumb of happiness I might have. You've always been the same mother."

Again she turned towards Nigel.

"My mother is not the woman you see before you now Nigel. She is an evil, domineering, old crone who has dictated every turn of my life. She ruined my father's life with her selfish ways that drove him to an early grave. Even now I suspect that it was the only way he could escape her."

She was now in full flow for at last she felt she wanted to disgorge herself of every bitter thought and memory.

"That woman!" she said thrusting a pointed finger like an unsheathed rapier in the direction of her mother. "That woman has never lifted a finger in this house as long as she had some idiot to slave after her. And there's nothing wrong with her Nigel. The Doctor can't find anything. He's told me that. Except that she is totally bone idle. It's laughable Nigel, laughable!"

She threw her head back and laughed in a wild hysterical flurry, then stood back looking from her mother, then back at Nigel and then back again at her mother.

Angela held each in a paralysing stare that absorbed all movement from the two objects of her mesmerising attention. So much was racing through her spiralling thoughts. Voices, unrecognisable were now becoming audible within her head. Strident, rumbling voices that sounded as if she was standing in a room of chattering people and only the sound, not the words could be defined.

And now images and sequences of events that she fought to understand and isolate into a time and a place. Dizzily they streamed behind her eyes as her piercing stare never faltered to control those before her. And as she stared, her eyes began to dance and bounce in their sockets losing focus and definition, gaining in erratic motion as if attached by elastic.

All this had now become a crucial and definitive moment for Angela as if it was confirmation to her that she was now adorned by a mantel of pure reasoning. That what was needed to be done was clear in her mind, and she would be the instrument of her own action, her own destiny. She stood throwing her head back, and from side to side as laughter erupted in hoarse, unrecognisable guffaws from deep within her breast.

"You're mad! Mad!" her mother barked in a fearful outburst. "Look at her Nigel she's mad!"

"Yes mother you are absolutely right, I am mad!" Angela screamed in a voice that was unrecognisable as belonging to her.

In an instant the laughter had ceased and Angela's words became soft and menacing in a quiet, very deliberate whisper.

"Mad for putting up with you for all these years. My whole life wasted.... Wasted!"

"You've never been a proper daughter to me," her mother said fighting back in her usual aggressive taunting manner. "Never!.... I wanted a son and look what I got, a painted Jezebel, an insolent slut of a daughter. You're father couldn't even get that right. All I ever wanted was a son. A son! You're father was like you. Useless...USELESS!" she shrieked.

"Don't you even dare to refer to my father like that, you evil bitch!" Angela screamed for she was now at a point of losing control completely. All her life long restraint was now in danger of escaping like some raging bull of retribution. "You sit there dictating my life, and cursing my father. God! How I wish it had been you that had died! That man was decent and hard working, and how he got landed with you I'll never know. But he did, and by God he paid for it."

"Get out you blasphemer!" came her mother's growling retort. "Get out of here. Get out! I will not have you in my sight, in my house one minute longer!"

"No it's you that's going mother. You!" Angela was now leaning over her mother so close that they could feel each other's angry breath. "YES! YES! YES!" she screamed. "That's what I came back to tell you. It's you that must go."

"Get away from me," her mother bellowed pushing Angela back with a renewed strength that contained a mixture of grating anger and fear. "Get away. Nigel is more of a son to me than you. He could be the son I never had. The son you're father deprived me of. He was never any use to anyone or anything. Just like you. Pathetic…. PATHETIC!. And you with your painted face and clothes that make you look what you are. A filthy tart! A whore, only fit for the gutter. Go back to the gutter you tramp..you...you!"

Her voice ebbed away as she finally caught sight of the growing expression on her daughters face. An expression she had never experienced before and which now sent an icy chill to run up and down her spine, gathering speed and intensity until her whole body began to tremble with cold fear. Nigel had sat totally frozen in his chair, witnessing in a silent aura of dread throughout each of the angry exchanges, but now he tried to sidle out of his chair, but the movement was too late.

Angela pushed between the two objects of her overpowering anger, and Nigel fell back into his chair as she snatched up the heavy poker that stood upright against the fireplace. The implement that had on so many occasions been used to taunt and to threaten, but which Angela had now chosen to administer the sentence her justice dictated.

"This is for my father!!!" she shouted

And with a low swinging arc of unbridled vengeance, the heavy poker struck with all the force Angela could muster at her mother's right temple. There was a brief look of fearful shock before the blow smashed into the side of the head with a sharp cracking sound. Blood spouted over the chairs antimacassar, and then in a red tide it flowed over the trembling shoulder and down the arm. And emanating from deep within the throat, there seemed to be a feint gurgling sound, but this grew less as the body sagged to one side and remained quite still.

Angela stood, devoid of any feelings, just looking at the motionless body before turning and facing Nigel.

He was in the process of frozen animation, half way out of his chair. His normally pale complexion had turned to a pure startled white of complete and utter terror.

For a few brief seconds neither moved, their eyes locked in a morbid fascination of what had happened and what each knew was to happen next. Nigel tried to plead for mercy with the pathetic expression that filtered into his face. But even as it did so he realised that Angela's face only seemed to display a ruthless loathing of him.

"She wanted a son!" Angela said in an almost childlike voice as she stared at the immobile, petrified Nigel. "But a brother," she added. "I never wanted a brother. No... Never!...I never wanted a brother!"

And she swung the bloodied poker at Nigel's head, but he managed to dodge it and the blow bounced off the back of the chair. This allowed Nigel to slip under Angela's arm as he made a dash for the door. But Angela was too quick, and lashed down on the back of his thinning pate, even as his hand secured around the door's handle. The blow sent him careering, with a deep grunt into the door frame.

"And you betrayed my trust!" Angela snarled in a tone completely devoid of any mercy.

Again she struck down with the poker at the already blood pumping head, and finally Nigel slithered to the floor. A series of slight groans accompanied a few twitches of his body as a pool of blood began to spread over the faded, worn carpet.

The room pulsated in time with the beating inside Angela's head as she allowed her eyes to focus, and then to dwell upon the macabre scene that had been played out in the sitting room of Rose Cottage.

A silence touched Angela like a forceful hand on her shoulder and moved her backwards towards the sideboard where she leant heavily against it. Her head sank onto her breast as she took a series of deep breaths whilst inhaling the significance of her actions. There were no tears, just an immense sadness that seemed to envelope her. Inside her there was a void, an emptiness of feelings. But there was no sense of remorse either. No flutters of conscience or guilt. No! Just a cold calculated resignation that bridged the chasms of her tortured existence.

Now for the first time in her life she began to feel a sense of peace and calmness, even tranquillity. Her mind felt at ease and free of any pervading sense of feeling or emotion, even when her wandering gaze settled on the sightless eyes of her mother, the great gash on the right temple still oozing blood that trickled down her face and neck to form a pool on her shoulder that overflowed down her arm and finally to drip to the floor. Angela gazed hard at that face, that face she had long ago come to recognise, not as her mother but only as her perpetual tormentor.

"My father never wanted a son," she said in a subdued whisper almost to herself, but in reality it was said in the hope that her mother could still hear.

"No Mother that's because he had me. I was his little angel. He told me so. And I never wanted a brother because I had my father. All I was ever destined for while I was caught up in your spider's web was to end up like dust on the shelf. A life totally wasted. But I have remedied that situation permanently, because I," she paused for a moment before whispering. "I have united mother and son."

There was a movement from near the door as Nigel made a slight groan and stretched out a bloodied hand. Pushing herself away from the sideboard, Angela moved with purpose across to the prone figure. She raised the poker and swung it down hard onto Nigel's head.

And Nigel moved no more.

Angela took one more cursory look around the room before allowing the heavy poker to slip from her fingers to the floor with a thud. So often it had been the taunting device of the wicked, hell bound she devil, now silent and just staring without seeing, her life blood merely a dark pool spreading over the living room floor.

Even so, it is ironic to think that the same poker should become the instrument of retribution, the dispenser of justice, thus allowing Angela's tormented inner soul to be cleansed of all the troubled thoughts, self doubts and contemptible abuse she had endured over so many years.

For Angela now felt nothing, at last her mind was at total peace with itself and devoid of all the torturous emotions and sensations that had dominated her whole existence. The only feeling she could feel now was that of finality, a conclusion, of this being the end. And with that feeling came such an abounding sense of relief that she had never experienced before.

And so picking up the telephone receiver, Angela dialled 999.

****

Angela Reed gazed down at the long, virgin white, clinically clean night dress she was wearing as if through a mist. She lifted her eyes to peer around at the white walls of a clinically clean room. At the bed she sat beside with the dazzlingly white sheets and at the white cabinet on the opposite side of the bed with the plastic water jug and plastic glass.

Then her bleary survey strayed towards the window with three vertical metal bars that attempted to obscure her need to see beyond them, to the pale blue of the sky with the few puffy white clouds. Her mind was trying very hard to understand where she was, but she felt so tired by the effort that the lids to her eyes hung heavily and she slowly bowed her head. But her head was filled with a continuous buzzing that only added to the dazed, woozy feeling she was experiencing.

A voice spoke her name through the buzzing. A man's voice that seemed to cut through the soporific haze that was engulfing her, but she forced herself to look up and seek out the speaker.

"Angela," the voice repeated. "I'll be back with your medication in a few minutes so you just relax now."

Her searching eyes fell upon a man in a doctor's clinically starched white coat. He held a clipboard, and had been standing by the door for some minutes, but until now Angela had not been able to focus on him and so he had remained unnoticed.

The anonymous man spoke again.

"Just a few minutes," he said. "I'll be back in a few minutes."

And he turned closing the door behind him.

The room seemed to hum within the clinical silence as Angela tried hard to identify her surroundings. The austere cleanliness fascinated her. Each object became subjected to an intense scrutiny, but without any real cognition as to what was being scrutinized. Obscure questions danced inside her befuddled mind to such a point that she tried to hide behind the hands that had raised themselves before her eyes. She strained hard to look at them. The cracked nail varnish, the blueness of the veins, the sinews and wrinkles that formed intricate patterns that seemed to bemuse her. Turning her hands over, she stared at the lines in the palms as if she were viewing the valleys and ridges of some far off planet.

Her eyes once again tried to zoom in on the room as the question materialised in her mind.

"Where am I?"

But it remained unanswered as she slowly became aware of another figure standing in the far corner of the room. At first the figure was unclear, a blur that contradicted the sheer white starkness of the room, for this figure was dressed in a dark brown suit and tie. She squinted her eyes, and rubbed them furiously with her hands. And almost immediately it was as if a veil had been removed from her sight.

"Father!" she breathed.

"Father!" she said again.

The figure slowly stretched out a hand, and without any movement of the lips a voice spoke words that seemed to tantalise her ears. Words from a voice she thought she would never hear again.

"Angela," it said. "My daughter.....my little angel"

Her mind was now trying even harder to understand what was happening, while fighting desperately against the intense weariness that seemed to engulf her. She desperately tried to lean forward, but the strength in her body appeared to be harnessed and she felt it was too difficult to try and coordinate her movements.

And yet, even as she watched the figure seemed to glide across the room to the door, where it turned and beckoned her to follow. She stared dumbfounded, all her instincts in total confusion with her inner thoughts subjecting her to a physical tussle of emotions. This was her father. How could that be, but there he was standing by the door, smiling and beckoning that she should follow.

So mustering every ounce of her weakened stamina and willpower she forced herself out of the chair as the figure seemed to melt through the door.

Then, in a stumbling trance Angela managed the short distance across the clinically white linoleum floor. Frustratingly, she found herself trying to follow the figure through the closed door, but she was thwarted in her efforts and could not understand why.

Angela's hand finally settled on the metal door handle and rattling it she felt it click. Because of her stupefied state of mind, it took several desperate attempts for her to negotiate the intricacies of opening the unlocked door before she found herself standing in a long corridor with doors on either side, but with not a soul in sight. Her head wavered dizzily from left to right searching without knowing what she was searching for.

Then a figure appeared at the far end of the corridor to her left, and through her blurred vision she saw it was the figure in a dark brown suit. It was the figure of her father with a beckoning hand summoning her forward, and so using the wall for support she edged her way towards him. But as she drew closer it was as if the fire door he had been standing in front of suddenly swallowed him up.

A distraught, agitated Angela reached the fire door and began to frantically hammer on it to open. But it refused to budge and summoning all her final reserves of inner strength to aid in her anguished plight she began kicking at it with her bare feet. Suddenly a flailing heel caught the release bar and with a rush of clean cool air that brushed her face like the fingers of a gentle embrace, the door flew back onto the fire escape gantry.

Slowly, unsteadily she looked down through the heavy mesh floor of the gantry and could vaguely make out the car park five floors below. She watched as ant like figures moved about oblivious to anything other than themselves. How small they appeared. How insignificant she thought.

It was then that she became aware once more of the figure of her father. She felt a warmth course through her veins. That same warmth she had always felt on seeing him walking up the path to the front door on his return from work. It always gave her a sense of relief and security when he stepped over the threshold. Now he appeared to float just beyond the railing of the fire escape with nothing below him for five floors. It was as if he was suspended in mid air.

Once again her father's voice tickled the membranes of her inner ear as words formed in her mind.

"Angela," the voice said "My daughter....my angel, I want you to come with me."

The words were so softly delivered, but they had an edge to them that required that they were to be obeyed. Angela stood bewildered, her mind straying in and out of a conscious state. She was struggling to respond to any sense of rhyme or reason for the strain of following her father, even this short distance, had drained the very last of her physical endurance and now she felt so weary that she just wanted to sleep. But the voice came again and this time it was more insistent.

"Angela!" it said. "There's nothing to be afraid of now.......All the evil upsets in your life are no more.....Come to your father!...... Come with me my little angel."

Angela moved towards the railing as her father held out his hand and smiled. She stretched towards it desperately wanting to touch it, but then breathed her disappointment when the attempt failed. She tried again, and stretched even further towards the hand that seemed to always be just out of reach.

Now her resolve to obey the words of her father was giving her so much comfort, that she felt truly at ease with herself and to what she must do. It seemed to be materialising in the deep rooted need in Angela to reach the outstretched hand of her father. And her life, her whole natural existence flashed before her in nothing more than a blink of an eye and in that instant she felt all that had weighed her down, throughout all of the days of her life were now being swept away into oblivion. She was being offered true freedom by reaching the outstretched hand of her father and everything else was of no consequence. Nothing was going to stop her reaching that hand. Nothing!

Somewhere in her consciousness she became aware of voices, anxious voices in the corridor behind her. She stretched that little bit further, never taking her eyes from that smiling, reassuring face, her father's face.

Still she stretched and finally finger tip to finger tip they touched, and silently... this little angel, devoid of wings, fell.

****

A MINOR DECEPTION

To see a police patrol car parked on the drive to a house in the residential enclave of Summerhill would be considered as an extraordinary event. But to see one at 2am on a Sunday morning had most certainly set the curtains twitching. Bedroom lights had momentarily been switched on and then off, leaving ghostly faces peering down quizzically. Some would disappear for a few seconds to give a report, or to update details, or to answer questions to other occupants who found the warmth of their beds too comfortable to leave.

Then living room lights had also come to life to demonstrate the fact that this had now become a serious community matter, with damaging implications on the areas so well guarded reputation, not to mention the value of the properties.

Now in the expectant silence that hung over these up market, spacious, detached residencies, phones would be setting the jungle telegraph in motion with all manner of theories and conclusions. Had there been a murder or a burglary or some unsavoury domestic? Would it reach the papers, or the radio, or television news? So many questions with, at this stage no answers but a gamut of opinions and conjecture.

The situation had also gravitated to a personal investigation by one couple. With the front door of their porch wide open they stood in their dressing gowns, bathed in the arc of the overhead security lights and gazing with intrigue clearly written all over their posture and stretching necks.

A man, still in his pyjamas, dressing gown and slippers and brandishing a cricket bat appeared in the doorway of a house further down, and immediately the three met in animated conversation at the bottom of the couples drive.

Soon the little huddle were joined by another man from a house opposite. This one had taken more time over his attire, for he was dressed in overcoat, white golfer's cap and wellington boots. Armed with a four iron, he also carried a large torch with a beam like a search light. The four stood, obviously debating all the known facts and adding their own possible conclusions, when the sound of a Big Ben mobile phone ringing tone interrupted the summit conference. Instantly, the over coated resident whipped the offending instrument from his coat pocket, and began a two way discourse with the members of his little committee and the anonymous caller.

It was now apparent that other residents needed to make their presence known, for up and down the avenue they appeared in all manner of hastily donned garb, from a variety of night wear, dressing gowns and coats, to one man in a pyjama top, jodhpurs, riding boots and wielding a swishing whip. To a casual observer, the absurdity of the scene that was being played out must have seemed like some nocturnal, fancy dress street party for the inhabitants of the now, well illuminated rows of pretentious mansions that was Cedar Avenue.

PC Ian Monkley sat totally unperturbed, indifferently observing from the driver's seat of his patrol car the developing interest of the residents of this particularly posh part of town. He had seen the little group as it had gathered a few houses down and had quite expected them to approach him for information. Whereby, he had prepared a number of suitably glib, noncommittal answers that would hopefully have seen any deputation on their way. Even so, he now started to feel a little concerned when other residents began to appear at the bottom of their drives, especially when he considered their many forms of dress and in particular the whip swisher in jodhpurs and riding boots.

He was also very aware that the Assistant Chief Constable lived not so far away, on an adjacent avenue. This brought a smile to his face when he thought that the ACC's property might be devalued with all the expected rumours of a police patrol car's appearance in the early hours of a Sunday morning.

The constable had been munching on a Mars bar, and had nonchalantly taken the opportunity to fill in some report details from a previous incident in a night that had for him, seen the mundane rather than the unusual. However, the thought of a report regarding this incident being placed before his high and mighty superior made him swallow the chocolate bar a little quicker. This also hurried him to make the decision to avoid any approach to disperse the gathering hordes, for fear of having to write that report. Least said the better he decided and dug deep into his pocket for a Twix bar.

PC Monkley had been in this job for thirteen years, and he treated it as a job. Promotion was not on his agenda. It was not for his partner either, who even now was dealing with the details of the current incident inside the five bedroom house, spuriously called Everglades. PC Monkley considered himself fortunate in having a partner who he not only liked, but he also trusted and with that as a starting point he felt they made a good team.

The incident they were now dealing with had a personal element to it for his partner and without any questions PC Monkley had accepted it for what it was, and that was good enough for him. Equally, it was not the major affair that he suspected the locals were now thinking it was and a broad smile widened on his face as he looked round at the growing number of figures in both directions up and down the avenue. There would be no need for a neighbourhood watch scheme round here, he thought, not with this amount of nosey buggers.

The porch light of Everglades blazed into life and two figures came out of the door, one in police uniform and the other in pyjamas and dressing gown. As they approached the waiting police car PC Monkley leant out of the driver's window to listen to the ongoing conversation.

"So you see Duggie," said PC Henderson in a low voice. "Your Mark won't be so lucky next time."

"I do know that Rob," came a reply.

"If any other car had received the call," the PC continued. "Then your Mark would have been arrested for being drunk and disorderly and criminal damage. It wouldn't have been so easy to get him out of that. Not with the clamp down on these drink offences."

"Rob I do know that. Mark's not a bad kid, but he's got some iffy mates," Duggie explained in equally subdued tones.

"I thought that, but a criminal record would just drive him further down," the constable advised. "And you've been a good mate to me Duggie, but I might not be on duty next time. Like I said inside, I've managed to square it with Mr Beddows, and I've said you'll go round in the morning to sort out the damage."

Turning he opened the passengers door of the patrol car.

"I know one thing though Duggie. Your Mark will have one helluva head in the morning!" he said with a broad grin on his face.

"And it's a good job he didn't throw up in the back of here," PC Monkley warned as he indicated the rear seat of the patrol car. "Or he would've been cooling his heels down the nick."

"No he saved that for Duggies hall carpet!" his partner joked while resisting the urge to laugh, but the humour was not wasted and the tension seemed to ease until PC Monkley chirped in.

"Well the ACC might have something to say Rob. Remember he lives round here somewhere."

"Oh Christ!" exclaimed PC Henderson. "I forgot about that. We'd better push off Duggie."

"Anyway lads, my thanks," said Duggie shaking the constable's hand. "I owe you, both of you."

PC Henderson climbed into the passenger's seat, and pulled the door gently closed with a subdued click.

"You can buy us a pint down the rugby club on Saturday," he said through the open window.

"You're on!" Duggie replied as the patrol car backed off the drive and then slowly turned to cruise past the lines of questioning faces, before accelerating away from Cedar Avenue.

Duggie stood watching it out of sight, before turning and peering around at the other houses and for the first time he seemed to realise the interest that had been caused. The gathered spectators had begun to disperse and he smiled ironically to himself as he gave a flamboyant royal wave to the original little group who still remained inquisitively waiting for any further developments. And then he broadened his wave into a salute to include all the twitching curtains, as one by one they ceased to twitch as the lights were switched out.

Duggie remained motionless for a few minutes, breathing in the cool air as he endeavoured to control the inner temper that bubbled deep within him. He stood waiting for Cedar Avenue to completely empty of quizzical observers, and to return to just the amber street lighting before turning and slowly walking thoughtfully back into his house.

A Minor Deception

****

To see a builders van parked on the drive of a house in the residential enclave of Summerhill would certainly have raised the eyebrows of the other residents. Firstly, with questions of what improvements were in progress, and secondly how those improvements would benefit the price of that particular property. For the residents of Cedar Avenue were in a permanent state of desperately trying to keep up with the 'Jones,' and any improvement to any property would automatically mean a setback for the other residents, a setback that would always be viewed with contempt and envy.

However, to see a latest registration white Peugeot Boxer van with Douglas J. Watson, Building Contractor proudly inscribed in bold red letters on both side panels parked on the drive of Everglades on a Sunday lunchtime, certainly did have the car washers, the lawn mowers and the hedge pruners stopping dead in their Sunday rituals. Especially as there was still a distinct air of speculation and intrigue with all the developments in the early hours of the morning for the residents to gossip about.

However, Duggie Watson now sat behind the wheel of his builders van just thinking about the problems that faced him on the other side of the door to his house, Everglades. He had not returned to his bed after the police had gone, as far too much had occupied his thriving thoughts.

Instead he had preferred to sit in the palatial conservatory at the rear of his house until the dawn light had begun to filter through the cultivated border of trees at the bottom of his extensive garden and the morning chorus of song birds had greeted the new day. But he had been totally oblivious to the tranquil ambiance provided by his surroundings as he had pensively sipped at a glass of neat whisky, despite the fact that he was not normally a drinker of spirits, much preferring a pint of real ale at the rugby club.

And yet, at that moment in time he had needed the whisky. He had needed the sharp burning sensation that it could produce to fire his tonsils and focus his thoughts. And in doing so it also gave a levelling effect and helped to quell the seething anger he had felt from the moment he had answered the door to his friend PC Rob Henderson.

It was an anger that although he was able to control, even now it still seemed to be fermenting deep down inside him as his mind called up the details of just a few hours before.

The constable had stood in the porch supporting the limp form of Duggie's son Mark so very worse for wear, who had then had to be carried unceremoniously to his bed leaving the remnants of his night out all along the hall carpet. Then with his tearful wife Anne in his arms Duggie had been required to stand and listen while his friend, sounding like the policeman that he was had recounted the events that had brought him to their door.

Rob it seemed, had received a call just after 1 o.clock that had been phoned in from a Mr Beddows of 37 Lancaster Road regarding intruders in his back garden. Rob's patrol car had attended to find a youth, obviously intoxicated dancing on Mr Beddows garage roof. Two other youths had disappeared very swiftly at the first sight of the patrol car. Rob and his partner Ian had managed to get the youth off the roof and Rob had recognised him as Mark, the son of his good friend Duggie Watson. But Rob had managed to get Mr Beddows to agree not to press with any charges if Duggie would go round next morning to make good any damages.

It had been fortunate that Mr Charles Beddows had known and remembered both Duggie and Rob as former pupils, and had regarded them as two who would make something of themselves when he had been their form teacher at the Malcolm Grove High School.

It was this endowed respect from others that Duggie Watson had nurtured in all his dealings since he had left the 'Malgrove' over 25 years ago. Alright, he had never been an academic, for the classroom environment had not been conducive to his practical ways. Even so, he had always tried to understand the processes that had been put before him and it was this that Mr Beddows and the school had recognised in him, that and his obvious talents in all sports.

For Duggie had represented the school as a team member in cricket, football, and even the field events of athletics. But it was at rugby that Douglas Watson had excelled and the school had found itself a talent to boast about the most. As fly half and captain for the 'Malgrove' he had also held those positions with the county combined schools team and had led them to two consecutive, inter county trophy wins in the two years he had been eligible. And it was this application and dedication that had given him the glowing reports from the school, and not for his hard earned but mediocre exam results.

But then it was his practical aptitudes that his potential employers had been looking for. And almost immediately from leaving school at sixteen, he had walked into a builder's apprenticeship with Hardy and Foulkes the main local contractors. Not for good wages, but he had learnt the various trades properly and with one day a week over four years at the local Technical College he had achieved good knowledge and results for the applied technical subjects. This was simply because those subjects had interested him.

It had crossed his mind on a number of occasions that if the school had identified his innate attributes and channelled his efforts down practical routes, then his school leaving results may have looked quite different. As it was, he had been taught as part of the collective, just one in a class of thirty or so that never had their individuality identified. Only when the strong in character had left those boundaries of the education system could their true spirits fly and express themselves, and Duggie had certainly used his wings to great effect.

He pressed a button on the driver's door arm rest, and the window dropped down with a slight humming sound. Duggie breathed in the fresh autumnal air. It felt cool on his lips and nostrils. His eyes slowly swept round and came to rest on Simmerson the accountant from two houses down, who was just emptying the cuttings from his hover mower into a barrow. He looked up, and Duggie gave him a wry smile and mock salute. Simmerson stood erect, ignoring the gestures before turning his back to continue his weekly routine.

His front lawn was immaculate, with the rockery, the precision of the borders and plants, even to the ornate sun dial placed central in the geometrically correct lawn. Each of the properties in the Avenue replicated each other in their desire to outwardly impress, rather than to give a more homely, individual appearance.

All along the avenue there were others, a solicitor, a bank manager, even a consultant surgeon either tending to their front gardens or preening over their BMWs, Jaguars or Discoverys that always seemed to be exhibited on the driveways on a Sunday as a show of status.

Duggie smiled to himself, this was the first time he had allowed any sign of his occupation, his business to be displayed or advertised on his drive.

Normally, it was either his old Freelander or Anne's Mini that were parked on the drive, never one of his vans. If these stuck up snobs needed any convincing of who their neighbour was and his position in their social grading then the activities of last night and his name sprawled over the side of his van would be a complete giveaway.

And if he needed any convincing that he was out of his depth living here, it was clearly being demonstrated to him in what he could now see and in the dismissive arrogance of his so-called neighbour. Without even looking he could feel the darts of animosity that were being aimed at him from so many of the windows and doorways and drives.

Duggie adjusted the wing mirror and gazed at the face that looked back at him as he pushed his fingers through his mop of thick, fair hair. It was a face just turned forty with strong lines and a purposeful mouth that still maintained an upward lift at the edges to indicate that he had retained a sense of humour. A sense of humour that had been so much a part of his childhood, and now something he was grateful for and needed when working with the lads in the building trade.

Apart from his time doing his National Service, Duggie's father had worked all his life on road maintenance with the Council, while his mother had been a cleaner in the offices of the local dairy. But each day had been a cheery event in one way or another, and it was these thoughts of his time growing up that Duggie's mind now seemed to dwell on.

"So long as you had enough, but never any more than what you deserved from honest toil," is what his father had preached, and that was so true.

Now Duggie had worked hard to build up his own business with his own yard, and eight men working for him. He was liked and trusted by all he came in contact with. Those he had dealings with on a day to day basis, those who spoke his language, who he understood and who understood him. And those were the same people he would also meet on a social level.

A sudden realisation was hitting him. He was coming to the conclusion that no matter how much he wanted it, Cedar Avenue was not for him.

When he had sub contracted on this very housing project fourteen years before, he had promised himself he would own one of the houses one day. And five months ago he had achieved his goal, but now it seemed it was to the detriment of his happiness.

Deep down he suspected that Anne was just as unhappy, although she had never mentioned it. But they knew each other too well to be able to deceive one another.

From childhood sweethearts they had always known that their destinies were closely aligned, and as soon as Duggie had found a flat and refurbished it himself, they had married. Soon after that Sophie had arrived, and a year later Mark. But what a difference in the two, Sophie was now at University studying Law, and Mark was a bloody layabout with no future unless Duggie would be willing to provide him with one.

Again he looked at the face in the mirror, but this time his attention concentrated on the eyes. At those deep set blue eyes, that on so many occasions he had submitted to close examination and always with the motive of seeking an answer or a reason for his inner thoughts or actions.

"It's all in the eyes lad," his father had said. "If you want to read a person, then it will always be in the eyes."

On so many occasions Duggie had made important decisions by what he had seen in the eyes of those he had been dealing with. Trust meant so much to him, and he had always worked with his own maxim....

"You will only cross me once!"

And those who knew him respected that, simply because they knew Duggie Watson, and they also knew he would never step over his own self-imposed threshold to cross them either. He had always held this in good faith and it made no difference to him who he had to deal with, providing they passed the eye contact test.

However, on the few occasions that he had encountered his neighbours he had always been left asking himself questions with regards to what lay behind their patronising manner and cynical smiles. Though mainly in their deliberate refusal to maintain eye contact with him, and when they did there was always a shadow before them to cloud any sincere intent.

Now their true colours were being flown for all to see and he was even more convinced that his first impressions had been right and they would never pass his searching glances. But whatever was in his mind now, and whatever he felt about his neighbours or what they felt about him, last night his pride and self esteem had been hung out for close inspection and he now felt the nudges of humiliation begin to impair his reasoning.

Slowly he moved the mirror back to its correct position and closed the window in preparation for sorting a problem much closer to home.

****

The kitchen door that led from the rear patio and garden of Everglades opened and Duggie stepped in. Anne, without looking round was pouring hot water and stirring a spoon of coffee into Duggies favourite mug. She would have sensed his return, even without being made aware of it from either sight or sound of his arrival. So close were the ties of their relationship.

Mark sat hunched at the breakfast bar with his head of long unkempt hair sunk low, and chewing a piece of buttered toast whilst being cocooned in his dad's favourite British & Irish Lions bath robe.

Duggie took the mug of steaming coffee without a word and casually leant against the work surface sipping gratefully at the black mixture. No one spoke for almost three minutes. Only the crunch and munch of the toast being consumed and the sip, sip of coffee being drank infiltrated into the heavy, imposing silence.

Mark continued to avoid his father's heavy stare, sensing that the dormant volcano was about to erupt. He was also trying desperately to control the inner vibrations of his stomach that seemed to be connected to the marauding throb inside his skull. To add to his brooding chasm of self pity was the burning sense of guilt and remorse that seemed to have a tight strangle hold on his throat and which made swallowing difficult. He knew quite well what was coming his way and deep down he realised he deserved it.

Anne stood stoically by the sink marvelling at Duggies sense of reserve at holding back the door of what she knew to be a smouldering furnace of anger inside him. She was very aware that on the surface he was always self-controlled and mild of manner, never showing her anything other than a gentle attentive nature, for that was her Duggie. But she had also seen the other side, the one that had certainly unnerved her at times, the one that she had witnessed on the rugby pitch. For it always seemed to her that it was there he allowed all his frustrations and anxieties to break loose to be cleansed, and where his pre-match cry to his team was...

"Take no bloody prisoners!"

The silence now seemed to pulsate on the ears of the expectant occupants of the kitchen and it was Duggie, who at last broke into the tension.

"And what do you intend to do now Mark?" he said calmly sipping his coffee.

There was a long pause before an answer was forthcoming.

"What!" Mark finally gulped with his mouth full of toast and his face staring at his plate, for he still feared the volcano within his father, and sensed it was still bubbling in a semi volatile state and just ready to burst forth.

"I think you heard me the first time Mark," Duggie stated dryly. "I said what do you intend to do now?"

There was a definite bite to this last sentence that made Anne look round for the first time, and for Mark to momentarily pause in his munching for he also knew the potential eruption was now beginning to dispense the first lava flow.

"And I want reasons not excuses. You are always so full of excuses," Duggie said, still in quiet tones but with menace edged in every syllable.

As far back as he could remember, Mark had never wanted to do anything constructive with his life. He had always been able to lay the blame anywhere except at his own feet. And Duggie was now realising that the anger that boiled inside him was at a very dangerous level.

"Well!" Duggie demanded.

There was no response, for even the munching had now ceased with the half eaten toast lying on the plate.

"Well!" Duggie fired.

The word rang out like a pistol shot that made both Anne and Mark look round with a start. But the word only seemed to ricochet off the tiled surfaces and then into the oblivion of silence as Marks head once again sank down even lower towards his plate.

"I'm sorry dad!" he finally muttered.

"Is that the best you can bloody do..... Is that all you can dig up," Duggie barked, placing his half empty mug down with a thud.

"It wasn't my fault!" Mark blurted out.

"Well who's bloody fault was it," Duggie said with words soaked in pure venom. "Please tell me. Please inform me who it was who poured all that beer down your bloody throat for you to then deposit all over the hall carpet. Because I'll go out now and fetch him back to bloody well clean it up. And who was it who danced on Mr Beddows garage roof causing what I estimate is going to cost me around six grand. Please tell me who's fault that was, because I'll fetch the prat back here and wring that six grand out of him that it's going to cost me to put things right."

"Six thousand pounds? Mark said looking up with something of shock on his face.

Duggie moved quickly across the kitchen, and crashed his hands down on the breakfast bar either side of Mark and stared down menacingly at the cowering head of his son.

"Yes Mark...Six thousand pounds! I've been round to see Mr Beddows this morning. My God you are bloody lucky. If you hadn't been picked up by my mate Rob then you would have been facing the beak on Monday morning. But that's providing I replace the whole garage roof and doors, and supply and fit a new greenhouse and plants. You know, the green house that was used for target practice with empty beer bottles. And who are you going to blame for that Mark, please tell me because I really need to take all this out on someone. So tell me! Or am I looking at him right now!"

"Don't keep lecturing me!" Mark finally snapped whilst holding his head in his hands. "You're always lecturing me. Always trying to live my life for me and telling me what to do. Always saying Sophie's done this! Sophie's done that! I've always had to follow in Sophie's footsteps. You've always had more time for her than me. You've put the money up for her to go to university, but not me. No, all you ever do is crowd me and hassle me!"

Not once during this whole pathetic tirade had Marks eyes looked up from staring at the debris of his unfinished breakfast. But this search for excuses and his efforts to push the emphasis away from himself, were certainly not impressing his father.

"Mark, believe me, I haven't started yet!" Duggie snarled, again slamming his fists so hard onto the breakfast bar that the plate with the remnants of the toast jumped a full inch from the surface.

"I....I....I'm sorry Dad," Mark stammered with a catch in his voice. And attempting to gain a little sympathy he turned his face towards his mother.

"Mum I'm sorry," he bleated.

"You're sorry. Sorry! I don't want your bloody sorry's!" Duggie said thumping the breakfast bar again in an uncharacteristic display of anger. Something he resented in others and equally in himself. "Sorry doesn't heal the wounds Mark," he persisted. "You sit there all innocent and expect me to accept sorry. You had better think again Mark, I've had too many of those meaningless gestures over the years to the point that it makes me sick to hear you stomping it out again thinking that it makes any difference. Well, all it means is a waste of your breath in saying it and a waste of my time in having to listen to it. I don't take it from the guys who work for me and I'm damned if I'm going to take it from you anymore."

Duggie moved away and picked up his mug of coffee from the draining board. He felt he needed to compose himself. He had come as close as he ever wanted to grabbing his son and giving him the hiding he knew he deserved. But that was not the answer. He knew that for he had never laid an angry finger on either of his children, and he hoped that they had respected that as a show of strength rather than weakness.

He turned and facing his son he continued in a calmer voice.

"I'm not accepting sorry. It's been sorry since you were at school. Sorry you were caught skipping lessons. Sorry you were caught smoking behind the sports hall. Sorry for being excluded from school for that graffiti antic of yours in the girls changing rooms. Sorry you flunked your A levels. Sorry for being caught with that creep Steve Lawson....the shop lifter."

"But I didn't take anything Dad." Mark said defensively.

"No.. but I will lay bets it was him you were out with last night. Him and that other waste of space from Lodge road. That Barry so and so...... Well!"

The Ballad Of Jessie Gray

"But you've never given me a chance. It's always Sophie!" Mark said reverting to his former defence line of throwing the weight of blame to where ever it may divert from himself.

"I've given you too many chances Mark," his father said brandishing a clenched fist. "And if you had given me one good tangible reason to back you, to finance you, then I would have done like a shot. But every job you've started was a no hoper, a dead end. Take the last one, McDonalds, what bloody good is that! Eight days that lasted. And the job before that in that Amusement Arcade, a whole week end! That's been the standard for you Mark, job after job after job. Tell me something, where do you see yourself in ten years time."

"What do you want from me Dad a clone of yourself?" Mark whined, now trying to find an approach that he knew would genuinely hurt his father.

Although, if there was one thing he respected about his father then it was the fact that he was a hard working and fair minded man. But he also realised he could never come up to those standards. He could never be what his father wanted him to be. And now he had said it.

"I'll never be what you want me to be Dad!" he stammered with a slightly contrived whimper creeping into his voice.

"No Mark. I don't want you to be like me. It's true I only want the best for you. But I just want you to stand on your own two feet, to be your own man without me and your mum standing by to pick up the bloody pieces. That's what I want Mark! That's all I want!"

"I'm sorry Dad," came the subdued reply. "I'm sorry!"

"Yes Mark. And I'm sorry, because I've had enough. This is the end for me. I've carried you through God knows how many lost jobs. At the last count it was well over twenty since you were 16. Well....Am I right!"

"They didn't suit me. I didn't like them," Mark mumbled, almost under his breath for now he was becoming very irritated by this continued inquisition.

"Is that really the best you can do," Duggie flared with an element of ridicule in his voice. "No, but you would expect me and your mum to carry you, and to fund you."

"I give mum some of my benefit money each week," came Marks excuse.

"And you have it back by the following Tuesday...And more!" Duggie said.

"Mum, you told him!" Mark shouted at his mother who was now standing with tears in her eyes.

Duggie looked at her, and he felt that bond that he always felt ever since their school days.

Everything he had worked for, had built up was here in his family and it burned deep inside him to act the way he was acting now. The one thing he had sworn to himself many years ago was the fact he would never allow any actions of his to bring tears to her eyes. And he would do his damndest to make sure no one else did either.

"No Mark she didn't have to," Duggie finally said in a much softer tone whilst he tried to swallow the anger that was still attempting to break through his self control.

"You just expected me to turn out like Sophie," Mark continued. "Always the swat, always the one everyone would praise. Five A stars, then University. You just wanted me to be like her."

Mark was now fishing hard for some plausible excuse that had any substance by which to form a coherent rebuff to his father's persistence, but it was to no avail.

"No Mark...I just want you to be straight and honest. Not a waster like those so-called mates of yours. I knew way back that you didn't have a head for learning. Just like me. But at least you would have the backbone to find something honest that would've given you a living and respect. I would've been prepared to back you in whatever you had wanted that was on the level, anything that would have set you up for life and given me and your mum some feeling of pride and satisfaction that we had done our bit. But you've just thrown all that in the dustbin as far as I am concerned"

Duggie had said this with so much depth of feeling that both Anne and Mark were left looking at him. It was strange for him to open up like this, so perhaps that had been part of the problem. Perhaps if he had spoken his inner thoughts more often, then this barrier that existed between father and son may not have been quite so impenetrable. But the die was now caste, and he must follow through with what he had decided.

"So Mark......In four days time you are twenty one. Am I right?" he said looking down at his son's, not too healthy countenance.

"Well!" he barked.

"Yes," Mark snapped with an essence of agitation in his voice that his father recognised, and which gave him the push to continue.

"Well Mark," Duggie went on. "By tradition you are entitled to the key of the door. But it won't be this door. Because Mark on Thursday morning, the day you are supposed to be a man, our responsibility ends. I want you out of here. Gone!.... And I don't care where that is!"

Anne caught hold of Duggies arm.

"No Duggie... Please!" she implored.

But she knew it would have been very difficult for Duggie to come to this decision. She looked from her husband with determination etched hard into his face and realised that his mind was made up, and then down at her son whose expression held both disbelief and hurt.

For the one thing that Mark truly knew about his father was his honesty. Many times he had heard people say that Duggie Watson's word was his bond and now that impression was so deeply ingrained in his mind, to the point that he believed his father actually meant what he was saying.

"And where do I go? Where do you expect me go?" Mark stammered.

"Quite honestly I don't give a damn. Because at midnight on Wednesday 23rd September is when I consider my responsibility to you ceases. You are then supposed to be a man and to act like a man and by god Mark you are in for one helluva bloody shock. Because out there is a vicious world waiting to gobble up the weak and unsuspecting and you fall into both categories. I had planned to give you two hundred quid as a present, well you'll get that when you leave on Thursday morning."

"You can't mean this Duggie," Anne said with a slight waver in her voice.

"I can, and I damn well do Anne," Duggie growled turning towards his wife. "If you think that I'm prepared to work and worry myself keeping him, and at the end for him to benefit from all of this then you are mistaken, love. I have no intention for you or me to be upset by his pratish behaviour anymore. And last night was the last straw."

"I've said I'm sorry. What more do you want!" Mark snivelled, feeling even more sorry for himself now that he could see, what deep down he had feared all along. He had been riding the crest of this wave of irresponsibility for so many years, that now to finally be beached in this way was frightening him.

Again Duggie came and leant over his trembling son.

"I want you to be a man," he said with so much conviction in his voice. "Not some delinquent overgrown school boy. I want you to accept that life doesn't owe you a damn thing. I want you to realise your life is in a mess and you need to clean your act up and get some decent friends around you. Not those bloody scumbags from last night. They showed their true colours. They got you on that garage roof and were laughing at you when the police turned up. Mark you don't need friends like that, and we don't need all this. So I want you out!"

"But dad I'm sorry," Mark bleated. "I really am. I do know what I've been like and I'm sorry for what I've put you and mum through. Last night I realised the state I was getting in and that Steve and Barry were just topping me up. But I also knew I was letting them do it. I don't want to be like this. I know I've got to change!"

"Duggie he needs our help, not to be thrown out," Anne said pleadingly.

She knew Duggie had a hard edge to his character, but she had seldom witnessed it. Even so she was quite sure that he never said anything that he did not mean. So this ultimatum that he was now delivering would have been the result of a great deal of thought. And certainly he would not have come to any decision lightly.

Anne once again scrutinized her husband's features but they seemed to be set firm and resolute with that harsh glint of fiery determination that she had only seen on the rugby pitch and it frightened her.

"Can't we sort something out?" she added meekly, again clinging to her husband's arm.

Duggie released himself from his wife's tight grip, picked up his cup of cold coffee and retreated to the kitchen door before turning to face them both. The anguish on his wife's face, and the obvious despair on his sons suddenly wrenched hard at his conscience.

Now was the time to make his move. A move that he had been deliberating on ever since Rob and Ian had cruised away in their police patrol car.

The Ballad Of Jessie Gray

For Duggie the deliberations had involved a problem that over the years, through the lack of care and attention on his part had been like a deep rooted thorn. Annoying, troublesome and painful at times, but he had always been able to override any discomfort through his stubborn resolve for self commitment and hard work. But instead of treating the irritating wound at an early stage it had now become poisoned and could develop into a gangrenous infection if left to fester.

Even so, by way of the move he now intended to make, he hoped he would be able to extract the offending barb without too much hurt and distress for all those concerned. And fully aware that two pairs of eyes were focused unblinkingly in his direction he allowed himself a few more seconds, as if he were still in deep contemplation.

Slowly he turned his face towards the distraught expression of his wife and the defeated scowl of his son. Each had their own reasons to feel anxious, and each had their own fears of what Duggie's next move might be.

"Alright," he said with a sharpness in his voice. "No one will ever accuse me of not being fair."

Thoughtfully he moved across to the breakfast bar and the two intently staring faces of his wife and his son.

"Mark. I think I know you well enough to read the sincerity in what you've just said. So Anne, I will give him a chance, but with conditions. You will have two options Mark, but with conditions that you have to accept. Is that agreed?"

"What options? What conditions?" Mark questioned.

"Neither of the options will leave you out in the cold Mark. But you need to think hard about what I am offering. I am offering you two options, the alternative to them is you leave on Thursday morning. As I've already said with your two hundred quid in your pocket. But two options Mark. Do you agree?"

"Duggie. What is this?" Anne asked hoping there was some kind of solution.

She had cried for days after Sophie had left for University, and whatever Duggie had done to console her had been futile. But she also knew that University had been what Sophie wanted and what was truly best for her future. But this was different.

"Well Mark!" Duggie said deliberately trying to ignore his wife's despair when his instinct was to go to her and comfort her. But he needed to do this without Anne interfering.

"OK.... I agree," Mark said with so much uncertainty in his words. But he knew his father was serious and he only had himself to blame for being placed in this uncompromising position. He had no choice whatsoever in what the future was to bring.

"Right!....Option one," Duggie said as he leant menacingly above his son before slamming a Yale key hard onto the surface.

"What's this? Mark questioned.

"That is the front door key to Flat 2b of 27 Monks Road. My lads have just finished refurbishing that place for Syd Fletcher. I know him well. He's alright. He's got a couple of these houses that I've done up for him. 2b is a one room bedsit with a shared bathroom, it's four hundred a month and if I give him a call now you can have it."

"But I don't want it." Mark stammered defensively.

"You agreed to abide by the conditions Mark, so listen on," his father snapped before taking a steadying breath and waving away Anne's unspoken objections and gestures.

"Hear me out Anne!" Duggie said and turned on his cowering son once more.

"I will pay the rent, utilities and damage deposit for the first month, and only that," he said in purposeful tones. "For one month Mark. Simply to get you started. You'll have your benefits for food, and any extras. But after that then you will be on your own. You can take what's in that mess you call a bedroom, and nothing else. So you'll have all your bits and pieces and your bed. And when I say on your own that's what I mean. After that one month you will be responsible for everything, rent, food, utilities. And I mean everything. You will find no back up coming from here and the only way you'll keep that place is by getting a job and sticking to it."

"Duggie you really can't mean this. You really can't!" Anne was now dabbing her eyes with a convenient tea towel, but her husband continued to ignore her.

"The second option is you stay here. But you come and work for me at the same rate as the other guys. But you will be deducted a fair amount for your keep. I will teach you the trades and I'm certain Geoff and the other lads will help. But the conditions for both options are the same. You mess up with me, and you are out. You mess up with Syd Fletcher, and you will most certainly be out. You mess up on either, and both options will be removed and you will fend for yourself. You will be out instantly without a second chance. Those are the options and my conditions, and think yourself damn lucky I'm giving you any chance at all after you humiliated us so badly last night. The other way of course, if you can't decide, is you are out on Thursday morning with two hundred quid in your pocket and no way back here...Well?"

"I....I....but," Mark stammered in shock.

"Duggie you can't do this. We need to talk about this," Anne said moving a little closer to her husband and trying to understand the man in front of her. She thought she knew him, but there was a stranger standing there that she had never met before.

"Well Mark!......Come on, surely you can make a decision."

"I can't.... I......I don't want to.....I," Marks indecision was making him stutter his words as he pushed his face into his hands.

"My God!....you can't make a decision. Well that's bloody marvellous. Should he stay or should he go and he can't decide. What are you Mark, man or bloody mouse. You can't decide! Well....I tell you what, let this decide for you."

Duggie delved deep into his trouser pocket and drew out some coins.

"Let's decide with the toss of a coin," he announced holding up a pound coin. "Well!......Do you agree?"

"No!" Anne begged. "No...Duggie you can't do this. No!" she cried stretching out her hands towards her husband.

And for the first time in their lives together, Duggie brushed her aside and stood over his son.

"Well!!!"

Duggie's voice was rasping and loud and Mark knew then that his father was close to breaking point. He had memories of that tone being used to good effect to goad his team mates on. For even they seemed to have a deep respect for the bottled up rage they knew he was capable of.

"Yes! Yes! Yes! OK!" Mark shouted while holding his head as a sign of the inner despair he was feeling. Not just at the position he now found himself in, but also seeing that the blame rested solely on his shoulders and nowhere else.

"And no going back. This is it Mark. You've pushed me into this.... Heads and I'll lend you a van to move your stuff to Monk Road....Tails and you come and work for me."

The coin spun in the air, and Duggie caught it and slammed it down hard onto the breakfast bar beneath Marks down turned face. Keeping his hand covering it he spoke softly.

"Look at it Mark!" Duggie growled. "I said look at it!"

Mark slowly leant back on his chair brushing the hair from his eyes, ready to face the inevitable. Duggie slowly withdrew his hand to reveal the coin, tails upwards. There was a sigh of relief from behind him as Anne began to show her fearful emotions.

"Tails Mark, it's tails," Duggie said with a hint of triumph in his voice. "What is it Mark?"

"Tails," Mark admitted in submission.

He had been beaten fair and square. He had tried his hand all these years. Pushing and pushing the sympathy button with his mother and now to come to this, for he knew his father would keep him to the conditions he had agreed to.

And all on the toss of a coin.

"I have to say that I am relieved," Duggie said over the bowed figure of his son. "Not just for your mother, but for you as well."

He bent forward, scooped up the pound coin and returned it to his trouser pocket.

"What about you, Dad? What about you? Are you relieved for me, or for yourself?" Mark said in the first show of defiance he had managed to conjure up.

"That Mark.....Remains to be seen!"

Duggie had continued to stand over his son as he answered this pointed question. He had wanted to say a lot more but he had returned to his normal taciturn approach for he refused to give his son any sign of weakness regarding the terms of his sons future.

"But your first job is to get yourself cleaned up," Duggie said with the merest hint of relief creeping into his voice. "You are coming with me, first to the yard to pick up what we need to secure Mr Beddows' garage roof, until I can get what's needed to replace it properly. Then for you to apologise to him, to thank him and to make him understand you really mean it. Just remember Mark, Mr Beddows could have taken it further and it would have meant a charge of drunk and disorderly and criminal damage. That would've followed you all your life. Remember that when you apologise. Then tomorrow morning I'll pull Kevin off his job and you can work under him to do the repairs. And Mark, Kevin won't stand any messing. Now let's get moving."

Mark pushed back with a scrape of stool legs on tiles. Reluctantly he dragged himself to his feet and without saying another word shuffled out through the door to the hallway, where his heavy defiant foot falls could be heard ascending the stairs.

"And one more thing Mark," Duggie called after the receding figure of his son. "You lose those so called mates of yours. Or I will do something about it. For your own sake, they're no good."

And with that he closed the kitchen door so shutting out any sullen reply.

He turned to Anne and gently kissed her on the cheek.

"Well!" he said in the soft, familiar voice he always used with his wife, who even now was looking at him and seeing the man she really knew.

"Duggie. You frightened me. You really did," she whispered.

Her husband lifted his head back so he could hear Mark moving about in the bathroom. Once again he pushed down into his trouser pocket and dug out the pound coin.

"I banked on him not being able to make a decision. So I couldn't miss," he said pressing the coin into Anne's open palm. "Found it on a site a few weeks ago."

Anne looked at the coin and turned it over in her fingers. Tails on one side and tails on the other. She looked at her husband in astonishment before a smile of understanding broke across her gentle features.

"The thing is though love," Duggie whispered in a low conspiratorial voice. "I've only ever seen double headed coins before and people sometimes question a toss coming up heads. But a double tailed coin. Well!!!" he said with a smile infiltrating into his previously serious expression.

"And what about the door key to 27 Monk Road?" she enquired sharing Duggie's smile with one of her own.

"My office key from down the yard," he said smiling with his eyes as well as his mouth for the first time that morning.

"Oh Duggie," Anne purred with a slight shaking of her head. "And what about all the rest of it?"

"Just a minor deception Anne.....just a minor deception," Duggie breathed with a mild air of satisfaction.

****

Duggie sat behind the wheel of his builders van waiting for Mark to make an appearance, while he pondered heavily over the events of the morning and the inner tussle with his mixture of emotions. He began to realise that many of his problems were self inflicted. All he had ever wanted was the very best for Anne and the kids. To that end he had devoted so much of his time and efforts into building his business, and against all the odds he had managed to succeed. The work was coming in nicely, mainly on his reputation. The social climbing was just a part of that success, but he glanced around at his surroundings and realised he just did not fit in, for his roots were far more lowly.

The family, on the surface had benefitted. Sophie had been the stronger character, very much like himself and almost unaided was moving towards a promising future via University. But Mark, the weaker sibling had fallen by the wayside struggling to emulate his father, but not strong enough to see it through without his father's help. And that help had not been forthcoming.

"Had he left it too late!" Duggie wondered.

"No!" he said to himself.

He continued to ponder positively. Six months under his wing and then if Mark made good he would reassess the situation and back him in whatever he wanted to do. If he wanted to stay in the business, all well and good, but it was up to Mark now to prove himself and this time he would be there for him, all the way.

"Yes," he thought. "That's the answer!"

But why had the answer been so simple to realise, had he been so blind all these years not to have seen the truth. This hurt him deeply and he threw back his head in a moment of silent regret.

Anne stood in the open porch doorway of the house and smiled at her husband. Duggie looked across at her and their eyes met. He smiled back, and in that instant he realised that he had been a success.

Even without the business, the house and all the trimmings, he was a success. That smile from Anne said it all. Something he deemed his most precious possession and it made him feel very humble.

And for Duggie that was a first.

****

THE CORNER SHOP

To many in the area, the shop that occupied the corner of Victoria Road and Chapel Street had always seemed to have been there in one form or other. Sitting snugly within the conurbation reputedly referred to by Queen Victoria as the 'Black Country,' it had served the occupants of the surrounding maze of two up two down terraced houses for many generations. To the working class locals it had become as important as the Methodist Church and adjacent Meeting Rooms, the Albert Street Junior School, and even the two local pubs, the Chainmakers Arms and the Unicorn.

It had been as much a part of the urban structure of the area as the canals and the coal mines and the interminable clouds of black, industrial smoke from the factories. As much a part as the ringing sound of hobnails on cobbles and the clatter of horse drawn vehicles before the asphalt had arrived. As much a part as the close knit community spirit that resulted from the common need for survival. Each then, in its own way had become a fundamental part of the everyday life for everyone, each being a constant in this now ever changing world of the 1960s

Though some of the older inhabitants could even remember when the shop had been a pharmacy, with its large bell like jars of coloured water and the pharmacists own concoctions of pills and mixtures proudly displayed in the windows either side of the door. Even then it had become something of an institution within the community.

For Mr William Lovelace, the pharmacist had come to be regarded by the people more as a philanthropist and Good Samaritan than just another shop owner. Coming from an austere Victorian family background that had encouraged, as well as financed the education of its children, he had come to appreciate the hardships of his less fortunate clientele. Assisted by his wife Clara, he would dispense his own mixtures and advice and would also attend the sick and needy, and only refer the patient to a doctor or hospital when he felt it necessary. Thus, the cost to the patient's family would be in pence rather than shillings or even pounds.

The respect that this achieved was well deserved.

Old Mrs Harrison from Langley Lane often retold instances of the pharmacist's generous nature.

"Oh yes I remember little Harry Watts, he was in my class at school," she was known to say. "Well he was really poorly with the chicken pox and his dad had been laid off. It was Mr Lovelace who called round, personal like, with medicines and ointments and told Harry's dad not to worry and to pay him when he had a situation."

And Mrs Dawson from Albert Terrace usually had some informed snippit to chip in with.

"Yes and there was Percy Hinchcliffe the coalman, when he was kicked badly by his horse." she would declare. "Well it was Mr Lovelace who got him back on his round, and all for a half bag of best nuts. Can you believe it!"

These conversations would not have been the same without Old Dotty Clover having something to say on the subject.

"I can still remember Mrs Peplow," the aging widow would recall with a great amount of affection. "She was Annie Jenks' grandmother. Well she took such a long time to go with the consumption poor soul, but every day that dear man was round there with his potions to make it easier. And not a penny would he take for it. Not a penny!"

There were even stories of William and Clara Lovelace acting as midwifes.

"I bet there's a few round here that saw the light of day at the hands of that dear pair," Mrs Turney often recounted. "And that includes me!" she would add with an element of pride in her voice.

In those days, in the early years of the twentieth century, the working class knew their place in society. So people like William and Clara where often frowned on by their peers, but looked up to and respected by those they had chosen to serve. As a consequence there are many more anecdotes that have been told and retold and passed down over the years, to be reminisced over by the patrons of the shop on the corner of Victoria Road and Chapel Street. So much so, that with all these colourful memories, William and Clara Lovelace have now gained almost legendary proportions.

And so for 28 years, up to 1910, William Lovelace and his good wife Clara had dispensed their medicines, pills and compassion in good measure. Until one morning Clara had come down from the flat above the shop to find her beloved husband dead behind the counter. He had worked tirelessly for the community he loved, and it was this devotion and exhaustion that had claimed him at the age of 63.

Mrs Simmons from Gordon Street would describe quite vividly the 'good man's' funeral.

"You've never seen anything like it, there was hundreds that followed that hearse. Hundreds! They couldn't all get in the church. They was all down the street. That was the measure of the man, and we ain't seen his like since. Nor will we I expect!"

And Mrs Simmons had been right on that point.

Soon after the funeral Clara Lovelace had departed for Manchester and her sister. And though fond farewells were exchanged with promises of visits, she was never seen or heard of again.

The shop did not stay empty for long. Within a few weeks it had opened as a tobacconist and ironmongers. Apart from the selection of tobaccos, cigars, cigarettes, snuff, pipes and such like, the shop had also displayed a useful array of household utensils such as brooms and brushes, galvanised baths of various sizes, buckets and kitchen pots and pans.

From opening time to closing Mrs Elsie Webber, the aging owner would sit and scrutinize from behind the glass fronted counter. With her wiry grey hair trapped within a course net and scarf, a wide shawl round her shoulders and thin, silver rimmed spectacles perched precariously on the end of her nose, she produced a forbidding presence as she peered above them to focus on her customers. This gave her a permanent frowning, staring expression which combined with the dim, depressing oil lamps had resulted in a very dour welcome. It was not helped by the short, stubby clay pipe smouldering continuously in the corner of her mouth, and hands that were feverishly in motion with knitting needles clicking like demented crickets.

Sadly, because of all this the shop was always thought of as being a miserable place to enter and as a consequence would only be patronised by a sturdy few.

Mrs Collins from Tipton Row had distinct memories of the strange shopkeeper.

"I've seen pictures of them hags who sat knitting and watching the heads being cut off by the guillotine," she would say. "Just like old Ma Webber. Ha! Just like em she was!"

Even so no one ever really knew Mrs Elsie Webber, or where she had come from. Of course when there is a lack of actual fact then the imagination takes over and the gossip and tittle-tattle flourishes.

One opinion had been that....

"She had escaped from being burnt at the stake as a witch!"

And another equally ungracious viewpoint was....

"She could sprout wings and at night she haunted the local cemetery and collected bodies!"

All that was certain was that two days into the new year of 1914 the shop failed to open and that was that. Mrs Elsie Webber had gone.

"Quite a mystery," Mrs Preece would insist. "Quite a mystery!"

But changes were on the way.

Early in May 1914 the shop on the corner of Victoria Road and Chapel Street had re opened, this time specializing on serving the local community as a general store. With its brand new sign displaying supplies and provisions it also announced the proprietors as being A and E Boyce.

Still utilizing the pharmacist's rich oak and glass fronted counters and shelving it now boasted gas lighting in place of oil lamps, which so instantly improved the whole ambiance of the place. It also retained a good selection of the ironmongers stock that had been left behind by Mrs Webber.

But most of all it provided all the necessary provisions for the local customers. From cooked meats freshly sliced, to vegetables, bread, milk, cheese and cakes, to tinned foods and preserves and all the other necessary needs of the community.

It had become an instant success with many saying....

"Why hadn't somebody opened a shop like this before?"

And so, Arthur and Edith Boyce soon became well liked and respected. Coming from a retailing family in Bromsgrove they had purchased the shop simply because it was cheap and well situated, with no real competition in the area to worry about. Though most of all they wanted to be accepted and it was how they struggled to supply their customers through the shortages of the next four years of war that really saw them taken to the heart of the community.

They shared all the fears and anxieties of those they served as they watched the enthusiastic young men going off to war, and then seeing the survivors returning, cynical and broken. Of comforting the families as the dreaded telegrams seemed to arrive on a daily basis to add despair to the misery that was already such a part of everyday life.

Those young men had volunteered in their droves, like sheep to the slaughter for King and Country. However, in 1918, when it was all over, it had been King and Country that had forgotten them, casting them aside, almost too embarrassed to acknowledge the sacrifices of a complete generation of young men.

But for Arthur and Edith Boyce, who had now risen from being 'Strangers' in the community to being accepted as friends and neighbours, found that their shop on the corner of Victoria Road and Chapel Street was now much more than a place to buy supplies and provisions.

A photograph that was taken outside the shop around 1920 still hangs in the backroom. It shows Arthur with his tall sturdy frame and starched white, ankle length apron tied round his ample paunch. The daunting appearance is all finished off with waistcoat, gold chain and fob watch, stiff white collar and tie, horn rimmed glasses and resplendent King George V beard and moustache.

All that and a well deserved respect for being the quintessential gentleman with his quiet, polite manner and air of forthright honesty.

"If I am to be straight with people," he had been known to say. "Then I can only expect the same in return."

At the beginning some had voiced the opinion that Arthur should have volunteered for war service until the truth had been realised. The truth being that he had tried to enlist, but had been rejected because of his withered right leg, a relic of childhood polio. But that did not diminish the stature of the man, for he was able to conceal his gait accordingly.

The photograph also shows Edith with her small demure figure that possessed an elfin daintiness, so much in contrast to the full, robustness of her husband. Even so, none would ever question the devotion that was shared between them and is so clearly evident in the picture. It also shows the warm, pleasant smile that was a remembered feature by all those who knew Edith, and the wide questioning eyes that, even in the photograph you felt would never miss a thing.

Many would also speak of the reputation she had for her formidable inner strength that was said to be an equal to any man, and which was so well disguised behind her quiet but no nonsense approach.

For Edith was the organiser, the book keeper, the motivator. Where Arthur provided the work force it was Edith who was the management. It was also said that without any effort at all she could draw respect and good manners from the coarsest of customers, especially those men who were used to strong tobacco and even stronger language who would refrain from both in the presence of Mrs Boyce. It was also not unusual to see them either touch or doff their caps in deference as if greeting royalty when passing her in the street or entering the shop. Then it would always be to the amusement of the other customers, especially the womenfolk drawing smirks and wry smiles rather than frowns.

"The only time my Syd ever takes his hat off to me is when he gets into bed," Mrs Horton would say with something of irony in her voice. "But then, not after he's been down the Unicorn on a Saturday night!"

In all senses of the word, Arthur and Edith Boyce became loved and respected by all.

So following the hardships and horrors of the war to end all wars the shop that occupied the corner of Victoria Road and Chapel Street continued to serve the community and to move forward with the times under the guidance of Edith, and the hard work of Arthur.

In 1922 the shop was given sub post office status and the pride and joy for Arthur was the bright red pillar box that was erected just along from the front window of the shop. In 1925 Edith introduced a 'slate' and though strictly administered it came to be of great assistance to many a family through the difficult times of the depression of the late twenties and early thirties.

To improve the shop a retractable awning was installed over the window and wider pavement of Victoria Road. This allowed for produce to be displayed and remain protected from the vagaries of the weather, and so relinquished more room inside. This extra space provided shelving for amongst other things, a selection of newspapers, magazines and especially the new breed of children's comics.

1934, and Edith introduced an agency for the Littlewoods catalogue. Customers would choose from the packed pages, and Edith would send for the items. The customers could then pay weekly for a small charge of interest on the price. It became very popular this idea of hire purchase or 'the never, never,' as it was referred to. But again Edith kept a strict account of all the dealings and the system was respected by the customers.

And so through the thirties and the shop moved with the times and installed electric lighting. Even so it was never bright enough to diminish the darkening clouds that gathered as the threat of war raised its ugly head once again. But the shop continued to be a servant to the area until that fateful Sunday morning in September 1939 when the world sank inexorably into the abyss of hostilities.

Now everything that had seemed to be in abundance and in reach was scarce and controlled under rationing, which only added to the misery of having to live with gas masks, air raids, blackout, the dreaded telegrams, the fear of invasion, the mounting loss of life and an uncertain future. Not to mention all the other devastations that war imposes on a civilised world.

Conscription was introduced and the men folk once more became the pawns in the political games of the warring governments.

Early in 1941 a new face appeared briefly behind the counter in the form of Edith and Arthur's 16 year old niece Alice. She had arrived from Coventry to escape the ravages of the Luftwaffe, after leaving her parents in the shadow of the city's St Osburghs Church.

Even so the war years dragged on until VE day in 1945 which saw the shop celebrating with everyone else. Once again Good Old Blighty had come through, weakened in many ways, but much stronger where it counted. Even Arthur could hold his head up as he handed over his Home Guard helmet, uniform and rifle and proudly know that he had 'done his bit'.

Now the shop that occupied the corner of Victoria Road and Chapel Street was able to progress through the austerity years of the late forties and to the enlightening new Elizabethan era of the fifties. However, this new era came with the sad, lingering, painful death of Arthur in 1954. Then Edith, her daunting inner strength finally quenched followed her beloved husband six weeks later. And because they had no other living relatives the shop had been willed to the very grateful niece, Alice.

Very little was really known about Alice prior to her arrival, other than at the age of sixteen she had arrived in early 1941 from her parent's home in Coventry to escape the bombing. Though tragically just a few weeks later news had come through to say that her parents had been killed in an air raid.

As a consequence a long period had followed whereby Alice was rarely seen in or around the shop, preferring to remain out of sight in the spacious flat above. There was very little speculation by the customers regarding this self instilled seclusion, although one reason that was proffered was that of the effect on the young girl following her terrifying experiences surviving the early blitz on Coventry in November 1940. That combined with the deaths of her parents.

The young Alice did eventually mature out of her self-imposed isolation to become as much a part of the area as the shop that she was later to gratefully inherit.

However, it has always been an accepted fact that Alice's surname was Boyce and this has never been questioned or commented on. Even so the truth, and it is not commonly known, is that Alice's mother had been the younger sister of her Auntie Edith.

And so Alice Boyce became the new proprietor of the shop on the corner of Victoria Road and Chapel Street and was able to keep the name A and E Boyce to proudly remain unaltered above the shop door.

****

And as the sun rose over the distant factory roofs Alice Boyce stood for a moment, leaning on her broom and gazing at the sight that she considered to be quite beautiful. She watched as the colours changed and filtered through the smoky haze that seemed to perpetually hang over the whole area in varying degrees according to the capricious moods of the weather. But this morning the effects were quite sumptuous and she felt it announced a bright day, even for early autumn. Here on the step of the shop that occupied the corner of Victoria Road and Chapel Street she liked to just stand and contemplate the world going by.

She continued to lean on her broom as she wistfully watched the occasional delivery van or lorry or bus or car or even cyclist going about their business as they did every morning. And all those who needed to be somewhere, passed by with either a "Mornin'!" or "Alright!" with some even adding her name "Alice," to their greeting.

Or some would just give a smile or a touch of the cap, but all were the folk that she considered as friends or at least acquaintances, the community that she was so proud to be a part of. It was all so heart warming to her to realise that she had been accepted by them, and to warrant a kind of respect that she found so precious.

She carried on with the morning chore of sweeping the pavement at the front of the shop in Victoria Road, and also under the side window and backyard entrance in Chapel Street. A chore her Auntie had called 'sweeping the step'. She then gave a few moments to rearranging the selection of fruit and vegetables that were displayed on the two trestle tables on the wider pavement of Victoria Road.

"No need for the awning today," she thought, for she took a pride in how the shop looked to any potential customer.

"It should be efficient and pleasing" her Auntie had said on many occasions to her niece.

Now Alice smiled to herself as she vividly remembered how her beloved Auntie would insist on how the shop should be seen and run by her own long standing way of doing things. And even now so much of the daily routine of the shop had been retained and had become something of a tradition, and it suddenly occurred to Alice that she was becoming part of that tradition also.

She caught her reflection in the shop window and smiled while she adjusted the turned up collar of her pristine white blouse and her black hair, short in the style of her heroine film star, Audrey Hepburn in her favourite film 'Roman Holiday.' She felt it seemed to compliment her small frame and features. That and her selective choice of clothes gave her a definite look all her own. And all though she would say she was not fashion conscious, she could still admire the tastes and trends of the day with a certain amount of subdued envy, and as a consequence this all went a long way to belie her years.

For now in her thirty ninth, she found that her tastes in many things had not been restrained. She could have a conversation with a sixteen year old as easily as a sixty year old. She could listen to 'pop' music on the radio with as much appreciation as listening to Frank Sinatra. Often in the shop of an afternoon 'Mrs Dales Diary' on the radio would stimulate a conversation on what 'Jim,' Mrs Dale's husband was up to. And brief debates about the 'Archers' were always good to help ease along the chore of shopping for the customers. Although her choice of television viewing indicated a broader scope of interests, for Alice could find 'Coronation Street' and 'Z Cars' as equally as absorbing as 'Thank Your Lucky Stars' and 'Panarama.'

"Mornin' Alice," a voice called to her from across the road.

"Oh!" she said turning sharply. "Oh, good morning Joe! How's your Beth this morning, still under the weather?" she called back, pulling herself out of her day dreaming.

"No....she's much better thanks," came Joe's reply.

Joe gave a wave as he continued on his way down Victoria Road before turning into Canal Street, where he would walk to the far end. And then to the canal wharf where he worked shovelling coal into sacks and then stacking them ready for delivery. But his whole swagger implied contentment. He had been doing the same job since his demob almost twenty years ago.

Alice watched Joe on his way, for he seemed to epitomise the whole philosophy of the people she knew and loved. They did not ask for a great deal, they only asked for a living wage and the opportunity to work for it. And Alice felt that that was what she liked about the people.

There was a generosity about them too that went further than money. For it was the nature of the people to give of themselves, to share with each other. If one family genuinely fell on hard times the community seemed to rally round. There were many stories that customers would relate to on that subject from the other side of the counter.

A radio was now playing some tune that Alice seemed to recognise, simply because it was played at least twenty times a day and youngsters would be singing it to and from school, and any other time in between. Alice felt she could quote all the words if she were asked to.

The title suddenly came to her, 'She Loves You' and strangely she had to admit to herself that she liked it.

All in all she felt her reclusive earlier years with her Auntie and Uncle had not been unduly detrimental to her, and she was thankful that her broad outlook was giving her life a true purpose.

However Alice did have a tendency to allow her mind to dwell on those thoughts and images that had contrived to haunt her over the years, those marauding dark memories that would sneak up on her during the day or taunt her in the night hours. Even now, as she swept the step and sought to find beauty in the morning sun rise, she found she had to physically shake herself free of those aspects of that past life that were still hurtful to her.

The song had abruptly been curtailed when the radio went silent, and it was with a wry smile that she found herself still humming the tune as she finished her morning tasks and ruminations. And so stepping back into the shop she closed the door behind her.

Now she was back in her world. A world that she had come to know so well and a world she felt comfortable in. A world she was very fond of and would always be grateful to her Uncle Arthur and Auntie Edith for leaving it to her.

For a moment her thoughts lapsed towards reminiscing as she once again visualised her Uncle standing starched and proud behind the counter and the meat slicer. And her Auntie fussing about in the back room, come office, come sitting room which then led through to the rear yard and the store room. And for a brief instant she closed her eyes and imagined she could almost hear her Aunties dainty steps crossing the floor of the spacious three bedroomed flat above. But then the moment had gone.

Just occasionally Alice would allow herself a few moments like this, as if to pay tribute to the kindness that was always so apparent in the shop when her Uncle and Auntie had been there. And it had been her wish to perpetuate that feeling in all her dealings, and she smiled to herself at the comforting thought that she felt she had come close to achieving that.

She looked at the clock above the door to the back room. It showed 6.57, and so she made her way behind the counter to the small cubicle with the glass window and hatch that doubled as the Post Office and unlocked the door.

The Ballad Of Jessie Gray

Mrs Patterson the postmistress would not be here till later, at exactly 8.15 on the dot in fact. Not a minute before and not a minute after. Alice had joked, even in Mrs Patterson's hearing that if that arrangement ever differed then time would stop altogether. But that kind of humour made for such a happy place for all concerned to work in, and Alice found that the shop ran smoother because of it.

Alice crossed to the main counter and the till and opened it to check the float. She knew it would be there because she had already put the money into the correct compartments when she had brought it in from the safe in the back room. So, taking one more cursory look around she walked to the front door, casually raised the blind and turned the closed sign to open, ready for another day. She gazed out into the street through the glass in the doors, and without turning she crisply announced.

"It's funny how the smell of fresh bread always makes me feel hungry."

"Don't worry!" came a voice from the back room. "The kettles on and the toast won't be a minute"

The voice belonged to Lucy Porter. Not merely Alice's best friend and almost equal in age, she was also her assistant in the shop though sadly a widow of nearly twenty years.

"A war bride to a war widow in six weeks," she would joke wryly with just a hint of bitterness to accompany a moist eye.

Lucy had been married to her childhood sweetheart on the 23rd April 1944 and widowed on the 9th June 1944 leaving her with a son that had been born in January 1945. Named after his father, John now worked in the local offices of the Pearl Insurance Company.

"He's a nice steady lad Lucy, his dad would have been proud of him," Alice had said on many occasions with something of a remorseful sigh.

It was a sigh Lucy had come to recognise but never question, though she had often pondered over what the answer would be. She also realised it was something Alice would share with her when, and if she wanted to.

In fact it had not been till 1950 when the infant John had started school that Alice had really got to know Lucy, for it was then that she had come to work in the shop. Almost instantly the two young women had hit it off together as firm friends that had grown over the years.

Firstly, it was with visits to the cinema or events at the local Methodist Church Assembly Rooms with Uncle Arthur and Auntie Edith as ready and willing baby sitters for the young John. But when they passed away the outings became more infrequent, and with the advent of the women's early thirties the outings had become slightly more mundane.

Wednesday was half day closing which allowed them both to join the local gossip circle at the Methodist Women's Bright Hour. This meant tea and biscuits, a bring and buy stall and the occasional speaker thrown in for good measure. But those Wednesday afternoons were mainly as an update on all the various intrigues of the community. It was harmless and merely informative was how Alice saw it, more to justify her continued membership than anything else.

Apart from the very occasional visits to the cinema, Alice and Lucy also enjoyed every second Saturday for the Sequence and Ballroom Dancing Sessions again at the Assembly Rooms which really doubled as a community centre, and which gave Alice and Lucy the opportunity to really dress up. Admittedly the ladies outnumbered the men and often resulted in women dancing with women, but this did not seem to matter for this informal occasion.

The music was on records provided by Mr Stevens the locksmith and he would place himself on the small stage and with great style and self importance, introduce each record and the corresponding sequence or dance.

In his younger days Ivor Stevens had been a professional dancer and teacher, but arthritis in his knees had forced him to retire and to reluctantly take over the family locksmith business. Even so, now in his sixties he was still able to demonstrate the various dances and sequences that went to provide so much enjoyment for those who wanted to learn.

The Methodist Church was a major factor in one way or another for many in the area. Not least Alice, for although the shop only opened from eight till twelve on Sundays it did not stop her from attending the evening service. She was passionate about her involvement, something she had willingly inherited from her Auntie and Uncle. Often she would take her turn to play the organ for the service, having been taught music by her Auntie. Also she would always provide the teas for the Sunday School Anniversary and the children's Christmas party. She felt it was her way of putting something back into the community that had supported not only herself, but her Auntie and Uncle before her over so many years. And it was these gestures that the community did appreciate.

And so life for Alice at least, had a meaning, a purpose, even if it did have a somewhat mundane routine about it. She was part of something sturdy and robust that cared about itself and for those who were a part of it. For many, the day to day existence was not easy, raising their families on low wages for hard work.

But within all of this there seemed to be a real contentment, a reason that provided them with the energy to get out of their beds each morning to face whatever the day was prepared to throw at them. And they did it with a stoical smile and not too many grumbles. Sharing each other's troubles and helping were they could in the knowledge that if they needed help they could expect it in return.

Now as Alice glanced at the clock once more, the minute hand flicked slightly to the upright position and she pushed the shop doors open so as to allow another day to begin, as it always had done on the stroke of seven.

Within seconds the first of the early workers rush came through the portal for either, tobacco, cigarettes or newspapers or bread or milk. Later these would gradually give way to school kids with their pocket money for sweets and comics, and later still would be the housewives for the groceries that would sustain the family on their return in the evening. A predictable cycle, that was important not only for the shop, but for those who relied on it. For knowing exactly what the customers wanted and expected, and conversely for the customers to know that the shop could always be relied upon to provide it, in many ways meant that the shop and the customers were working together, in unison.

But at this moment, now that the door was open Alice had managed to move into the backroom where jam, toast and tea awaited her. This was part of the routine. While Alice prepared the shop for opening Lucy worked in the back, and when the shop opened the roles were exchanged allowing Alice time for her breakfast.

"Teamwork," Lucy would say.

"Yes teamwork," Alice would agree with a smile.

Now Alice sat munching her jam and toast between sips of her cup of tea while scanning the Daily Mirror for the conversational pieces of the day. So absorbed, she was oblivious of a figure standing in the doorway, although she should not have been as this was all part of the daily routine as well.

"I bet if I came back at five this afternoon, I'd find you here!" the figure said smiling.

"Oh come in Ben, pour yourself a cuppa!"

Constable Ben Clements took up the offer and sat down opposite Alice, scrutinizing her features without interrupting. This was a daily stop for him on his beat. He would put his head round the door perhaps two, maybe three times a day just to say hello. But this early morning call was important to him for it meant Alice would be on her own.

Since he had transferred to this area nearly eight years ago after his wife had tragically died miscarrying what would have been their first child, he had found the genuine welcome from behind the counter something he had come to look forward to.

At first he treated it as part of his community duty to keep in contact and show a presence. But that had grown to a need to see Alice. He had a fondness for her which he had desperately tried to conceal. It had been Lucy who had recognised the obvious, even if Alice had not. However, above all else he was a gentleman and would never have presumed to make even the slightest of moves, fearing outright rejection and embarrassment. For now he was more than content in just knowing that Alice considered him to be a friend, even if that was amongst so many others.

"You're staring Ben!" Alice observed.

"No...just sneaking a look at the headlines," he said rather sheepishly.

"Uuuum!" Alice conceded.

Then with a knowing smile she continued her scrutiny of the news.

"I see you've started coming to the Sunday evening service." she said from behind the paper.

"I used to be very regular at my previous posting," the constable admitted sipping his tea. "That was until.....well!.....I sought of lost the need for it after that. But recently, well as you get older you start thinking things a bit deeper."

"I'm sorry Ben. I didn't mean to pry," Alice said, lowering the paper and looking directly at Ben attempting to see if she had upset the man.

"No that's alright you weren't prying. It was a long time ago."

So the conversation continued through its usual two cups of tea. General in content, but with a sense of abstraction for both Alice and Ben, engrossed for a few moments in each other's company.

But then duty demanded attention, and with a "See you later," Constable Clement replaced his helmet to its rightful position on his head and disappeared through the door and back onto his beat.

Lucy came and stood in the doorway of the backroom and looked down at the table where her friend sat, now studying the Daily Mail.

"I wish he was as sweet on me as he is on you Alice," Lucy said as she had often said before. "Tall, good looking and he thinks the world of you."

"Don't be daft. I like him. I like him very much, but that's as far as I want it to go!" said Alice with a certain degree of conviction creeping into the words.

For a brief moment Lucy thought her friend was about to allow her a glimpse of her real feelings but then as Alice looked directly towards her a cloud seemed to appear across her eyes and her mood changed in an instant.

"You don't understand Lucy! You just don't understand!" she said in a brusque, off hand tone as she crushed the newspaper closed to leave it crumpled amongst the crockery before brushing past her friend on her way into the shop.

Lucy had thought that she knew Alice, but it was at times like this that set her wondering. Those few words that had been spoken with such a depth of feeling and the reaction to her quite innocuous comment had confused her. It had also prompted her not to pursue the conversation at that point. Rather to wait for a better opportunity, even though the words not only puzzled her, they also concerned her. After all Alice was her friend and friendship accepts these fluctuations of temperament.

Later that morning with the early rush now over Alice knelt down to rearrange the newspapers that had been dislodged on the display. Quite subconsciously she glanced at the heading of the Daily Sketch and was quite taken aback to see the day was Wednesday. She had woken that morning convinced that it was Tuesday, and that notion had remained with her. Even as she had prepared the shop for opening, and then when she had glanced through the papers at the breakfast table she had been blind to the glaring references to the day and to the date that should have been so obvious to her.

For Alice, in some ways it was easy for her days to simply melt into one another, for there was such a set format to them that seemed to defy any acceptance of the passage of time, or even the hard fact that this was all there was to life. But then there was the consideration that although the shop meant everything to her it could exist quite well without her. All this can have a slight jolting effect when it becomes necessary to sit back for a moment, as Alice was now forced to do and take stock of herself after being brought back to the present so abruptly.

But immersed within her repressed mind set there were other shadows lurking, conflicting shadows that had a tendency to surface at unguarded moments to upset her normal equilibrium and logical pattern of thinking.

On one side she had the irksome, nudging feeling that there was something missing from her life, but she was unable, or unwilling to identify exactly what it was. She would try to place Ben into this equation, even though she would instantly reject any suggestion that she did care deeply for the man. However, the sheer nature of her self-imposed isolation instantly rejected any idea that her future could possibly lie in that direction.

The fact being that over the years she had resisted a number of opportunities to form a relationship, these had always been quashed, even before any possible inkling of a development could occur. It was as if she had built an impenetrable wall around herself that withstood all emotional intrusions. As a result there was a certain resignation in Alice's mind that a lonely spinsterhood would be the inevitable course that her future would take.

She was equally and profoundly aware that certain elements of her past greatly influenced her present and her future, and this had become a controlling factor in her pervading sense of denial. There were dark shapes and forms that she knew resided ominously in her memory. Even so, she was reticent about acknowledging them or facing them full on and to treat them for what they were, merely unwelcome instances that should be relegated and placed firmly in the past and out of sight.

However, when these opposing shadows of her past, her present and her future infiltrated into her consciousness, to materialize like floundering images in her mind she would instantly revert to simpler, every day considerations. Such as rearranging the newspapers or confectionary stand, purely to divert from the anxiety that would well up inside her and result in a distant look of a dreamy vagueness on her features

But now as Alice placed her mind securely back into the present she was able to contemplate what the day entailed for her. It was Wednesday and that meant half day closing and tea and biscuits at the Methodist Assembly Rooms for the Women's Bright Hour. It meant a convivial cuppa and a gossip with Mrs Humphreys from the Haberdashery shop in Gordon Street giving a talk and demonstration on handkerchief embroidery.

So really the days as they passed could never be considered as anything other than routine. But in truth, it was a reassuring routine that suited both Alice and Lucy and to a lesser extent young Malcolm Phipps, the third member of the shop staff, who doubled as errand boy and store man.

Just sixteen, he had worked for Alice since he was twelve. At first it was after school, then Saturdays and school holidays, and now for almost a year as a full member of the staff. Polite, hardworking and reliable was all Alice wanted and that was exactly what she got in abundance. Malcolm had left school at fifteen knowing he had a job he liked in an environment that suited him and one that would teach him a trade. That was because Alice trusted him and bit by bit allowed him more responsibility.

Of course there was also Mrs Patterson the post mistress, who even Alice referred to as Mrs Patterson and not by her Christian name of Joan. Middle aged with a sombre outlook on life she was a law unto herself. Though efficient beyond reproach, who had sold stamps and postal orders amongst all the other requirements of her position for over fifteen years.

And without much effort and only minor irritations to the ingrained routine, the shop on the corner of Victoria Road and Chapel

Street ticked by as a stable institution within the community, always with an outlook not to become complacent, and always willing to revise and modify if it felt like a secure move for the future. Though reluctant ever to admit that change was in the slightest way participant in any of the considered decisions that were made.

Hence with the passage of time, on the surface all seemed to be as it always had been and that was how it should be.

****

Even so the days continued to pass and to slot neatly into weeks. And from there the weeks matured with comfortable ease into months without any significant alteration to the structure and purpose of the shop on the corner of Victoria Road and Chapel Street. However, with the passage of time change inevitably does come, being that inexorable movement forward that has no conscience for sentiment or emotion. It merely trundles on without ever looking back to view the damage it has laid bare. It can be subtle and lie unnoticed, fermenting within a situation or a person, dormant yet stealthy all at the same time, until it permeates to the surface to either resolve or ruin.

However, change can also have the potential to materialize in a second, without an introduction, or invitation. It can be thrust on you without any prior warning and then be the dominant factor in your existence, for the good or equally, for bad.

And so it was for Lucy, who had thought long and hard in an effort to pinpoint the exact moment that she felt there was something very different, a defining change about Alice. For a change had most certainly manifested itself in her friend. It had not been a gradual metamorphosis so imperceptible as to be unnoticed for a space of time, it had occurred almost as an abrupt invasion on the normal formation of things. So much so, that the whole normally friendly atmosphere that existed in the shop had been shattered as cleanly as if a brick had been hurled at the plate glass front window. And the repercussions of that change had reverberated now for almost a week.

Lucy had long ago come to realise and accept that Alice had the ability to exhibit a rather remote side to her character and had often caught glimpses of these pensive moments. Whereby Lucy would stand back and observe with a real element of concern. Though she would also tentatively try to draw her friend out of her abstractions with some innocuous but calculated comment like.....

"Cuppa tea Alice?" or "How do you fancy some chocolate?"

And Alice would dreamily acknowledge the suggestion with....

"Oh yes," or "That would be lovely."

And instantly the spell would be broken, and the Alice that her world recognised would step forward with that smile that held so many secrets and so many welcomes.

And yet, in those moments Lucy had also come to realise how little she really knew about her friend. All that she actually did know was what was generally known anyway, that she had been evacuated out of Coventry a few months after the heavy bombing of November 1940, and that her parents had been killed a little later in April 1941. Lucy had often wondered if any of her past experiences still plagued or tormented her mind. For that early period of Alice's life was never spoken about or even alluded to. It seemed that the door was firmly locked on her life before her arrival at the corner shop.

But then Lucy also thought that Alice had been so close to her Auntie and Uncle and that their passing might still be a reason for the lapses into her dream world.

Lucy had been witness to how distraught Alice had been when her Uncle had died, and then to be followed so soon by her beloved Auntie. She could also remember the genuine sense of shock and disbelief Alice had shown when it was revealed that she was the only beneficiary.

"It would never have crossed my mind in a million years that they would leave me everything," Alice had tearfully admitted to her friend.

Lucy had shared that distressing time with Alice and had come to realise that there was a deep emotional soul concealed beneath the somewhat hard and at other times dreamy exterior. But even through that sensitive period Alice had managed to draw the curtains across the windows to those inner depths that she guarded so meticulously. Even so Lucy had managed to snatch, albeit by the briefest of glimpses, insights which went a long way to confirm the true honesty of her friends character, if not any details of her mysterious early life. But this did not detract one iota from Lucy's love for Alice as the sister she never had.

Even now, as she looked across the shop towards her friend, all she could see was the plain prettiness of her features that men certainly did look twice at, to the style and cut of her black hair, to the firm slim lines of her petite figure. And as she did she wondered what it could be that had changed her friend from sometimes being easily distracted, easily caught in a day dream, to this now deeply sullen shadow of herself.

For now the dreamy, somewhat easily distracted Alice had been shut away and in her place there was this Alice with such a petulant and intensely, morose broodiness about her that had certainly not gone undetected, not by Lucy and not by a number of the customers and even Ben. Her whole manner had changed almost overnight it seemed and Lucy was genuinely worried. For she had striven hard to understand her friend but now this Alice of late was so very different, constantly on her guard, remote and distant and very reluctant to even leave the confines of the shop.

But for Alice, change had come in an instant, a shock moment that had been as fleeting as a flash of lightening. It had been that one brief glance that had set the fire beneath the steaming cauldron of all the torments that had surrounded her life for all these years. Torments she had struggled so hard to contain, but which had betrayed her on those brief slips from reality that she knew Lucy had come to recognise and accept as being part of her personality.

For Alice it had been the merest tenth of a second out of the corner of her eye that had now come to haunt her. For many days now she had tried to dismiss it as a materialising of her own lingering apprehensions and fears that had simply constructed the moment.

She realised that her own imagination was quite capable of being deceptive and misleading and able to convince her of the details of what she thought she had seen. But was it the truth and the truth is what she needed to know.

And even later still, after the shop had closed, the all pervading silence found Alice sitting on the side of her bed as she began the process of persuading herself all over again, either way, merely to grasp the truth by tentatively delving back and scrutinizing the instant and also the moments that had led up to it.

It was a process that took her mind back to the previous Saturday evening and leaving the Methodist Assembly Rooms after the sequence dancing. Of strolling down Chapel Street with Lucy and Maureen Thompson, chatting and laughing after a good night out. When across the road, outside the Unicorn, in the circle of light from a street lamp Alice had noticed four men standing in a huddled group in deep conversation and smoking.

Alice very rarely felt unsafe walking at night along the streets, and that Saturday night was no different for she had even recognised and could name three of the men. However, the group may have become aware of the women for they seemed to close ranks, but one, the fourth man in the group just for a moment had looked across towards the gossipy voices. And it was in that moment, that fleeting glance of instant recognition, that Alice had seen a face, a face from her past. Or at least a face she thought she had seen from her past, for as she continued on down the street some doubts almost immediately had begun to materialize in her mind.

As the initial shock of the moment had steadily subsided she had tried to participate, though awkwardly in the gossiping of her two friends. But even Lucy had given Alice a sly searching look out of concern for the guarded change in her friend and had also noticed one of the men still watching the retreating trio.

Alice had desperately tried to hide her confusion, yet all the time she could still see that face, a face she had dreaded seeing ever again, either in her dreams, her nightmares or in reality.

Now as she examined into the furthest recesses of her memory for the minutest of details it was becoming clear enough to convince her of what she had thought she had seen was in actual fact true.

Details like the lean pale face with the inevitable cigarette dangling from the corner of the mouth, the thin black moustache that followed the line of the top lip and the black, wide brim trilby hat that had always seemed to hang nonchalantly for effect over the right eye. It was as if each detail had always been indelibly forged into her memory with red hot pokers.

Doubt and believe had fought an ongoing battle in her subconscious mind from that Saturday night until this moment, and as she sat on her bed pondering on what it all meant, the room seemed to close in on her to leave her feeling vulnerable and afraid.

And the accepted reflective side to her nature, which had always been construed as dreamy and distant, could now only be identified as being as deeply troubled as her furrowed brow was now testifying to.

****

Alice casually pottered over the confectionary display, rearranging the disorder caused by the onslaught of school children, the expression on her face giving little indication of the inner conflict of uncertainty still churning in her reasoned arguments like a perpetual dose of Epson Salts. It had been three weeks now since that Saturday night, and finally she had begun to cautiously think that she might have been mistaken, or maybe he had not recognised her. But then, once again an undercurrent of murmurings from her own conscience sought to grow louder and louder and inflict disturbing contradictions in her mind.

"No! It's him!! It's him!!" her inner voice screamed. "He saw you!! It's him!!!!

When these instances occurred she would slyly look about to see if her confusion had been noticed, for she was becoming adept at her own self control in these moments. However, it was not always successful and then it would be necessary to find an escape route by whatever means was available.

On this occasion she was able to control the fever pitch her emotions had reached and to calmly allow them to subside, and a subtle glance around the shop gave her the reassurance to think her inner turmoil had on this occasion, fortunately gone unnoticed.

But the most upsetting part of all these deeply disturbing spells was the fact that Alice realised the changes that were happening to her, and also the consequential demands they were making on those around her. But she also realised that she was becoming unable to think and feel rationally and this was now a governing factor on her mood structures.

It was sad to think that the morning 'cuppas' with Ben had now been forfeited because of the brusqueness of her attitude to him. Even her one remaining point of stability that she prized above all others had been reluctantly curtailed. That of her involvement with the Methodist Church and Assembly Rooms, a decision that she deeply regretted, but found so necessary to be able to maintain a fragile control over her sanity and her twisting emotions.

Lucy looked across at her friend who seemed to be totally absorbed yet outwardly calm. But from recent experiences Lucy knew this could be deceptive and in the blink of an eye this could all change. It need only be the most innocent of comments or actions on the part of anyone within range that could set Alice off. All too often Lucy had intervened in these potentially difficult situations and had found it necessary to placate with erroneous excuses and apologies to whoever was involved in the unfortunate incident.

Or then it could be the trance like state of complete abstraction that Alice was now capable of sinking into, and which was getting harder to bring her out of without some adverse reaction.

She accepted that Alice had always seemed to succumb to her dreamy, thoughtful diversions, but now there was such a depth to her moods that Lucy was finding them so much harder to cope with. And when Lucy did manage to break through the defence lines of those dream like stupors, then the colour would drain from Alice's face as if in shock and invariably she would scurry away into the back room or even into the flat above.

Each time it happened Alice would become totally unapproachable in her inaccessible shell, leaving Lucy to wonder what exactly she could do to help.

Even so, she was completely unprepared for what was to happen next.

It was later that same day and Lucy was in the back room making some tea with Mrs Dales Diary on the radio. Mrs Patterson was her usual conscientious self, closeted behind her Post Office window, completely oblivious and unaware of anything other than matters relating to the Royal Mail. And Malcolm was at the front kerb having just returned from his deliveries on the shop bike.

Alice stood in the window casually watching him as he checked the chain of his machine, obviously deciding that it might need adjustment. For once her mind seemed untroubled and at ease from the continuous distraught meanderings it was inclined to take and there was a rare tranquil feeling within her as she absentmindedly looked up and gazed out across Victoria Road.

Suddenly a chill like ice water ran the full length of her spine sending a cold shudder throughout her whole frame. Her hands instantly came up to cup her face, hiding and supporting her jaw as it dropped uncontrollably. A silent cry welled up in her throat as her eyes blinked at what her mind was now confirming to be true as her whole frame began to tremble.

Her stare was firmly focused across the road towards the man in the dark suit with the lean pale face and the thin moustache that now seemed to crease upwards into a smug smile. It was only for the briefest of moments before he touched the brim of his black trilby and obviously reassured that he had been recognised, turned away and strolled off down the street leaving Alice staring into his wake.

"Alice!...What's the matter?" said Lucy in a concerned manner as she held two cups of tea in her hands. "God! What is it, you've gone white. What's the matter?" she fretted loudly.

She put the two cups down heavily onto the counter and grabbed at Alice's elbows fearing she was about to fall. Slowly she led her into the back room as she called out.

"Malcolm! Come in here and look after the shop!"

Sitting Alice down at the table Lucy stared at the pallid complexion and gaping frightened eyes. Holding both of Alice's hands in one of her own, her other hand gently stroked away the tears that were escaping down bloodless cheeks leaving her friends eyes dark smudged with spoilt mascara.

Malcolm appeared with the two cups of tea.

"Is she alright Mrs Porter?" he said in anxious tones as he placed the cups of tea on the table.

"Yes....she's alright. Just a bit tired, doing too much I expect," Lucy said with a contrived calmness in her voice. "Now be a good lad and watch the shop. And tell Mrs Patterson there's nothing to worry about."

Malcolm took one last glance at the lady he had come to like and respect and then turned back into the shop.

"Drink this," Lucy said placing Alice's hands around her cup. "What happened? Shall I call the doctor? Malcolm can get him here in a few minutes," she continued as she gently stroked Alice's ashen cheeks.

Alice glared absently into Lucy's eyes for a long moment before she appeared to realise where she was and what had happened. She was in shock. Everything she had feared, everything that her mind had said could be true had confronted her through the plate glass of the shop window. Fighting to control her erupting emotions she tried to stammer an explanation before Lucy asked her any more questions.

"I..I...a..dog...it was a dog!" she said falteringly. "It ran across the road, nearly got killed by that car. I thought it had been killed!" she blustered. "I was frightened for it!"

"I didn't see any car!" Lucy queried.

"No..No!...It...It was just before you came with the tea!" Alice answered quickly trying to divert from this inquisition. "I'm alright now. I just thought it was going to be killed," Alice said taking a deep gulp of air. "Really Lucy I'm alright," she said staring blankly at the ceiling.

Then with an unconvincing smile that seemed to insist on no more questions, she lowered her head to sip at her tea.

Lucy stared at her friend. She did not believe a word of what she had just been told. But she also realised that this was one of those moments that she should not try to pursue her concern.

But as she picked up her own cup of tea and sipped at it pensively she began to wonder what had really caused such an effect. Lucy accepted her friend's dreaminess, but now this had gone far deeper and far more disturbing.

Too many times of late the expression on Alice's face would show a complete separation from the reality of the moment. It was so noticeable how easy it was for her to become preoccupied, even in conversation she could lose the thread of what was being said. Then, it was as if what her mind was absorbed with completely shut her off from her surroundings and leave her to the sharp irrational awakenings into the real world, as though from some nightmare. And this was now becoming so noticeable to customers and friends alike.

"All that is one thing," Lucy thought to herself. "But now this!"

For even with her normal stoical attitude to life, this was now beginning to unsettle even Lucy, for the expression that had filled her friends face bordered on sheer terror. An expression that Lucy could imagine would fill anyone's face if confronted by a ghostly apparition or a spectre from the supernatural.

Lucy decided that she would ask Malcolm if he had seen or heard anything, as he had been at the front of the shop when this supposed dog incident had occurred.

She also concluded she did not like what was happening, for there was something so deeply ominous and malevolent disturbing the whole fragile ambiance of the shop and her friend. With this thought firmly placed in her mind she made a firm resolve that she would find out exactly what was causing it.

****

Lucy stood in the open doorway of the shop.

"Malcolm's got the trestles and veg in round the back and it's all locked up," she announced, and with a cheery "See you later!" the door closed behind her.

Alice pulled down the last of the window blinds then walked across to the door, her heart pounding with the weight of her anxious buzzing thoughts. For now she was facing the inevitable that had been confirmed the instant that the figure touched the brim of his trilby just a few hours earlier.

Without thinking she turned the sign on the door from open to closed and drew down the door blind. She wanted to shut out the world from seeing what she knew was about to happen. Backing away from the door she positioned herself in trembling anticipation in the gap in the counter that led to the back room.

The minutes passed in an ominous silence that could almost be felt. Alice turned her head to look up at the clock, it showed 5.46. Fifteen minutes had passed since the shop had closed, when she noticed the door being slowly pushed. Finally, it was fully open and the lean figure of a man entered and slowly closed the door as his eyes devoured, first the shop interior and then Alice who stood staring at this ghost from her past. Perhaps a full minute went by before the man spoke.

"Well well well! Little Alice Turner!"

The voice seemed to have a rusty, bronchial edge to the broad cockney drawl as he continued.

"After I saw you outside the Unicorn I've been looking for you Little Alice Turner, never thinking I'd find you in this shop and that you'd changed your name to Boyce."

Alice did not answer straight away. She was stunned at the appearance of her visitor who was now standing only yards in front of her, so allowing her a closer scrutiny.

Gone was the suave, self confident, well dressed young man who had arrived in Coventry in late September 1940. Here stood a man in a tired dark suit shiny with wear, scuffed black shoes crying out for a polish, black tie and off white shirt that matched the pale, slightly gaunt features with that trademark pencil thin moustache gripping the top lip like some malnourished caterpillar.

It was still there, that growth that at one time had been an elegant piece of facial adornment made so popular by the 30s and 40s Hollywood stars like Errol Flynn and Clark Gable, but here in 1963 it looked ridiculous and seemed to epitomise the tardiness of the man. That and the black trilby worn cockily over the right eye, and the final touch of the cigarette stub tucked behind his left ear. It was the overall picture of a man succumbing to years of over indulgence of alcohol, smoking, a questionable diet and constantly living off his wit and wiles.

"God! What did I possibly see in him!" she thought, and with a slight shaking of her head she realised she could not answer that, all she could do was to hear her father shouting as if from the grave.

"Keep well away from him. He's nothing but jail bait!"

The voice sounded so close and familiar as it echoed in her agitated mind. But no, regretfully she had not listened to those warnings all those years before, or to her mother who had pleaded with tears pouring down her face.

Alice saw the man staring at her for an answer.

"The shop was my Uncle and Aunties," she guardedly said at length not wanting to give too much away. "I came here in 1941."

"Ah" he said smiling and displaying a row of nicotine tarnished teeth. "So where are they, your nice Uncle and Auntie?"

There was so much hidden derision in those few words that it ignited a furnace of anger deep inside Alice.

"They're both dead," she answered biting back what she wanted to say.

This was a game he was playing and Alice was not going to fall foul of it.

"I see," came a reply that seemed to be loaded with so much knowing. "Both dead you say, and this little goldmine is all yours I take it?"

"What do you want Jack?" Alice said with venom beginning to taint her replies.

"So you do remember my name Little Alice Turner, as was!"

"How could I forget Jack Corfield. The man whose sole purpose in life is to destroy every one he comes in contact with. Still doing your best in that area, are you Jack?" fumed Alice surprised at how she formulated the words so easily.

145

"Now! Now! Little Alice Turner," Jack said though the words were spoken as more of a taunting ridicule. "And what became of that old man of yours, the one who chased me through Coventry, threatening to kill me. That was until a couple of my lads kinda....dissuaded him," he said with a smirk creasing his face.

"My parents were killed in bombing in April 1941," Alice said pointedly and with a hint of regret sneaking a passage into her words.

She was losing this battle of wits, and it was all due to the emotional upheaval that was now simmering to boil over within her, as her whole life had always seemed to have been, and even more so over the past few weeks.

"And amongst the old fools threats he said something about you being pregnant," he said flinging the words dismissively as he gazed absently around the shop. "So where is this kid?"

"This kid!" she gulped. "Was your daughter! She lived exactly six days, eleven hours and forty two minutes, and was christened Rebecca!"

This was said with an angry sigh that held so much feeling that she felt she was going to allow herself to cry.

However, she stiffened her spine and repeated her question.

"So....What do you want Jack?"

But Jack made no effort to answer, simply skipping over the particular details regarding his deceased off spring with a question of his own.

"And I can take it that no one around here knows that Little Shirley Temple is not the virgin queen she would like everyone to think she is. Yes Alice Turner I've been finding out about you!" he smarmily concluded with a pointed finger.

"So that's it," Alice retorted angrily at the realisation that Jack now thought he had landed a big fish at last.

"You would do that to me!" she declared "After you're pound of flesh are you Jack. The vulture has come to pick the bones!"

She saw the smile broaden on his face.

"And to think, that once I thought I loved you Jack!" she said as she stared directly into his eyes whilst at the same time thinking to herself just how pathetic those words now sounded.

"Though God knows why!!!" she fumed, giving the subject of her remark a sardonic up and down scrutiny of sheer disgust.

Even so this final declaration was made with the slightest of tremors in her voice. And though it was a tremor born out of emotion, it was, never the less a tremor.

But, it was a tremor that Jack recognised as a potential weakness to be exploited and he smiled once again at the realisation that she was now hooked.

"Love!" he said mockingly. "Is just a tool to be used when and where it's needed Little Alice Turner."

"I was sixteen Jack. Sixteen! And you did say you loved me," Alice said, again disbelieving that she was actually saying what she was saying, and which was now leaving such a vile taste in her mouth.

"I more than likely did tell you that. Mind you Little Alice Turner, it got me what I wanted," he said moving closer to Alice. "It worked in the past. It worked on you, and I dare say it will work in the future."

Alice took the opportunity and slipped back from the gap in the counter and pulled the flap down as a gesture of separation from any possibility of physical contact. It also gave her time to regain her composure, because the actual thought that Jack might actually touch her, filled her with a growing feeling of repulsive nausea.

"What do you want Jack?" she finally said with a deepening of the tone in her voice.

"I don't know yet," he replied turning away. "I haven't decided."

Jack strolled away from the barrier and across the shop where he leant over the counter to the shelves of alcohol and lifted down a bottle of Bells whisky. He then went to the cigarette display, stretched over and took two packets of Senior Service cigarettes.

"This'll do for know," he said as he walked towards the door. "It's been so nice seeing you again Little Alice Turner."

Smiling he opened the door.

"But make no mistake, I'll be back."

And he was gone.

Alice stood transfixed for many minutes, just staring at the closed door. So many images crowded her mind, her parents and their trust that she had betrayed with her lies and deceptions. Then there was her Uncle and Auntie, who had shielded her from everyone during that first year after her arrival. A desperate feeling of guilt wafted over her as she remembered how they had paid for and supported her all through her pregnancy and the birth of her daughter, and then through those few sad days of Rebecca's so short life. In fact, throughout all those desperate months of self imposed isolation until she was ready to face her new life and future, and not least with her new adopted surname.

Jack had been right about one thing at least, the secret had been kept. No-one, not even Lucy knew the truth. The whole community, her customers, her friends and even Ben all believed the Alice they knew, to be the Alice she wanted them to know. And they all would be devastated if the truth was to come out.

But this meant a continuation of a lie over twenty years old, a lie that had tormented her all that time, awake and asleep. So many times the past had crept up and tapped her on the shoulder, and this was when Lucy had suspected her friend of being 'a bit of a dreamer.' But Alice knew that she wanted it to remain like that, she could not allow herself to be any other way. She was very fond of Ben, and she knew he was fond of her, but nothing could ever come of that, simply because she could not face what was the truth. How could she possibly try to build a relationship with anyone knowing that it would be founded on so much deception in her past.

That was it, even though the truth had walked in to confront her, she still could not accept it for what it was, the past. Like everyone the world over she innocently thought, they all must have something in their past, some skeleton jangling its bones in their cupboards. But the sensible ones would confront it, bury it and then leave it where it should be, in the past. It was this that Alice knew she was unable to do, simply because her past was daubed in so much self assumed guilt.

The door was opening again, and for a moment she thought Jack had returned, but the head that peered round it was not Jack's.

"Aren't you ready yet?" Lucy said peering hard at her friend.

"What!" answered Alice snappily.

"Don't tell me you've forgotten?" Lucy said stepping into the shop.

"Forgotten!" Alice said in a confused tone as if she was fighting hard to sort through her tangled thoughts.

"Don't you remember you said you might come to Maureen's with me? She's altering my dress," Lucy said peering hard at the obvious dilemma her friend seemed to be in. "What's the matter Alice? You're head seems to be up there with that Russian space woman they're all talking about, that Valentina what's her name."

For a few moments the relevance of this remark seemed to fall on stony ground and Lucy felt she may have over stepped the mark.

But the tension was eased as Alice accepted it as a joke and a smile emerged on her face to hide her drawn, worried expression. But most of all it brought her back from the tautness of her heavy thoughts with the realisation that she had been standing on the same spot, staring at the closed shop door for more than forty minutes. She glanced quickly at the clock and it pointed to 6.35.

"Yes....Well... I'm back on earth now," she said taking a deep gulp of air as she subconsciously tried to climb out of her pit of despair.

However, the weight of her recent, torturous encounter began to crush her mood once again and for a few moments she found it difficult to get her voice to respond to the words she wanted to say.

"But....really Lucy....I don't feel like it.....I think I'll have an early night."

And with that she turned her face away and scurried into the back and up the stairs to the flat above.

Lucy followed her with her eyes and concern began to filter into her mind. She thought back to her conversation with Malcolm out of Alice's hearing, and his words only seemed to fuel her deep sense of foreboding.

"No Mrs Porter," the lad had said. "There was no car or a dog, just some bloke standing across the street."

Slowly, thoughtfully Lucy walked over to the gap in the counter, to the light switch board just inside the door to the back room. Flicking the switches, the shop and back room were plunged into a sombre darkness. She stood for a moment adjusting her eyes and listening to the footsteps of her friend as she crossed and re-crossed the floor of her room above Lucy's head. It seemed to Lucy that even those footsteps reverberated with such a contained agitation that seemed to permeate throughout the whole building, such was the effect that Alice's black moods were having on the place and the people within it.

Lucy shook herself free of the creeping feeling of morbid curiosity that had come back to tantalise the fevered thoughts that were constantly lodged in her mind. And once again she tacitly vowed to find out what was causing these inexplicable changes in Alice.

Moving back to the shop door she dropped the latch and pulled it locked behind her.

The Corner Shop

****

It was a week to the day that Jack Corfield made his next appearance. Like the week before he must have watched until he saw Lucy leaving, and after a few minutes he slowly pushed the door of the shop open.

Every minute that had passed over those seven days had been a minute filled with anguish and apprehension for Alice.

Now, early each morning she would be waiting in the doorway of the shop peering up and down the still empty Victoria Road in tentative anticipation of Lucy's time of arrival, and would then scuttle back inside, a pale shadow of her normal vibrant self.

It was becoming clear to Lucy that Alice was not sleeping properly. Her whole appearance, instead of the primness and neatness that she was so careful about, was now looking as tired as the red in her eyes would indicate. And she would often be wearing the same clothes that she had been seen in the day before, something that was totally unheard of before all these changes.

And to epitomise the deterioration in Alice's whole declining attitude was the fact that the long standing routine of "sweeping the step" had now gone, along with the trestle table and the vegetable display. Simple tasks that Alice took so much pride in that were now being allocated to Malcolm as his first chore of the day on arriving for work at 8 o.clock.

And all the other duties of preparing the shop for opening that Alice accepted as her responsibility were now being ignored. She had derived such a satisfaction of following her Auntie Edith's example of personally arranging the newspaper stand, the dairy and bread deliveries, and of checking the till and float and all the normal details necessary before the first customer should walk through the door.

But now all Alice was capable of was to be fretful and short tempered to such a degree that Lucy would take charge and discretely insist that her friend should....

"Go in the back and make some tea!"

And Alice would slink away like a zombie, deep within her own thoughts and remain hidden from view for hours. For no matter how hard she had tried to avoid the way her behaviour was encroaching on what everyone expected of her, and no matter how hard she tried to curb her hostile reactions to what normally would be brushed away with a smile and a wry comment, the changes were all too obvious to everyone. So much so that even Alice had recognised all this in herself and which was now dwelling so heavily on her sorely pained conscience.

Even so, the long periods of sombre seclusion that Alice was adopting came as something of a relief for Lucy, although not for one second was she free of worry and concern for her friend.

For Lucy it had become more and more difficult to always be in the right place at the right time to avoid problems for her friend. Problems with the way Alice was dealing with customers, for instead of the cheerful face behind the counter, customers were being greeted with a surly, dismissive attitude. Then it could be the morose trance like states Alice found it so easy to sink into, and the extreme problems caused by drawing her out of them without the flaring repercussions.

And the all too many times Lucy had found it necessary to step in as her friend began to admonish the harmless Malcolm over some insignificant mistake. And in all these growing number of instances Alice had merely shrugged her shoulders, and had retreated into the backroom or the flat above, where she would allow the day to day running of the shop to fall onto the troubled shoulders of her friend.

Ironically, Lucy considered this new development in Alice, of escaping for long periods from the reality of her own actions as a definite breathing space. It allowed her time to manage the shop and to mull over the problems that seemed to be seriously challenging her friend. However, it only stirred the desire in Lucy to unearth the reasons for her friend's distress and wretchedness. In this, Lucy was now fully committed.

But for Alice it was every minute of her wakeful hours and nightmare filled nights that images of her life and the faces of those she felt she had betrayed, combined to torment her already disturbed mind. It was as if she had been waiting all these years for the door of the shop to open and for her past to enter and deliver the final blow.

Now, the instrument of her guilt ridden conscience and self torture, the instigator of all those searing, irrational mind games stood before her, exactly as he had done a week ago. However, this time he had a more measured confidence about him. The smirk that filled his whole pale face just oozed contempt. The sheen on his pale cheeks was evidence that he had been drinking, and the slight control to his speech confirmed it.

"Looking good Little Alice...as always." he said with the merest of wobbles in his stance.

"What do you want Jack?" Alice retorted bravely. "What's this all about?.....What is it you want?"

"Want!" came the answer. "Want!....What I want is a bit of what you've got here my Little Alice."

"And what is that?" she said curtly, but with a sense of unease creeping into her response.

Jack stood for a moment wavering uneasily. But then with an effort he leant across the counter and retrieved two packets of Senior Service cigarettes and a bottle of Bells whisky.

"This is for the old time's, let's say. But in future I'll need a little more consideration."

"What do you mean consideration?" Alice questioned. "What do you mean?"

"Consideration my Little Alice is a two way process," came a reply that for the first time contained a hint of menace. "For me to consider whether or not to open my mouth down the Unicorn will mean for you to consider greasing my palms with twenty quid a week. And also my Little Alice, it's for you to consider the complications if I don't keep quiet. That's what I mean by consideration."

"Twenty pounds!" Alice answered enraged. "Twenty pounds!"

"Such is the price of silence, my Little Alice," Jack said with a smile that indicated he felt he was winning.

He moved towards the door before turning.

"Twenty quid a week is the price of my silence..... I'm not greedy," he smarmily added. "But that's my consideration. And the first instalment is this time next week. It will give you time to make sure it's here, and then my Little Alice twenty quid each week after that."

He concluded this little speech with an annoying snigger creeping into the last few words as he pulled the stub of a cigarette from behind his left ear and placed it between his thin sneering lips. Dipping his free hand into his trouser pocket he retrieved a match and with a deft flick of his thumbnail he ignited it and brushed the flame along the tip of the cigarette. Blowing a contemptuous smoke ring he delivered his parting blow.

The Ballad Of Jessie Gray

"Remember my Little Alice, this time next week. Twenty quid, and telling the bogies will only mean I deny everything, but my mouth will most certainly not stay shut down the Unicorn!"

And with that he mockingly touched the brim of his trilby and slithered through the door leaving Alice standing open mouthed and lost in a mixture of shock, despair and disbelief.

Alice felt her brow and the fine beads of sweat that had congregated there and hurriedly wiped them away. She was relieved that she had not weakened while Jack had been in the shop for she was sure he would have suspected that she was in fear of him. And as she continued to stand and stare at the closed door she could now almost feel the silence, an almost ethereal silence descending and surrounding her like some invisible cloak.

She stood frozen to the spot listening intently to that silence, that throbbing silence that seemed to gradually increase in volume. It was as if she was standing in a vacuum where no other sound could infiltrate from beyond the shop door. Her gaze wondered aimlessly around the stock filled shelves and fittings merely looking without seeing, merely a blank survey of the familiar without any understanding or reaction. Her mind was closed to everything beyond the instant of the moment, almost as if she resided in some kind of emotionless void.

For how long this lasted she was unable to say, but eventually she managed to lean against the counter for some kind of support. And with this, as though for the first time, she became aware by way of a stark realisation of where she was and who she was. And then as if waking from a deep shock induced nightmare the truth of what all this was about.

Slowly she regulated her laboured breathing and steadied her trembling frame, for every muscle in her body ached from the tension and anxiety she had been feeling. And as she did so her wits began to reassemble and she was able to contemplate all the options that were open to her. Her thoughts were now tentatively beginning to focus, not so much on the painful depths of self pity and recriminations of her past but on reigniting that strength of will that she believed she possessed and which had been such a feature of her Aunt Edith's character.

As if by some magical insight she knew she was not going to allow this dark apparition from her past to beat her and she also felt that a remedy to all of this was but a finger touch away.

A strange calmness that she had not felt in a long time seemed to sweep over her and brush her brow with a tingling coolness that at once quelled her fire storm of torments and yet stimulated her dormant logical outlook and reasoning abilities. For they appeared to combine and gel together, almost as though she were reading the way forward from the pages of an open book.

In her mind's eye the words on the pages were telling her, if she was to pay Jack what he wanted then there would never be an end to it. He would just bleed her dry, and then move on. And if she refused to pay him then her life would be in ruins for she could never bare the truth being known. The gossip, the sniggers, the taunting, the humiliation was all something she had feared over the years and had purposely guided her life to avoid.

And the option of going to the police had been removed by Jack's adamant threats of reprisals.

But now all this was confronting her like the hand of the Reaper stretching forward to take her. Everything that her Auntie and Uncle had worked for would be gone, the shame of it. The hurt that her parents had taken on their shoulders for the daughter they had loved, and then had died with no word of regret from Alice, the shame of it. And of Rebecca her baby daughter, eternally innocent and yet destined to live a mere six days, the shame of it. All these disturbing impressions leapt from the imaginary pages and crowded Alice's mind to overflowing. And Jack was the perpetrator of all this shame and now Alice was totally absorbed in that shame, and the consequences of her own actions within it.

Alice moved away from the counter and pushed the latch on the shop door, and suddenly she felt an inspired serenity of thought. Looking round the shop at the shelves full of the needs of the community that she loved, a desperate sadness seemed to overwhelm her and mentally she closed the book, for in that moment she knew that there was only one solution to the situation.

****

Alice opened the lid of the ottoman chest that stood at the bottom of her bed, and delved down between the layers of blankets and sheets. Finally she could feel the thick canvas bag she had been hunting for.

Lifting it out with its weighty contents she closed the lid of the chest and placed the bag on top. For long moments she stood back looking at the bag before giving a deep, thoughtful sigh of resignation, for the process to put an end to all her fears and demons was now in place.

Stooping forward she carefully opened the bag and drew out a .38 Webley service revolver and a small cardboard box of cartridges. She handled the cold metal of the revolver with a sense of growing familiarity. It had been her Uncle Arthur's when he had carried it on his Home Guard duties during the war. It had not been issued to him and she never knew where he had acquired it from.

However, he had made it his responsibility to show Alice how it worked, and how it fired with the imminent threat of invasion in those early years of the 40s.

Even now she could hear the voice of her Uncle making her repeat his instructions regarding the weapon. With the revolver sitting comfortably in her right hand and her left hand supporting it under the butt, she held it at arm's length sensing its weight against the strength that it seemed to give her.

Quite methodically and without any sense of emotion creeping into her actions, she closed one eye to allow the other to peer along the barrel at some imaginary target. Then as she continued to take aim a face seemed to appear beyond the notch of the barrel sight. It became a pale face with a sliver of a black moustache above the mouth that had a mean, sinister smile painted on it as the eyes mocked her. Slowly she squeezed the trigger until she felt it pull and the hammer clicked as it fell. The face disappeared as she lowered the weapon and for the first time in a very long time she felt a composed conviction of purpose.

There was no sense of apprehension at the prospect of the consequences of the actions she was planning, just a quiet acceptance that there was no rational alternative.

"It's twenty past five Alice!" Lucy called from downstairs. "I'm starting to close up!"

"I'm coming!" Alice replied easing herself out of her thoughts.

She bent down and opened the box of cartridges, then filled the chamber of the revolver before clicking it securely back into place.

"Remember Alice," her Uncle had calmly instructed. "The only safe gun is an unloaded gun. So only load it when you mean to use it and then keep it safe until the need to fire it."

With an air of finality she placed the weapon back into the canvas bag and out of sight from any possibility of prying eyes and laid it carefully on the top of the ottoman chest.

Quickly she busied herself in a side mirror, and then took a longer look at the face that she was staring at. It seemed different now that she had come to a decision on what she needed to do. She felt that some colour had returned to her cheeks. That the deep furrows in her brow had almost faded completely. That the creases that had begun to form either side of her nose and mouth had almost gone. She felt the face looked younger as if a great weight had been lifted from her shoulders.

"Tonight at a little after 5.45 it would be over," she thought.

Almost immediately she felt a sadness grip her and tighten across her breast and into her throat like a strangle hold. In an instant she knew it was not because of her intentions, for she knew that what was to happen was an inevitable conclusion to all the pain her mind had suffered all these years. But it was because of all those she had hurt and betrayed and simply because of her own selfish and foolish actions. Her parents, who had always stood by her, supported her and had died before she could tell them how much she loved them, and how sorry she was. Then her Uncle and Auntie who had taken her in without question and would have been wonderful to the daughter Alice was destined to lose so early in its short life. The daughter she had only been allowed to hold in her trembling arms, just once.

In that instant she had a momentary desire to enfold them all in one long, abiding embrace as a sob tried to manifest itself deep inside her, but she managed to contain it and in so doing she was able to stabilize her emotions.

But only for a moment for there was Lucy. Dear Lucy, no better friend could a person ask for. Always there when needed, but Alice now felt she had even betrayed her for not confiding the real reasons behind the difficult moods she had been in. And there was Ben, for Alice knew deep down that her chance of happiness with him had now gone completely. He had obviously taken her adverse attitude of avoiding the early morning 'cuppas' together as a sign she wanted nothing to do with him. She had not seen him, even by his occasional appearances during the day, since the morning of the Friday before, almost a week ago and it was only now that she realised just how much she missed him, wanted him.

Once again Alice considered the tragic common bond they shared with each other, that of them both losing a child so very early on in their lives. It was a common bond she could never admit to, least of all to Ben. This thought brought with it a deep resounding regret which was instantly discarded into its rightful place of out of sight and out of mind, so that she could concentrate fully on the job in hand.

She glanced around her bed room in full knowledge that it would be for the last time. Nothing was out of place as her gaze settled on the large white envelope sitting on her dressing table. It was addressed to her solicitor and to be opened only by him. The envelope contained her final instructions, for she had firmly decided that she did not wish to face the consequences of her actions. It had taken many a long sleepless night of deliberation to come to such a determined conclusion. But there was not one iota of regret in that decision, just a deep seated resolve that it was the right and only decision that could be made.

Again she looked briefly into the mirror and touched a few loose strands of hair back into place and then picking up the canvas bag with the loaded revolver inside she started down the stairs. She stopped for a moment in the shops back room and looked for the final time at the framed photo of her Uncle Arthur and Auntie Edith. For a few fleeting seconds she felt a mixture of churning emotions from remorse to sadness and from despair to anger, but finally those taunting sensations corrected themselves and the iron resolve she had so often seen in her Auntie Edith surfaced once more in her niece.

Lucy was just pulling down the last of the window blinds as Alice came into the shop. A quick movement secreted the revolver under the counter where the gap led directly from the back room.

"Everything is away from outside and the back's locked up so I let Malcolm go a bit early tonight Alice," Lucy said as she struggled into her coat. "And I want to get John his tea before meeting you. So if you still feel like it I might see later at Maureen's."

And with that she was out of the door and gone.

Alice crossed over to the door and turned the sign from open to closed. Pulling the door blind down she turned towards the clock, it showed 5.29

Standing with her back to the door she began to ponder on the hurried departure of Lucy. Had she been so upset by Alice's moods and attitude of late that she should want to rush off in such a dismissive manner. Then she remembered Lucy's parting comment.....

"So if you feel like it," she had said, almost assuming that Alice would not want to go to Maureen's.

But that was true she had not wanted to stray beyond the threshold of the shop doorway for many weeks now. So Lucy was right to assume she would not want to go and how she must be hurting at the way she was being treated. Alice sighed such a long sad sigh of deep regret as she considered how she had abused a real friend so badly.

Deep down she felt so sorry for her actions, and at the same time she also felt a brooding sense of being alone and exposed. For one split second she actually felt helpless and wished that she had confided her innermost thoughts and fears to Lucy. But that chance had now gone, like the chances she had missed with Ben.

And a deep sullen thought scurried across her mind. It had suddenly struck her that the final impression, the last abiding remembrance both Lucy and Ben would retain of her was how they had last seen her. Argumentative, bitter and in all respects not a very pleasant individual. And this sad thought brought her careering back to the present.

Once again she looked at the clock, 5.37. Slowly yet purposefully she made her way back through the gap in the counter and positioned herself so that her right hand would be in easy reach of the revolver. Opening the bag she placed the weapon down on the shelf under the counter with the butt facing her hand. She ran her fingers over the cold metal, imagining that it would soon feel warmer after it had been fired. It was then that she also considered the enormity of the actions she was about to undertake, and instantly she felt absolutely calm and at peace with her resolve. After all, she would not only be ridding herself of her lifetime of demons, but on a larger picture she would be ridding the world of a devil.

And so, the minutes ticked ponderously by and Alice waited in silence.

The door slowly opened, and Jack Corfield once again slid, snake like into the shop. He stood staring across at Alice. It was clear on this occasion he was reasonably sober as he moved to the counter and confidently leant over to take two packets of Senior Service cigarettes and a bottle of Bells whisky from the displays which he then placed on the counter.

Alice remained motionless, watching, waiting.

"We'll call this a little bonus, shall we," Jack said with a smirk creeping across his face.

Alice did not reply, she just kept her gaze firmly fixed on Jack as he slowly paraded round the shop space in what could only be described as a swagger, with arrogance and self confidence oozing from him in every step he took. It was as if he felt he had the upper hand and he was wallowing in the knowledge.

"Do you know what I think?" he remarked casually while looking directly at Alice, anticipating a reply.

But no reply was forthcoming from Alice who was desperately trying to contain herself. She wanted the right moment to produce the revolver from under the counter, and then to relish every fear filled twitch from Jack before she pulled the trigger. She so wanted that 'evil part of her past' to suffer the way she had suffered all these years. She wanted to openly delight in the depth of desperation that this bullying coward would obviously show the instant his fate was revealed.

He was of a type that benefits from other people's misfortune. His whole existence had been to prey on the gullible, she could see that now. And he had taken advantage of her innocence and naivety all those years ago in Coventry when his silver tongue had simply talked his way past the crumbling guard that she had tried to put up. All the lame reasons that she knew were the right reasons, but had been totally ineffective against this man.

Once again in her mind, flashed the faces of her parents, her mother weeping and her father bruised and battered by the louts Jack had set on him. There before her now, was the coward who could not face the older man, who then had run and had been running ever since. But now she was impervious to anything he might try to say or do.

"You've got quite a nice little set up my Little Alice," he continued while picking up the odd item to examine, and then quietly replace it. "Yes," he said. "There's more money here than I thought. Much better pickings....Umm," he muttered thoughtfully. "I do believe I've been under pricing myself. Its twenty quid this week, but next time it really has got to be thirty quid a week. Think of it Little Alice, every penny will be well spent in securing my silence," he said coming up so close to Alice that his face was no more than six inches from hers.

She almost choked on the mixture of stale tobacco and beer on his breath and the pungent aroma of sweat filled clothes from his unwashed body. With a great effort she managed to hold herself together, for fear of allowing him any sense that he might be intimidating her. She held firm, and it was Jack who finally backed away under her penetrating stare.

"So! Little Alice Turner," he said moving away towards his stash of cigarettes and whisky. "Where's my money?"

There was a long pause as they both stared at each other before Alice replied with so much purpose in her delivery.

"There is no money!" she stated in a composed tone. "And there will be no money!"

To say Jack was shocked at this refusal would be an understatement. He had convinced himself that he had Alice on the ropes, at his mercy.

"Well!" he spluttered seeking to add a grin with his response. "You do know the consequences don't you. You'll never be able to hold your head up round here when I've finished with you my Little Alice," he said with his voice beginning to grate in anger.

Alice's right hand slid and caressed the butt of the revolver as her forefinger curled around the trigger, now even more convinced that her actions were correct. He would never let go not until he had bled her dry.

"No Jack. I'm not going to give into you or your threats. Ever since I met you and I fell under that devils spell that you weave wherever you go, the things and the people I love have always suffered because of you. You had a daughter who never lived long enough to see even a week of life. My parents died with my shame on their lips. My Uncle and Auntie would turn in their graves if they thought I would allow you to take the shop away from me. I suspect that your whole life has left a trail of human destruction behind it, and in ridding the world of scum like you would be seen by all as a blessing."

She felt the weight of the weapon in her hand as she began to lift it from the shelf as her heated determination flooded into her eyes and her lips squeezed together in a firm embrace.

"That's done it," Jack shouted with a pointed finger aimed at Alice. "That has done it. You are finished!" he growled, hoping even at this late stage that Alice's words were a bluff.

"No Jack. It's you that's finished," Alice said calmly as the revolver came level with the counter top.

Suddenly the door swung open and Ben in his civilian clothes came smiling into the shop.

"Oh I saw the light, but I didn't know you had a customer," he said in his normal cheery manner.

Alice slowly lowered the revolver back onto the shelf and quickly covered it with the empty bag.

"What are you doing here?" Alice questioned completely taken aback.

There was a slight waver in her voice as she grappled with so many inner emotions, for she had been absolutely prepared to shoot Jack with no sense of regret whatsoever. She had been just a split second away from dealing out her justice, being judge, jury and executioner. And her own subsequent demise was something she had certainly come to terms with, had planned for down to every minuscule detail and now all that had been foiled. And her heart sank like a foundering ship on a rocky shore with the overwhelming prospect that the misery and torment over so many years, was now destined never to end.

Alice stood, staring at Ben as she trembled with a myriad of sensations dancing wildly behind her eyes.

"Where have you been?" Alice said in a light conversational tone, but not really having any idea of what she was saying. "We've missed you," she added without thinking.

"Oh I've been away for a few days. I needed a break," he said deliberately facing Alice while he kept his back towards Jack in an obvious gesture of ignoring him. "So I spent a couple of days in London at the Police Headquarters in Southwark. That place took a pounding in the war. I did some research at the coroner's court as well. Some very interesting facts came out. Spoke to some of the locals who've lived there all their lives. Found this lovely pub...now what was it called?"

Ben stood rubbing his chin thoughtfully, though he appeared to be intentionally holding back with the information. Behind him Jack was seething as he fidgeted with frustration and anger not only at this interruption on his business dealings but also by what this intruder seemed to be alluding to.

The suspense lasted a few long moments before Ben spoke again.

"Ah........yes that's it," he said at last. "The Tyburn!"

The change in Jack was now nothing short of amazing. He had come to the shop fully confident that he was onto a winner. He felt that he had Alice so much in fear of him that he could conclude the business of the money very quickly. And even when he had been presented with Alice's stubborn refusal he had been prepared to knock some sense into the woman. But with every syllable of the final sentence that had left Bens mouth a fierce fury could be seen to flourish in Jack's once pale cheeks, to such a point that on the last word 'Tyburn,' the flood gates burst open.

"Ben!... He's got a knife!" cried Alice as she scrambled to retrieve her revolver.

A switch blade had appeared in Jacks fist, but before he could thrust it between Bens ribs, a short ebony, life preserver had slid down from the constables coat sleeve into his waiting palm, and in one swinging motion had crashed down onto the wrist of the knife wielding assailant.

With a wild squeal of pain, the knife went spinning across the shop floor.

Instantly Jack, clutching his dangling, injured arm flew at the gap in the counter, pushing Alice aside as he headed towards the backroom and the yard beyond.

"He's getting away!" cried Alice.

"He'll be back," said Ben confidently.

Seconds later Jack came bursting back into the shop pursued by two trench coated men, though his head long flight for the shop door was instantly halted by Ben's powerful punch into his midriff which sent him gasping into a heap on the floor. Quickly handcuffs were clicked on Jacks wrists, securing his hands behind his back by one his pursuers. Then he was placed in a crumpled sitting position against the counter, gasping for breath and cursing all within earshot.

"Don't worry Alice, these are two of my colleagues from the CID in London," Ben said crossing to the startled woman and placing a kindly, reassuring palm against her now wet cheek.

"You can have the honour Ben. This is your call," said one of the officers.

"Thanks Kev," Ben replied as he walked across to the sorry figure on the floor. "Cyril Oswald Blunt I arrest you on suspicion of the murder……"

The rest of Bens reading of his prisoner's rights were lost on Alice as the enormity of the words bounced around her head defying any sense of reality whatsoever.

****

A little under an hour later, three cups of tea laced with a good measure of whisky sat steaming on the table in the back room of the corner shop of Victoria Road and Chapel Street. Alice and Ben had now been joined by Lucy, and each sat quietly pondering over the events of the last hour. Jack, or should we now say Cyril was speeding on his way to London accompanied by the two detectives seconded from the Met to help with the arrest.

Ben had just finished his explanation of his part in the episode and the words still hung in the air like the conclusion of some dramatic feature film that Alice and Lucy would watch at the cinema.

He had said that following the mythical incident of the dog almost being run over by a car, Lucy had questioned young Malcolm, who had confirmed that there was no dog, only a man with a black moustache in a dark suit and hat just watching the shop.

Next morning Lucy had told her suspicions to Ben. She had related what Malcolm had said and also informed him of the incident after the Saturday night sequence dance outing. She had said she felt Alice's problems had started there, with the recognition of the man outside the Unicorn. Lucy also confirmed she had also caught a brief glimpse of a man with a black moustache.

Ben had then approached his friend Norman the landlord of the Unicorn, who had recognised the description and said that it sounded like Jack Corfield, a very dubious character. He also told Ben that the cockney "spiv" had talked openly in his broad accent about his roots in Southwark in London and a pub called the Tyburn. It had struck Norman that even though Jack Corfield had spoken fondly about his roots it was very odd when he had also admitted that he had not been back to his patch since the blitz of 1940.

Also, Ben had then managed to obtain a beer glass that Jack had used and had then been able to have lifted a good set of fingerprints. Also Norman had furnished a couple of photos of the darts team. Typically, the slippery, over confident Jack Corfield had managed to place himself in the pictures, even though he was not a member of the team. It was obvious that he felt so comfortable that whatever past he had, was now well and truly behind him now.

Armed with his concerns and his evidence, Ben's superintendant had given him permission to go to London as it was decided that there was some urgency about the case when it was discovered by Lucy that Jack was coming for his money on this very night. Ben and Lucy had been convinced that Alice was being either threatened or blackmailed and it also seemed that somehow it had something to do with this stranger Jack Corfield being in the area.

Apparently, nobody knew where he had come from, only rumours of shady deals with no hard evidence. But Jack's sudden appearance had also coincided with the distinct changes in Alice's moods and behaviour, from her acceptable, endearing dreaminess, to this uncharacteristic rude and abrupt manner of late.

Ben had found the Tyburn pub. There was still evidence of the bombing the area had suffered in the early months of the blitz. He had also come across six locals who quickly recognised the man in the photos as 'Slippery Cyril,' the local 'fly by night.' His full name was Cyril Oswald Blunt and they had believed that he had been killed in bombing sometime in September 1940. However, one man, who had served as an ARP warden had said there had been suspicious circumstances surrounding his death, which had led to the coroner's verdict of.......

"Death was caused by person or persons unknown."

At this point Ben had been even more convinced that Jack, now recognised as Cyril had a past that needed investigating. So then he had been given access to the police files and coroner's report.

Ben discovered that the body found in the cellar of a bombed out house had not been physically identified. No fingerprints were on file and the face was so badly mangled as to be unidentifiable. All that could be used was the identity card, some letters, a call up notification letter and a lucky sovereign signet ring Cyril had often been seen wearing. He was also dressed in a suit that had the name 'C.O.Blunt' sewn into the maker's label.

The Ballad Of Jessie Gray

However, a post mortem had concluded that death had occurred from a blow to the back of the head. It was also in the report that a bloodstained length of lead piping that had been found in the cellar had been confirmed as the murder weapon. The damage to the face that had made it unrecognisable had been caused after death and then rubble had been clumsily dumped over the body in a feeble attempt to make it look like the result of the bombing. Even so, a good set of fingerprints had been taken from the lead piping, but as they did not appear on file they were merely kept on the coroner's report and police records.

But for Ben it was the fingerprints that sealed the case, for whilst they had not matched those taken from the victim, they did match exactly those taken from the Unicorns beer glass.

In 1940, the police realised that the death was so obviously contrived and were immediately convinced that the death was suspicious. The theory at the time, was that due to the amount of circumstantial evidence Cyril Oswald Blunt had been murdered by black market rivals over some dubious deal. For it was common knowledge that he had trodden a very fine line with other individuals in the illegal trade. However, due to the bombing and all the resulting confusion, little time had been spent on the case after the coroner's verdict.

Even so, in conversation with some of the drinkers in the Tyburn, Ben had also found out that they seemed to remember that a young friend of Cyril's who had acted as a kind of runner, had disappeared around the same time. It was assumed by the police, it was because his boss had been murdered and he feared he might be next.

The drinkers also recalled that the young man had suffered from epileptic fits, and although he was fairly sturdy he was exempt from military service. He was also remembered as being good natured and likable, but was also described as being not very bright and impressionable and an easy target for the likes of 'Slippery Cyril' to use.

The young man's name had been Jack Corfield.

With this final piece to the puzzle Ben, with the two detectives had headed home in time to make their rendezvous with Lucy, and for them to make the arrest.

It was clear from the Tyburn customer's recognition of 'Slippery Cyril' in the photographs from the Unicorn, that an exchange of identity had taken place. That Jack Corfield was the victim and Cyril Oswald Blunt was the killer. And the fingerprints on the lead piping and the beer glass merely confirmed this.

So it was understandable that a murderer, now with twenty years of a new identity and keeping hundreds of miles away from his crime should feel confident of not being found out.

"And you did all this for me," Alice asked in a whispery tone as emotion tended to affect her words, for she was still feeling stunned from the recent chain of events.

"Yes," Ben said firmly. "But nothing would have happened without this lady."

He beamed a smile in the direction of Lucy.

"She's the one to thank!"

Alice looked at her friend who had sat silently listening to Ben's account.

"What does he mean?" she queried in a quiet questioning voice.

"Don't be shy about it Lucy. It took a lot of nerve to do what you did," Ben declared as he leant across the table to place a reassuring hand on Lucy's.

"Let her explain in her own words Alice," he said warmly.

There was a pause before Lucy looked up, and straightening her shoulders she began to unravel her story.

"Well," she stated with a sense of excitement creeping into her words. "That Saturday after the sequence dancing I did catch a glimpse of that man outside the Unicorn. It was obvious that it had stirred something inside of you Alice, but at the time I could not put my finger on it. I thought from the expression on your face and the way you reacted and have been reacting ever since, that it was a dark part of your past. So I determined to go along with the way you were, and if you wanted to confide in me I would be there for you. As it was, until that Thursday and you saw him outside the shop, I had begun to wonder if I had misread the situation. But that incident with the dog in the road only confirmed my suspicions. And then young Malcolm, first of all saying there was no dog and then his description of the man when I questioned him, only added fuel to the fire."

She stopped for a moment to take a mouthful of the whisky laced tea before continuing.

"Anyway, that Thursday night I was walking home up Victoria Road when I caught a glimpse of the man I had seen that Saturday night outside the Unicorn standing in the doorway of Mortimers the Undertakers. I didn't let on that I had recognised him and I carried on past and stood by the bus stop as if I was waiting for a bus. I kept my back towards him but I managed to watch him by using my compact mirror. It was obvious he was watching the shop because after a few minutes he strolled down and went inside. Next morning I managed to tell Ben about everything and he told me to keep an eye on you and he would make some enquiries starting at the Unicorn. After that I made it my business to walk up Victoria Road at the same time each night after the shop closed, and the following Thursday, bingo! I saw him in Mortimers doorway again."

She stopped again for a few moments to take another sip of her whisky laced tea. Now the excitement of her adventure was beginning to show in the glint in her eyes as she resumed her story.

"So, I waited by the bus stop and again after a few minutes he sauntered off down to the shop and again he went inside. But this time I followed him down and when I knew he was in here I came in by the side entrance into the yard and then crept into here. I was just in time to hear him say he would be back next week, that is tonight for his money. I heard him leave before I scuttled back out of the side gate and I caught a quick glimpse of him going down Chapel Street and into the Unicorn. The next morning, the Friday, I told Ben everything. I also gave him my John's telephone number at his office and a message came today for me to meet Ben outside the Assembly Rooms at five thirty. And from there I let the two detectives into the yard, and the rest you know."

With a sigh and a smile she leant back in her chair with a sense of relief at her evening's exertions.

"I can't believe it!" Alice stuttered at the enormity of what she had just heard. "All this was going on while I was wallowing in my own misery and you two were protecting me."

She stretched out her hands and clutched both Ben's and Lucy's in each of her own.

"I don't have the words to tell you how grateful I am and how sorry I am as well for the way I've been." she said huskily trying to hold back her emotions.

"There's no need," Ben replied with a smile.

"That's right," added Lucy. "But you could answer just one question."

"What's that," said Alice almost guessing what the question would be.

"What is your real name? I've always had a suspicion it wasn't Boyce," Lucy stated with a smile that literally glowed in Alice's direction.

"Turner," Alice answered after a long thoughtful pause.

She looked deeply from Lucy to Ben and then back again. Something welled up inside her, an overwhelming need to talk, to explain everything, all those things that had haunted her mind and her memory for over twenty years. And now she felt it was the time to unburden this heavy mantle of self inflicted guilt that she had endured.

Her words when they came were now spoken in a softly controlled manner that demanded the attention of the listeners.

"Alice Mary Turner," she continued. "That's why Jack...I mean Cyril couldn't find me at first. When I first met him in September 1940, he had only just arrived in Coventry and nobody ever really knew where he had come from, though his accent was something of a giveaway. But he revelled in his man of mystery label. He knew me as Alice Turner, I knew him as Jack Corfield and everyone here knows me as Boyce. It was always assumed that it was my surname and I suppose it was much easier for me and for my Uncle and Auntie to leave it like that."

She stopped for a moment. At last she thought, she had the chance to unburden herself of all that had tormented her over the years. And to two people who not only deserved to know the truth, but two people she trusted implicitly. Smiling, she took a deep breath before continuing her story.

"When I knew Jack I was just sixteen, and I make no bones about it I was swept off my feet by him. This was completely against my parent's wishes, for they warned me what kind of a person he was, and it is something I deeply regret. When I realised I was pregnant my father went after him and was badly beaten up by Jacks mates, and soon after that he disappeared. Early in 1941 my parents bundled me off to here, with the excuse that I was escaping the bombing. Uncle

Albert and Auntie Edith were wonderful, they hid me from the world and paid for all the medical care so no-one ever knew the truth. I had a daughter, Rebecca, but she was so very ill from birth and only lived for six days."

Alice stopped to look for a reaction on the faces around the table, but received nothing other than expressions filled with empathy and understanding.

"All my life I've lived this secret, in many ways it's controlled every minute of my day," she continued. "I cannot tell you of all the regrets I have, for my parents and how I hurt them, for my daughter Rebecca who never had a life, and my Uncle and Auntie for giving me everything. And I've had to live with all of this as a giant cloud hanging over me. I've always feared the truth coming out you see, and then when Jack, I mean Cyril turned up I was lost with his threats of exposing my past. I didn't know which way to turn."

She leant back in her chair and took in a long slow breath as the weight of all her admissions finally evaporated into nothingness.

"Well!...It's all over now Alice," said Ben with softness in his voice. "It's all behind you with a clean future to look forward to."

"That's right," agreed Lucy. "No one knows any different and it certainly won't come from me and Ben. And that creature Jack or Cyril or whatever he calls himself will be too far away to do you any harm."

"Lucy's right. His trial will be in London," confirmed Ben. "And the news of it is very unlikely to reach up here."

"One thing I don't understand is what happened in that cellar in 1940," queried Lucy.

"Slippery Cyril was a small time racketeer or spiv living off the black market," Ben said leaning forward on the table. "But at the time it was really unfortunate that he had managed to avoid being arrested for anything so no fingerprints were available, otherwise it would never have got this far. Now he had a runner, Jack Corfield who was something like an errand boy for Cyril and because of his epilepsy he was exempt from military service."

For a few moments Ben sat back in his chair as if he was confirming the details correctly in his mind before he continued.

"It's my guess Cyril had big trouble with other villains, possibly because he was working some other spiv's patch. And then he received his call up papers and he panicked. So for a number of reasons he needed to disappear."

Now it was Ben's turn to refresh himself with the whisky tea before continuing.

"It's also my guess that he lured Jack Corfield into that bombed out cellar, killed him by smacking him over the head with the lead piping and then disfigured the face beyond recognition. He then, clumsily pushed rubble over the body to make it look like he had been killed in the bombing. Before that he swapped identities by dressing the body in an old suit with his name in it. Then he placed his own identity card and possessions into his victim's pockets, and his signet ring on his finger. And taking Jacks identity papers, exemption from military service letter and anything else to help with the deception and quite simply Cyril Oswald Blunt was recorded as deceased and Jack Corfield disappeared, apparently to reappear up in Coventry."

Ben stopped and looked from Alice to Lucy and then back to Alice.

"So thinking that with all the fuss of the blitz, the bombing, the threat of invasion and everything else that was going on, one more dead body would cause little interest. And in that he was right for the only mention was a few lines in the local paper and the coroner's verdict and report."

Ben relaxed for a moment as he looked at the intrigued expressions of the two women.

"Since then he has lived this other man's life. And it was only because of his arrogance and over confidence that made him think he had got away with it after all these years. Stupidly, that conceit was his downfall because he allowed himself to be photographed when he crashed in on the darts team photo. And those customers at the Tyburn instantly recognised him, even though they had thought he was dead. Apart from that one man who had been in the ARP who had remembered the suspicious death. I think that was the turning point for me. Being pointed towards the official records like that. So there you are my friends. What a story this will make for my memoirs," he concluded with a smile.

"It's still a lot to take in. But I cannot tell you how relieved I am that it's all over and I've been able to explain everything to you," Alice sighed. "And I can't tell you how grateful I am to you both."

"It's all over now Alice," Ben said reassuringly

"But will I have to give evidence?" Alice asked.

"We'll cross that bridge when we come to it," Ben replied. "But I will need a statement."

"It will all fit into the past quite nicely from here on in," said Lucy with a strangely, philosophic tone to her words. "Now then who's for another cuppa," she added rising from her chair and wandering over to the sink to fill the kettle.

And as Lucy fussed over her task Ben leant forward and clasped both of Alice's hands in his.

"Tell me," he said in a confidential voice that was almost a whisper. "Would you have used that revolver, the one you had hidden under the counter?"

Alice blushed, and for a moment her grip tightened on Bens hands. But then she said in a firm, determined voice.

"Yes...I would," she replied without any hesitation. "But afterwards, well I don't want to think about afterwards." she conceded as she gripped Ben's hand even tighter so that he winced.

For the briefest of moments he caught an expression on Alice's face that made him question the significance of her use of the word 'afterwards'

"You need someone to look after you!" Ben said smiling.

Alice pulled Bens hand up to her mouth and gently kissed it before she answered.

"Yes Ben....I believe I do."

****

And so the shop on the corner of Victoria Road and Chapel Street had weathered another crisis, but this time it would never be the same again. Life goes on, and that is as much information as you will be given. You can assume that every one lived happily ever after, and you may be right in thinking that. On the other hand the pessimists amongst you might decide that it was all doomed to fail and that might be right.

But for now the shop on the corner of Victoria Road and Chapel Street is once again open for business.

So we will leave it at that.

****

THE BALLAD OF JESSIE GRAY

The narrative that follows was found in a small wooden chest that my father kept in his wardrobe for many years. After his recent death I retrieved the box as I had always been intrigued by what it might contain. As it transpired all it contained were personal mementos of nostalgic significance from a very full life, such as photos, his school tie, a die cast model of a racing car, copies of the Hotspur from1933 and the Beano from 1938 and his corporal stripes from his war time national service. There were other items, including the engagement and wedding rings belonging to my mother, who had passed away 12 years earlier in 1996.

But perhaps the most poignant of all the items in that wooden chest were two bundles of letters, one tied round in pink ribbon and the other in blue, which I have to say have remained unread.

However, one final item was a folder that contained the pages that make up what follows. It had been written by my grandfather in the thirties and after his death in 1971 had been kept and treasured by my father.

I had always been aware that my grandfather had liked to write stories and poetry, but this was very different being a personal account of something he had actually experienced. So I will relate it to you in its complete form and although it was written in long hand there is neither, alteration or correction only the sincere hope that it brings to the reader as much enjoyment as it has done for myself and my family.

****

The Ballad Of Jessie Gray

Sunday 25th July 1937.

As I sit down to write this strange story I am at once reminded of just how unbelievable it might seem to the reader. Nevertheless, I must insist that the truth of the matter is entirely indisputable. The events that I will put before you did in fact happen, and did unnerve me severely at the time as I will explain. Even so, I will leave it to you the reader to judge for yourself what it all meant and in so doing I merely ask that you never dismiss the truth of how I saw it, and how I interpreted it.

I was holidaying on Exmoor during the late Spring of 1937. A kind of pilgrimage for me since my dear wife Jessica, or Jessie had suddenly passed away some five years earlier.

We had first met when I was invalided out of the front line in France in August 1918 after being wounded by shrapnel in my right thigh and calf and was convalescing at a retreat in Somerset in the last few weeks of the war. Jessie had been a volunteer worker there, and quite simply we fell in love.

On March 8th 1919 we were married at a simple service and had discovered the rural beauty of the Exmoor area on our short honeymoon. Hence, we came to love and fully appreciate it on our many subsequent visits there.

So out of the army and the war over I took up my position in the family printing business in Bristol, but soon after my father had died and so the job of running it became mine. And yet, life had been idyllic with a wife that I was devoted to and later a daughter, Catherine in 1923 and then a son, Steven in 1925. This happy situation all combined with the enviable position of being the boss of my own thriving business.

And it was this business that provided our growing family with a very comfortable life and the chance to holiday each year touring the wonders of Exmoor. From that first visit on our honeymoon it continued right through our marriage, sometimes with the children but quite often it was just the two of us when the pleasures of looking after our little brood had been willingly taken on by Jessie's parents.

However, just into the New Year of 1932 after a short illness my Jessie had died leaving me to the devastating future of a widower.

Although I retained overall control of the business I allowed the day to day operation to be taken on by a manager, who was only answerable to me. I was content to stay very much in the background and I am pleased to say that it has proven to have been a very sensible decision. For John Dyer has not only turned out to be a good, trusted friend, but has also been someone with the acumen to help move the business forward.

As a result this has given me the time to take myself away to the little corners of Exmoor that I had explored in the company of my dear Jessie. I sometimes have the children with me when their holidays coincide but at other times I just like to get away on my own.

And so it was that found me in the corner seat of the snug bar of the White Horse Inn just outside Barbrook near Lynmouth on Exmoor. It was early evening and I had just finished devouring a large bowl of beef stew with a doorstep of crusty bread, and for once I was leaning back thoroughly pleased with the world. A tankard of the local brew sat with its frothy head slightly curling over the brim, and I quite absentmindedly scooped it up with my finger and licked it away wanting to savour every drop.

A young couple came in with their drinks and sat close to each other in the light of the glowing inglenook. I wondered if that was how we had appeared, Jessie and I on the numerous occasions we had stopped at this inn. I was even staying in the same double room, the only double room the inn boasted of. Some might think it to be somewhat morbid, but I did not. Deep down I found it necessary to touch something familiar in that way. It did not make me feel sad it only gave me a sense of the richness that our marriage had been built on.

A large round bald head with a cheery face that sported a monstrous drooping moustache appeared through the frosted glass hatch that was the only contact with the rest of the inn.

"You all right there Mr Kempe?" the gruff voice said concealed behind that formidable hedge.

"Yes thank you George," I replied. "And my compliments to Aggie that stew was beautiful!"

"Thankee! I'll tell her," the landlord said with a slight bow of his shining dome. "By the way, I hope you don't mind me asking Mr Kempe, but do you know how long you'll be staying?"

"Why.....Do you need my room?" I answered.

"No no!" was the apologetic reply. "It's Aggie, she likes to know so she can plan you see."

"Would three more days be alright with you?" I said. "I'd like to get back this weekend so I'll leave Saturday morning."

"That be fine Mr Kempe. Thankee."

And the hatch closed with a soft click.

I slowly dropped back into my thoughts. The warmth from the fulfilling stew, the strong beer and the honest glow from the fire all contributed to a very pleasant sense of tranquillity. The young couple, totally oblivious to their surroundings whispered their sweet nothings with no fear of being overheard, and the muffled murmurings from the main bar sounded distant and far removed adding to a strange feeling of remoteness.

I must have allowed my eye lids to drop with my contentment, because the first I knew of the figure standing in front of me were the words that he spoke.

"Good evening. I wonder if you would care to purchase a copy of the parish magazine?"

The speaker was a slender man of medium height who seemed lost in a long, heavy brown overcoat but with a face that can only be described as one that truly suited the dog collar around his neck. For it was a pleasant, clean shaven face with an air of sincerity that you could easily trust and confide in and with strikingly blue eyes that peered down at me from behind a pair of round horn rimmed spectacles. The hat that sat jauntily on the mop of unruly fair hair was a cream, straw panama that had certainly seen better days.

As he had been speaking he had produced from a brown leather shoulder satchel, a wad of what I assumed were the parish magazine.

"Oh yes of course," I said straightening myself in my seat.

"That will be thruppence," he said. "If you would be so kind."

He placed a copy onto the table as I fumbled through my coins. I pulled out a florin and handed it to him.

"No need for the change," I said. "For the collection plate," I added with a smile.

"That is most kind of you sir, most generous," he said dropping the coin into a small dark velvet pouch, which he returned to his pocket. "You would be surprised how long it takes to collate the various articles and contributions each quarter. And it is invariably left up to me to distribute the latest publication by the required date. So I thank you again sir for your consideration, and I bid you a pleasant evening."

With a hearty doff of his hat he turned to leave and flourishing a final 'good evening' to the young couple, who I could now see had also bought a copy and probably without knowing it, the gently spoken clergyman slipped out of the door, closing it carefully behind him.

Once again the room sank back into its semi soporific state, although now I supped at my beer feeling a little more awake than previously. It happens like that sometimes, that you can be stirred from restfulness into restlessness in an instant, and so it was with the interruption to my musings by the dog collared apparition.

Normally, for me to pick up and read a parish magazine would be like most people who are cajoled into buying them, as alien an act as shaking hands with a leper. Although this analogy might upset those souls of a truly caring disposition, I have to say that the copy of the parish magazine that now lay on the table in front of me was all at once, tempting and repellent.

Some minutes passed as my eyes swept the room, at the pictures, the horse brasses, the crossed sabres over the fire place, even to a closer inspection of the young couple lost in their own company. But then boredom raised its finger and pointed directly towards the innocuous publication, and so finally I succumbed to impulse and picked up my purchase.

At first I flicked through the pages with a professional eye and decided that for a cheap run it was of a fair quality. It even boasted some illustrations of a sort, but if it brought money into the church coffers then it was worth it. Finally I committed myself to spending a few minutes to browse through the twenty or so pages of St Michael's parish magazine.

The front cover was of a sketch drawing of the church and the contents were the normal contributions of the ardent parishioners with a penchant to display their limited literary skills.

There was a diary of the coming events, a whist drive, a summer fair with stalls, a cub and scouts jumble sale and so on. There was also an article relating to a talk and slide show featuring Lynmouth, and of course the inevitable minutes of the parish council. All of which bordered on the mundane, but each so very important to the integrity and stability of the community life.

Sifting through I came across one or two more interesting items, including a description of some coins that had come to light at a local

Roman site. But as I placed the meagre volume face down on the table thinking I had read all that there was to read, something caught my eye that made me sit back in my seat with a cold chill embracing my body, even in the cosy warmth of that room. I looked towards the young couple to see if they had noticed how my demeanour must have altered, but they were too engrossed with their own company.

Again I allowed my gaze to fall onto the back page of the magazine. It was a poem, or I should say a ballad and I found myself mouthing the words of the title 'The Ballad Of Jessie Gray,' for they seemed to flare up at me from the paper.

I stared long and hard at the thin booklet, for this one item on the back page had truly set my heart and my mind racing. My dear late wife's maiden name had been Gray, and though her full name had been Jessica Anne Gray, all those that knew her and especially myself, never ever referred to her by any other name than Jessie. Not Jess, not even Jessica. It was always Jessie, Jessie Gray.

Tentatively I steeled myself to read on.

The Ballad Of Jessie Gray.

She waits with her lamp on the quay,
Eyes firmly fixed on the sea.
So much sorrow so much pain,
Lines the face of Jessie Gray,
For the man her heart yearns to see.

Each night come fair weather or storm,
She keeps her sad vigil alone.
Tight wrapped in widows shawl,
Tattered skirts to the floor,
Bare feet on the cold cobblestone.

She died by her own trembling hand,
Flotsam in the surf and shifting sand.
Her last wish was to join,
The man she loved from a boy,
And carry his seed and be damned.

The Ballad Of Jessie Gray

A few weeping friends gathered round,
As her body was laid into the ground.
Like all that sturdy breed,
Being slaves of the savage sea,
Fearing nought, but Gods mighty hand.

A stone cross marks the simple grave,
But time will soon erase the name.
Twixt the constant rolling swell,
And the chiming warning bell.
Yet cold comfort for this sweet maid.

Now she waits with her lamp on the quay,
Alas no one has seen her, but me.
So I tarry a while to pray,
For the wretched Jessie Gray.
Will her restless soul ever be free.
Anonymous.
1859.

Leaning back in my seat, I could still feel that icy chill filtering through my whole body making me shiver visibly, even though the logs in the fire still glowed and crackled out their homely warmth. I looked around the room and discovered I was alone. The young couple must have gone while I was so engrossed in my reading, and the realisation only added to my feeling of isolation.

I had read the ballad through three times absorbing every syllable, every nuance of the text and each time I had felt drawn into the emotion of the writer for the unfortunate Jessie Gray. I could almost sense the depth of overwhelming grief that lay between those simply formed but tortured lines. Even so, it also seemed clear to me that it had been written as some kind of epitaph, a memorial to someone the writer had known.

And whilst I was considering these notions it also came as a jolting thought to think it had been such a defining coincidence that had dictated the good vicar should find me here, and then to sell me this flimsy publication. It would have been so easy for those precious lines to have been lost to me forever. But questions were now tormenting the curiosity impulses in my brain, for I wanted to know who had written this intriguing set of verses and who and what events had been the influence for them to be put down onto paper. So many questions demanding answers I thought pensively.

I sensed someone standing over me, and I looked up to see the large rotund figure of George the landlord gazing down over that bush of a moustache.

"What's this I sees here!" he said with an impish, throaty chuckle that I imagined would be accompanied with a hidden grin. "I comes in here to collect glasses and finds somebody actually reading the parish magazine," he continued still chuckling at his own joke.

"Yes....well there were one or two items of interest," I answered rather sheepishly. "Tell me," I added. "The vicar who brought the magazine in, where does he live?"

"Ohh, you means the Reverend Millican," George said crossing to the fire place table, and retrieving two empty glasses. "A really nice gentleman is the vicar. He lives about mile down the road in the small cottage next to St Michaels Church. You can't miss it, straight down the road. Can I get you another drink Mr Kempe?" he offered as he opened the door into the corridor.

"No thank you George. I'm going up in a few minutes," I said fighting back a yawn.

"Well if you needs anything just give a shout...Goodnight to you," he called as the door closed behind him.

Once again I was alone, with my mind in turmoil. But one thing was certain I was now intent on discovering more about this ballad, and my first call in the morning would be on the Reverend Millican.

****

It was early afternoon before I finally got to meet the good Reverend. I had left the White Horse soon after demolishing one of Aggies truly hearty breakfasts to drive the short distance to St Michaels Church. It was already familiar to me as Jessie and I had visited the church on one of our numerous forays into Exmoor.

It stood there, as it had done for many centuries with its square tower dating from the 14th century. Although, the main part of the church dates from the 15th century with evidence to show that it now stands on the site of a previous wooden Saxon church, before being rebuilt in stone as seen today. I also remembered the adjoining elliptical graveyard which probably had pagan origins to it. Standing there I gazed at it for many minutes with memories of happier times flooding through my mind.

However, my first visit of the day, and the subsequent two others over the next few hours had been fruitless, with no sign of anyone in or around the church or what I assumed was the vicarage. Finally on my fourth attempt at unearthing some form of occupation, my knocking on the cottage door had brought out a rather unresponsive and surly middle aged woman who had stated very sternly that.

"The vicar's out on Church business. Come back later!"

And so I did, and just after four in the afternoon I was in time to catch the elusive clergyman dismounting from a forlorn looking three wheeled cycle with a large wicker basket housed between the rear wheels. He stood for a moment unhitching the tails of his cassock from his belt, and I was able to call to him before he entered the cottage. Turning, he greeted me with as warm a welcome as I could ask for, and smiled as he must have discerned the curious look that I gave his mode of transportation.

"Ahhhh!" he said doffing his well worn panama. "The generous gentleman from the White Horse, you've noticed my trusty stallion I see. Well," he said patting the saddle of the cycle affectionately. "I retrieved it from the garden shed when I took up residence three years ago, and being without the benefit of other means of transport, I adopted Trigger," he said smiling again at this allusion to the horse ridden by the film star cowboy Roy Rogers. "Anyway kind sir, it is good to see you again," he added offering out his hand to me. "I trust this visit will allow me to be of some service to you?"

"Well vicar I certainly hope so," I replied whilst my hand was still being shaken vigorously.

"Millican," he said. "Reverend Thomas Millican, and if we mean to get on I prefer plain Thomas."

"Well.. yes..of course Reverend....I mean Thomas!" I stammered taken slightly aback at the informality I was being offered. "Yes well I would like to speak to you about a little problem I have."

"Certainly, but may I ask who it is who has this problem."

The smile that accompanied the enquiry dismissed any formality in the words, and hinted merely at the vicars truly amiable nature.

"Yes of course...Thomas!" I replied warming to this man. "My name is Kempe. Paul Kempe. Or as I prefer it plain Paul."

We both smiled.

"Well...Paul. I'm due for my scones and a cup of tea, so perhaps you would care to join me?" he said opening the door to the cottage and showing me in. "Mrs Gibbs, my live out housekeeper will have it ready for me."

"Yes," I said with a wry smile. "We've already met."

"Ahhhhh!" was his knowing reply as he ushered me into what I assumed was his study.

Two of the walls of this spacious hideaway were designated bookshelves crammed with books of all shapes and sizes and ages. Even the table and desk seemed to have been commandeered to accommodate the over spill. But the two armchairs either side of the fireplace, the couple of frill shaded standard lamps and the pair of glass doors that opened onto the patio and the spacious rear garden, provided a homeliness that somehow complimented the owner.

"I have to confess to a passion for books, mainly I'm afraid with a tendency to relate to my own chosen vocation," Thomas said with a hint of apology and explanation. "But I won't bore you with that. Now how can I help you," he concluded going to a side table that had the pot of tea and scones and miraculously two cups and saucers already placed on it. This Mrs Gibbs must seem like a godsend to this establishment.

Then sitting opposite each other before the flickering contents of a small cast iron surround fire place, I began my explanation.

Without interruption my new found acquaintance allowed me to relate a little about myself and my dear wife, and what had brought me to this area of Exmoor. I then told him of my amazement at reading the ballad and exactly what it meant to me. I also spoke with not a little emotion of how it affected me, and now my desire was to try and trace its origins.

As I completed my narrative I looked across at my companion, at the honest lines of his face, the blueness of the eyes behind those heavy spectacles, and the unfashionable mop of tousled fair hair, who even now lounged in the chair opposite digesting every word I had spoken. All of which seemed to epitomise this rather unkempt, though deeply sensitive and devoted man that I was building a fondness for. I could easily imagine that underneath the rather languid but approachable appearance, beat a heart that was true and a brain to respect.

However, his first comment took me of my guard.

"I'm surprised you reached the back page," he chuckled. "Nobody ever seems to. Normally it's only those who contribute to the publication that ever seem to read it. Never mind though," he said sipping his tea. "The ballad you refer to turned up in the pages of a book I purchased recently, but I have no history for it whatsoever. It merely intrigued me enough to include it to fill up a page."

"And you have no idea where it came from?" I asked.

"No I'm afraid not," he said thoughtfully. "It was in a copy of Explanatory Notes Upon The New Testament, by John Wesley. It was first published in 1755 and reprinted many times since, but it was this first edition that I had come across quite by chance, and I am convinced to my shame that the seller was totally unaware of its true value and significance."

"Why was that?" I queried.

"Because I was able to buy it for half a crown," he stated. "Which I must say was a truly meagre amount for such a rare volume, admittedly not in the best condition, but worth infinitely more."

"May I ask where you bought it," I said excitedly leaning forward in my chair.

"Of course," he replied. "I bought it on a recent visit to Dunster. Yes it was a few weeks ago now. I went to see my very good friend who is the incumbent of St Georges Church. I served under him before this, my first parish. We share a glass of wine and he is always open to give me advice, and when I do get the chance to visit him I always allow time for a browse through the shops."

"And one of the shops sold you this book?" I said with a little hint of frustration creeping into my voice.

"Yes...That's right," he said bringing himself back to the context of the conversation. "Yes it's called Digby's Emporium," he continued smiling broadly. "A rather large title for quite a small establishment I'm afraid to say. But that is the place. I'm sure you'd find a visit there very enlightening,"

THE BALLAD OF JESSIE GRAY

This last sentence was accompanied by what I could only assume was the merest suspicion of a chuckle. He was still smiling to himself as he stretched across to his desk and reached for a book.

"This is the offending volume of my embarrassing admissions," he said opening the large, heavy, calf bound book, and from within its pages he retrieved a folded piece of paper.

"It's not in the accepted classic four line stanza for ballads," he advised. "More like the five line stanza or cinquain, I believe it's called. In this case a kind of shanty ballad that you might hear in harbour taverns. Though really a ballad can take many forms, it's the content that identifies it as a ballad. And on this piece of paper is truly written a ballad. It has the storytelling, the emotion and the simple sincerity of the writer's heart. Unfortunately, there being no clue to the identity of the writer other than the year 1859, I found it necessary to assign it as anonymous. However I digress." he concluded handing the folded paper to me.

Gingerly I took it from him and carefully unfolded the somewhat brittle, yellow with age, scrap of paper. I gazed, intrigued at the almost intricate yet childlike scrawl. Each letter it seemed had been formed with great effort and thought. And I wondered if this was due to some infirmity or to the age of the writer or could it have been that the complexity of the word structure of the ballad that had taxed the writer's ability to formulate the words onto the paper.

For many minutes I seemed to be transported back all those years, to 1859 when the ballad had been written. I could almost feel and hear the scrape of the pen slowly shaping each letter onto the paper, as if each one was being torn from the very soul of the anonymous author. In a silence that I could almost sense was now enfolding me, I read and re-read each word, each line and each verse, totally absorbed in the images and pictures that they were conjuring up in my imagination.

Then as if awakening from a deep dream filled sleep I looked up and into the kindly features of my newly found friend. So deep had been the depth of my distraction that I had completely forgotten where I was and equally to the existence of my host.

"I'm sorry," I said apologetically. "I seem to have been lost for the moment."

"Yes," Thomas said with something of a knowing smile of understanding.

"I feel very humble," I said. "As if I've shared someone's very intimate emotions, and it's made me feel very humble indeed."

I leant across and handed the folded paper back to Thomas who replaced it inside the book.

"Now Paul," he said looking me firmly in the eyes. "What do you intend to do?"

"Well... tomorrow I will drive up to Dunster, and visit this shop," I said shaking myself out of my musings and at the same time considering the rather long drive. "And with your permission I would like to take the book so as to be to be able to remind the owner of where he got it from. That is if you've no objection Thomas."

"Of course you can," he said before adding. "But I would ask that you don't remind the proprietor of how much I paid for it, or for that matter what it is probably worth."

I smiled inwardly to myself at the deadly serious expression this last sentence had brought to the good Reverends normally so honest features.

"Of course not," I said suppressing my instinct to laugh. "I can keep your little secret."

We both saw the funny side of our little conspiracy and laughed out loud. What a bonus it was to meet a member of the clergy with such an open mind, and equally a sense of humour.

Now the business was out of the way we spent the next hour or so chatting generally, just trying to put the world to rights. Only once were we interrupted when Mrs Gibbs brought a fresh pot of tea into us before adding.

"I'll be off now vicar."

"Yes...Good bye Mrs Gibbs and thank you," was the reply before he added to the closed door. "A bit gruff as you probably experienced earlier today. But an absolute treasure. Does my washing and cleaning, and provides that feminine touch so vital I think. But the cooking I do myself. So tomorrow evening you must come here for something to eat. Even though it will be Thursday, it will be fish, freshly caught off Lynmouth," he confirmed. "Friday should be the day to eat fish, but my verger Harold Bevan always goes to Lynmouth on a Thursday and brings me back either herring or mackerel or even lobster. So this week we break with tradition so you can savour a freshly caught delicacy and in return provide me with an update on your adventures in Dunster."

"That's very kind of you. Thank you," I said with a genuine feeling of gratitude.

****

I slept a very restless sleep that night. My mind was in a whirl with questions and a gamut of contradictions that were all intermingled with images that left me somewhere between slumber and awake.

So it was, after one of Aggies mammoth breakfasts that I found myself, with the borrowed John Wesley book by my side, in 'Mable', my trusty Austin 6 Saloon. It had been my Jessie who had fondly named our first car back in 1920 and the name had somehow stuck on all our subsequent motor vehicles.

I was now heading towards Lynmouth, where I would join the Minehead coast road to travel eastward and my ultimate destination of Dunster. The morning was now beginning to brighten with the promise of a clear, sun lit sky and I felt in good heart at the prospect of my impending mission.

Reaching the junction I turned right along a road that had become so familiar to me over the years. I then began the climb towards Countisbury Common with the countryside opening up to reveal the sparse outcrops of occupation and the wild isolation for which the area was renown. However, I was soon bracing myself for the test on the brakes and gears and the two and a half mile, one in four descent down into Porlock, where I made a stop for petrol that was followed by some welcome refreshment in Sophie's Tea Shop, so often visited by myself and Jessie in those halcyon days together.

Then it was ever onward, passing through Allerford, Brandish Street, Buddle Hill, Venniford Cross and so on. Until, with Minehead and the distant Bristol Channel prominent on my left, I finally turned right at Marsh Street. From there it was now inland towards the picturesque town of Dunster, with its stunning castle, its church, its Yarn Market and its history.

I parked just outside the town so as to be able to take a quiet stroll up towards the Yarn Market and Hotel. It was a stroll Jessie and I had enjoyed once before, and it did bring a catch in my throat when I reached the top and stood in the shade of the Yarn Market and gazed thoughtfully down the broad, sloping main street with the little shops and cottages on either side.

Beyond the roofs of the shops on the right was the impressive square tower of St Georges Church, and further away still and rising up from a distant mantle of trees was the castle, dominating the higher ground as it proudly overlooked the town and countryside around. Originally of Norman origin, this later imposing pile was thought to have come from the early 16th century.

The town had been prosperous since the middle ages for the wool trade, and as I continued my stroll down the main street I could almost sense the antiquity of the place. With the wood burning smoke that curled upwards from the numerous chimneys, the absence of motor vehicles and the faces that glanced inquisitively at this stranger within their midst. For this was still something of a remote destination for the traveller, even though Dunster was now succumbing to the fact that it had been discovered.

Reaching the bottom of the road I looked round and caught sight of a dowdy little shop brandishing the dingy sign, Digby's Emporium. Windows either side of a wood panelled door displayed all manner of dusty items from books, pictures, hats of all kind to a hunting horn, cooking utensils and much, much more. All of which were tightly crammed in with no thought of presentation and looking as if they had not been disturbed in many a year.

For a few long moments I stood steeling myself with a series of deep breaths whilst rather hesitantly fingering the weighty John Wesley book, under my arm. I had taken the precaution of leaving the precious ballad in the care of the good Reverend.

Then opening the door I entered and was quite overpowered by the mustiness and the mixed aromas. The impression given on the outside by the distressed and dusty window display now continued inside and I remained in the doorway adjusting my senses to the odious atmosphere, and my eyes to the dimness of the lighting. I wondered how this place had remained unnoticed by Jessie and myself on our previous visit to the town. But then, we were not looking specifically for it, and quite honestly it was a shop that could be so easily overlooked.

Moving further in, I found myself stepping over and moving between the clutter of chairs, cupboards, stacked picture frames, rolled up carpets, stuffed animals, crockery, books, ornaments, clocks and a myriad of other items too numerous to catalogue.

The place seemed to be unattended at first, but then I caught sight of a glowing cigarette in the far reaches of the shop. Carefully approaching and peering through the murky light a dark shape began to take form. Now I was able to discern, sitting behind a small table strewn with books, papers and parts of a dismembered clock, what can only be described as a voluminous heap of coats and scarves surmounted by a large, completely bald piggish head. Perched precariously on the snout, sat a pair of pince-nez spectacles with two, round, jaundiced eyes peering over them. The whole of this daunting, sallow countenance clearly indicated it as being the result of a completely sedentary existence.

"Ah.. Good afternoon," I said trying to avoid a cloud of cigarette smoke that had swirled my way.

Being only an occasional pipe smoker, the aroma was nothing like I had ever smelt before and it left me with my eyes watering and also wondering exactly what the cigarette was made up of.

"Are you the proprietor?" I asked, but no answer seemed to be forthcoming and so I repeated my question. "Could you tell me if you are the owner, please?"

Again there was no response only another cloud of smoke that this time made me take a step back into a table with a stuffed chimpanzee on it. I turned in time to steady the wobbling monkey as a voice called out from the smouldering mound.

"Be careful with the merchandise if you please, sir," breathed a voice in a husky whisper that was probably a consequence of this evil, polluted atmosphere.

"I apologise!" I said. "Forgive me!"

"Just be careful," the throaty voice grunted, as another cloud of the thick odious smoke was emitted in my direction. "In answer to your question, I own this place. So what do you want?"

I was beginning to feel like an intruder. That this was not a shop, but a private residence that welcomed no-one and tolerated no interruptions, and this feeling made me uneasy and unwilling to continue the interview. I was also aggravated by the surly response to my innocent enquiry, but I had a mission to complete and this made me speak with a contrived authority.

I lifted the book from under my arm and laid it down heavily on the table.

"This was purchased from you approximately three weeks ago," I said forcing the words out as if there was a specific reason for asking the question.

Moving the book further under his snout I spoke in more forceful tones.

"And I'd like to know where you obtained it?"

"Why?" was the steely retort.

The whole deplorable ambiance of the shop and the continuous smog that emanated from behind the table all added to my taut sense of anger and contempt.

"Because...I want to know!" I said with a pointed finger jabbing only inches away from his shiny, sweat smeared face.

But then from somewhere, perhaps by inspiration I added.

"My enquiries have brought me here, and I would suggest that what records you may keep of your dealings, would be of great interest to us!"

"Who are you?" came the hoarse response. "Are you the police?"

The whole of the ragbag form quivered visibly, and the bulbous head swayed in obvious agitation as these words were spoken. Perhaps it was now being confirmed in his befuddled mind that my grey suit, collar and tie and trilby hat all measured up to how he envisaged authority.

Further inspiration seized me and I pursued my ploy by thrusting into my inside jacket pocket and fiercely flashed my driving licence into his face, but before the flickering eyes could focus for an opportunity to see through my deception, it was back from whence it came.

"Now then a simple question requiring a truthful answer and I will have no need to bother you further," I said leaning forward over the table.

"What do you want to know?" was the reply in a much more subdued manner. "And you'll leave me alone?"

"I've no business with you other than this," I said with an authoritative edge to my voice. "So where did you get this book from?"

A thick podgy hand appeared from within the folds of the clothes, and the sausage like fingers flicked the book open and began to leaf through the pages.

"Well!" I said.

The Ballad Of Jessie Gray

"I'm thinking!" was the mumbled response. "I'm thinking!"

For a few moments I stood watching the fingers pouring over the pages. I did not want to force the issue too much as I was now beginning to doubt the deception I had invoked. I was on the point of picking the book from his sticky grasp and exiting, when the face lifted towards me allowing the layers of jowls to wobble as he spoke, this time with a little more subservience.

"It was brought in by one of my regulars," he said throatily midst another cloud of the poisonous haze. "A job lot in a box."

"A name!" I demanded. "A name and full address!"

I was still assuming my role as a member of the constabulary, for it had seemed to have impressed this cantankerous pile of rotting humanity. But as I stood there waiting for an answer the mixture of unwashed blubbery flesh and sweat ridden clothes, the rank tobacco smoke and God knows what else all contrived to waft towards me in ever increasing waves, to the point that I felt my stomach begin to heave in revolt.

With considerable effort I forced my self control to take charge.

"An answer!" I barked. "Now!"

"Well, as I said it was in a box, a job lot of books. I bought the lot," he muttered contritely "Never said from where they got them from."

"Who sold them to you, and the address. That's all I want!" I said thrusting my fist onto the table so that it shook, dislodging some papers onto the floor and causing the shop keepers bloated features to wobble again as he fidgeted on his chair. Where was I getting this strength of such a dubious character from, even though it seemed to be obtaining the desired effect.

"Came in one day and was sold two days later," was the somewhat mumbled, guarded reply. "His name is Pentilow. Isaac Pentilow of Wooton Farm four miles from here on the Porlock road," he said breathing heavily into the scarf that had crept up around his face.

"If that information is wrong," I said in purposeful tones. "I shall be back and the worse for you. So be warned!"

And with the name and address burning into my brain I snatched the book up and made a hurried exit, closing the door behind me with a bang.

I walked briskly up the street, taking deep breaths to clear my clouded mind and to get the odious smells and tastes from my nose and mouth. I soon passed the Yarn Market and did not stop until I was sitting in the comfort and security of my car. I scribbled the name and address onto a scrap of paper before I allowed myself time to sit back and relax.

It was then that I became fully aware of the deception that I had employed, something that under normal circumstances I would never have dreamed of using. Being a devotee of the popular novel since boyhood I felt a sudden thrill surge through me when I compared my little adventure with some of those fictional creations of John Buchan and Ryder Haggard amongst so many. But deep down there was a certain satisfaction in acting like the suave and intrepid Bulldog Drummond, of more recent literary and film fame and a smile creased my face at the thought.

For a few more minutes I allowed my mind to consider the details of my little exploit as I tried to imagine what goings on did go on in that vile smoky atmosphere, behind that wooden door. Equally I could only surmise what kind of clientele actually frequented that musty pit of what I can only describe as junk.

And with these thoughts came another question into my mind, what on earth was the good Reverend Thomas Millican ever doing in a place like that. With this intriguing notion crowding my senses I started my car in preparation for the journey back.

Two and a half hours or so later and I was again motoring along, having concluded my undertaking in the most agreeable terms possible. I had soon found Wooton Farm and a tall, friendly middle aged Mr Isaac Pentilow had invited me into the farm house. His amiability had even extended to offering me a glass of homemade cider and to freely provide me with the information I was looking for. It transpired that he had been visiting relatives in Lynbridge and had attended a school fete which had featured a white elephant stall. The fete had been run by a Mrs Dempsey and the box of books had been left unsold.

"And I bought the lot for tuppence," he had confirmed. "But that's all I can tell you." he had concluded rather apologetically.

From there he had resold them for a modest profit to the proprietor of Digby's Emporium and so thanking Mr Pentilow profusely I had taken my leave and was soon well on my way.

Now with the steep climb up Porlock Hill behind me and crossing the barren wastes of Countisbury Common before the long drop down to Lynmouth I began, for the umpteenth time to recite the ballad in my mind and as always two lines in particular resonated harshly against my senses.

> *She died by her own trembling hand,*
> *Flotsam in the surf and shifting sand.*

****

Once again I had been subjected to a restless night. After I had returned from my dinner with the Reverend Millican, I had sat at the window of my room until almost daylight staring at the clear sky and stars. The freshly caught delicacy that had been hinted to at our first meeting turned out to be mackerel fillet, served with all the requisite trimmings. Rather than with wine the meal was accompanied by a good few glasses of local cider plus a genial host and conversation that had gone a long way to ease the tensions of the day. The Reverend had turned out to be an accomplished cook, and I had congratulated him on his prowess.

During the evening, I had recounted my day in detail and he had been intrigued with how I had deceived Mr Digby with my driving licence scam. He had laughed out loud, and had joked that I would not go to heaven.

However, I had managed to parry this jibe by saying in a mock accusing tone.

"I must say though Thomas, I was a little concerned about a man of the cloth ever entering that pit of very questionable moral intentions."

He had leant back in his chair and openly laughed at my scornful expression.

"I expected that you might comment on that," he had said still between his guffaws. "The books!" he continued. "Merely for the books my dear friend, would ever induce me beyond that ominously doubtful portal."

It was this openness of character that was endearing this man to me, and the ease and lightness in our conversation. He was nothing like the image of the parish priest that you would expect. And at one point he freely admitted to the fact. He had also said that his only wish was to serve the community as best as he could and the way to do that was to be totally approachable. Unfortunately, this was frowned on by those above him, though he had admitted to me that he had no ambition of climbing the ecclesiastic ladder and so he was more than content with his lot in life.

But leaning forward in his chair he had looked me straight in the eye's and said.

"Paul, we are all aboard the same ship on the same ocean of life, with all the same tempests or calms to contend with. And no matter what diversity there is in our beliefs, our faiths and our religions we are all trusting in the one captain to see us to our save anchorage."

And that was the only time he ever expressed himself in that manner, though he had also added.

"I have no wish to burden you with my calling, my friend, for that is a matter for my conscience, as yours is to you. But, if you come to church on Sunday, then that is my place where I am able to speak freely."

Although I had momentarily felt the significance of this statement and the way it had been put across to me, it was soon put to one side when Thomas had asked me about the box of books. Whereby, I told him that it had been bought as a left over item on a white elephant stall at a fete to raise funds for some local school. He had then asked if my informant had proffered a name and I told him that Mr Pentilow had mentioned a Mrs Dempsey, whereby he had grimaced and had sat back in his chair with a deep felt sigh.

"She's the local Post Mistress in Groscott," he had finally announced. "A formidable lady indeed, so I would suggest, if you have no objection, that I accompany you so I can act as a mediator. Because, believe me Paul, I think you may have need of one."

Now I was sitting in my car outside the vicarage waiting for the good Reverend. I had breakfasted at the White Horse, confirming I would be staying an extra day or so and had telephoned home to inform them of my change of plans. I was now even more adamant that I wanted to trace the story of the ballad to its source.

"A very good morning to you Paul," came the jovial greeting. "Ready for your expedition into no-man's land?"

"Why?" I said smiling. "Is this Post Mistress that daunting?"

"Could be," Thomas declared as he adjusted himself into the passenger's seat. "Could very well be!" he chuckled mischievously to himself.

The drive took no more than half an hour with the Reverend acting as navigator. It was a very pleasant excursion with the conversation hearty and the passing scenery as picturesque as you would expect.

As we entered the small village of Groscott the Reverend was instantly recognised with a wave by the two or three people that we passed. It occurred to me then that this man, with the approachable outlook on his vocation was indeed well liked and respected. Following his pointing finger I drew to a stop outside the little shop with a sign that also indicated the Post Office.

Inside the shop however, the elderly woman behind the counter and the two customers seemed to be somewhat reserved and guarded with their greetings, which the Reverend tried to brush over with his naturally exuberant and friendly manner. Their response to me was to say the least, rather chilly, but it was not as frozen as the countenance that greeted both of us from behind the grill that represented the offices of His Majesty's Post Office. It belonged to a large lady with piercing eyes, scowling cheeks, and the hint of a moustache above the upper lip of the mouth that curled downwards at the corners from permanently being pushed in that direction.

"A very good morning to you Mrs Dempsey," Thomas said cheerily with a mock bow of the head.

"Less of the flannel vicar," came the curt retort. "I'm not one of your congregation!"

"Yes of course Mrs Dempsey," he said slightly humbled yet coming straight to the point. "This gentleman is Mr Kempe, and he is interested in a box of books that was left over and sold after the recent school fete. He was wondering if you could tell him where the books came from."

"Why!" was the stone wall reply.

"Well," Thomas continued. "Mr Kempe is very interested in tracing where one of the books came from."

"And you expect me to know where every single item on that stall came from. Is that it," she said puffing herself out with importance.

"I was far too busy organizing the event with little or no help from anyone to be bothered over one book. People don't realise how much work it takes"

"Yes I'm sure," Thomas said trying to placate the onslaught, but it was to no avail as Mrs Dempsey continued undaunted.

"I have the responsibility of this Post Office. I have the Parish Council. I have the Womens Institute, amongst all my other responsibilities. And you come here asking me about one book. Well I never!" she said. "Well I never!!!!" now with an obvious rouge filtrating into her cheeks.

"A good day to you Mrs Dempsey!" Thomas responded dryly and turning sharply away he cut the conversation short. Lifting his panama politely to the occupants of the shop he led the way out onto the pavement.

"I'm sorry Paul, but I did warn you of the intractable nature of Mrs Dempsey!" Thomas said with a deep sigh of frustration in his voice. "Thank goodness she is not a member of my church!"

For a few moments we stood looking at each other, with the same thoughts of 'what to do next?' humming through our heads, and both feeling the disappointment of reaching this momentary dead end.

"I suggest we head back to the vicarage, perhaps Mrs Gibbs might know someone who could help us track down one the fete's committee members." Thomas suggested.

And with that we turned away with a slight air of defeat in our step.

However, as we walked towards the car a hand shot out from a side passage to the shop and caught the Reverends arm. In the shadows could be seen the elderly woman who had been behind the counter of the shop.

"Never mind that miserable so and so, vicar," she said with a quick, furtive glance back along the street to the shop entrance. "The person you wants to see is Miss Fletcher down at Bramley Lodge. She was in charge of the white elephant stall. She can help you."

"Mrs Luscombe," Thomas whispered, quietly taking the elderly woman's hands. "We are truly in your debt. We thank you and a very good day to you Mrs Luscombe" he said with a tilt of his head as he once again lifted his panama in an exuberant display of our gratitude.

Now armed with this information we drove the mile or so to Bramley Lodge, a cottage smaller than the title would imply where we

The Ballad Of Jessie Gray

were made welcome by the tall, willowy, tweed suited figure of Miss Ethel Fletcher.

There was a brusqueness in her manner that seemed to be in keeping with her status of spinster and retired teacher, but it also belied her willingness to offer us tea and biscuits and to furnish us with the details regarding the donator of the box of books. She remembered it particularly because it was the only item left over, mainly because of the age and dusty condition of the contents.

She also seemed to display a fondness for my companion, who became a little flustered when each time a comment was referred in his direction it was always accompanied with a beaming smile which seemed a little grotesque on such severe features.

It was not until we were on our way to our next point of enquiry that had been provided so cordially by Miss Ethel Fletcher, that my new friend confided in me by saying that the good lady actually terrified him. Equally he also admitted that she was, and always had been a very well respected member of his congregation and the community, but that she had taken something of a "shine" to him.

To me it seemed that it could be useful, as today had proven. And my observations made us both smile when I mentioned this to Thomas.

****

Killimoor Farm was something of a rambling, ramshackle affair with the farm house in need of a complete overall and a varied selection of out buildings that pointed to more prosperous days. Across the undulating fields towards the north could be seen the silhouetted spire of Saint Andrews Church, and beyond that about a mile, the rugged northern sea coast of the Exmoor downs.

"I know Mr Coates, Paul," said Thomas putting on his serious face. "He's a bit of a recluse as you can see from the state of this place. So it might be better if I go in and clear a path for us."

So I agreed and watched the affable clergyman, armed with the John Wesley volume housing the ballad as he strode towards the farmhouse.

Sitting back to wait for the path to be cleared, I was now able to ponder on the whole of the last few days. Up until the moment that I had read the ballad my stay had been pleasant, nostalgic to a point and uneventful. I liked the White Horse and the affable George and Aggie. The food was always good and homely, and the room held memories for me that could never fade. And the long, meandering lanes where each bend had offered a fresh insight into the way of life of the inhabitants had always held a fascination for my Jessie and equally for myself.

For we would use the drives that we took, to explore all the nooks and crannies of the sumptuous countryside, stopping to take in the views or to absorb the quiet ambiance of the scattered little hamlets and villages as we came across them. It had been quite easy to lose ourselves in our own companionship, and the isolation that we encountered. Now in my musings I could almost feel the gentle touch of my Jessie's hand on mine, and detect the fragrant aroma of the perfume she loved to wear.

But then I was spiralling down the verses of the ballad, now so familiar in my consciousness that I was able to recite each line. And with each line I could almost dissect the emotion that had controlled the pen in the writing of each individual word on that aging scrap of paper. And as my mind continued to mull through these deep thoughts I was once again confronted by the grotesque image of Digby's Emporeum and its equally obnoxious owner, which abruptly brought me back to reality with a start.

Fortunately, I was able to replace that brief but odious encounter with more pleasant thoughts before becoming aware of agitated tapping on the car window. The Reverend Millican was standing there, smiling and indicating that I should follow him.

As we approached the door of the farmhouse he turned to me, again wearing his serious face.

"Listen," he confided. "Mr Coates doesn't like visitors, and certainly not outsiders. Unfortunately you are an outsider. But he respects the cassock I wear and has agreed for you to hear what he has to say. If he offers any hospitality accept it gracefully, but let me do the talking."

Giving the door a respectful knock the Reverend pushed it open and we entered. It was like entering a time capsule. The dark oppressive interior boasted panelled walls and a beamed ceiling with a large inglenook fireplace housing a substantial, black, cast iron range and wooden settle. The lighting was provided by a number of strategically placed oil lamps, for little sun light was allowed to permeate through the heavily curtained window. Central to the room, resting on the floor of slate slabs was a large oak table that could easily have sat a dozen or more people on the benches that ran either side of its length.

Standing in the shadows on the far side of the room I could make out a tall slim figure, dressed as antiquated as his surroundings. The heavy tweed suit and plus fours all looked as if they had been made for a fuller figure. The narrow, grey chinstrap beard that seemed to follow the jaw line of the long, aquiline face and the thinning grey hair parted in the middle all combined to testify to the unapproachable, austere, hermit like existence that I imagined the gaunt figure followed.

"Mr Coates," Thomas said in somewhat humble terms as if he was aware of breaking some kind of intimate silence. "This is Mr Kempe."

"How do you do Mr Coates," I said as lightly as I could muster whilst resisting my natural instinct to offer my hand for shaking. My instant thought had been that it would not have been accepted.

The reply when it came was merely a grunt and an acknowledged drop of the head.

"Urm!" Thomas continued. "I wonder if you would tell us what you know of the ballad that I showed to you a few minutes ago. It would be of immense interest to Mr Kempe and myself."

After a few moments the figure moved to a huge, dark, ornamented sideboard and looked towards us over his shoulder.

"You'll take cider!" he said as more of a command than an invitation.

"Why yes...yes thank you Mr Coates," my friend flourished. "Thank you!"

"Then sit, the both of you," he said while picking up three tankards and a large jug before approaching the other side of the table where he stood looking from myself, and then to the Reverend and back to me again. The probing dark eyes seemed to be examining every fibre of our beings, and I for one was totally engrossed by the scrutiny.

So we sat down with a tankard of the strong brew in front of us and waited for our reluctant host to begin. He took a long pull at his drink, then in his rough tones he began a narrative that was as strange as it was poignant, as moving as it was so obviously true in every detail. It was a narrative that would have been a credit to any skilful raconteur or storyteller. It concerned the sad story of two brothers, Jacob and Joseph Baunsall.

The father of the Baunsall Boys had been a fisherman scraping a living in the wake of the Napoleonic Wars, fishing for herring or lobster either in his small boat or as a crew member on the larger vessels plying out of Lynmouth. It is also very likely that he could have been involved in avoiding the Revenue Men whilst earning from the smuggling trade.

One day however, like so many before and since, he had gone out as a crew member with the herring fleet from Lynmouth and never returned. This left eleven year old Jacob and nine year old Joseph to support their invalid mother.

Like numerous other tight communities all along the coast their small cottage was one of a dozen or so that formed a small hamlet a few miles to the west of Lynmouth. Being remote and insular and overlooking the steep cliffs with the rough cut steps that led down to the sheltered inlet with the name of Stepdown Cove. They were also left with their fathers two man fishing boat. So the boys, who had the strength of character and the will to survive took up where their father had so prematurely and tragically ended.

However, still too young to work as crew with the fishing fleet they eked out a living for themselves and their mother as runners on the Lynmouth quay, and also for the dubious occupants of the Rising Sun Tavern, notorious for the smuggling trade. But the mother soon fell victim to the hardships of her existence, and had died cursing the God that had given her that life.

And so now the Baunsall Boys were alone, and in some respects it made it easier for them for now they were answerable to no-one, but themselves.

Life continued very much the same for the boys, each day was a test of survival by whatever means was available to them, including to taking their fathers small boat out from Stepdown Cove to lay lobster pots. And for over two years, Jacob and Joseph Baunsall showed that they were trusted survivors and had become men in the eyes of the fishing community.

But into this conundrum came Jessica Mary Louisa Gray then at the age of ten and known to those in her world as Jessie, Jessie Gray.

Jessie's family had moved from Minehead to take over a small coaching inn on the coast road eastward out of Lynmouth, the family being her father, mother and Clarence her older brother by five years.

As her father began to develop his business it became necessary for him to take his small dogcart down into Lynmouth harbour to buy fresh fish and lobsters, and on some occasions he would allow his daughter to accompany him. Jessie found these little diversions so exciting with the fishing boats, and the hustle and bustle of the busy quay side. She would sit and watch, fascinated by all the comings and goings along the harbour while her father completed his business, invariably ending in the Rising Sun Tavern before starting for home.

It was on one such morning that her father had taken the young Jessie to Lynmouth, that she had caught sight of the waifish and roguish Joseph Baunsall. He had been standing near a group of fishermen with their clay pipes burning, discussing the days catch, but his interest had been taken by the fair young girl with the demur bonnet and cascading auburn ringlets, sitting on the seat of the dogcart watching him. She was dressed in a long, pale, high cut muslin dress with a pink crocheted shawl round her shoulders. At her feet lay a mastiff who snarled menacingly at any over inquisitive passerby who should show interest in the dogcart, its occupant or its contents. Even at their tender ages of ten and eleven, both Jessie and Joseph seemed intrigued by the diversity of each other's backgrounds, and as a consequence an attraction was born.

Jessie saw beneath the ragged clothes and impish good looks, a boy that seemed to have the strength to be the strong man that she did not see in her father, who even now was in The Rising Sun doing his doubtful dealings while addressing his thirst. She also saw in the boy's gaze, a worldliness that all at once intrigued her, bewildered her and made her slightly fearful of. And although there was a distance between them she felt she could describe every miniscule line on his face and every strand of his hair.

Equally, she was totally unaware that the feelings that were setting her pulse to race, and the breath to catch in her throat should not be happening to a young girl of ten years old. Without knowing why, she could not detract her fixed study of the boy even if she had wanted to.

And for Joseph, in his eyes he saw in Jessie a vision of subtle beauty, like the flowers he had seen opening to the sun along the cliff tops he walked daily to and from Stepdown Cove. In his passing he had seen them, but rarely appreciated the splendour of these little miracles of nature. Until now, as he gazed on the vision that was Jessie Gray.

There was no poetry in any part of young Josephs life and he found it difficult to think, let alone speak what he would like to have said. For this boy on the verge of manhood was also very unaware of the feelings that were gripping him as he peered longingly at something he never thought could exist in his world of the smugglers runner and herring boats.

But even though the attraction was instant for both, it seemed at that time to always be destined to be from a distance. On the occasions when she accompanied her father all Jessie wanted was to catch a glimpse of the boy. And for Joseph it was the same, all he wanted was to stare, mesmerised from any vantage point that he could find at what he came to believe was the true conception of an angel, here before him. For Jessie would sit, either in the dogcart or on the bench outside the Rising Sun Tavern and lower her eyes, but always managing to keep the handsome boy within her eye line and all the time being well protected by her mule sized, canine protector.

Inevitably the curiosity, the mutual fascination became more profound and obvious until smiles began to nervously filter into the surreptitious glances. For almost two years Jessie would use any ruse to be able to accompany her father on his excursions down into Lynmouth, to the point of even taking her pad, pencils and watercolours to sketch the various scenes on the quay, merely as an excuse. Almost without exception, Joseph would appear and the two would converse almost telepathically through their eyes and their smiles. And that was how it could have remained, but for another twist of fate.

Now with Joseph thirteen, and Jessie twelve they began to view each other differently and were able to adopt an understanding of their maturing emotions. It was also more than apparent to both that even though not a single word had passed between them, the attraction was stronger than either could endure. It was also apparent that their situation was totally reliant on Jessie, and her father's business dealings in Lynmouth.

Then suddenly, for whatever reason and without warning her father's business excursions ceased.

For both Jessie and Joseph it felt like their worlds had collapsed into infinity without trace. Jessie could not confide to any member of her family and her circle of friends was so very limited that it meant all mention of her deep emotions had to be painfully contained.

And for Joseph without his angel to gaze at longingly and now believing that he was not worthy of her considerations he delved into the hard work of survival with his brother.

However, with the passage of time the Baunsall boys enterprise began to expand and grow. They found a profitable business by delivering their herring and lobster catches by handcart, directly to the growing number of small hotels and restaurants that were emerging in Lynmouth and Lynton and the surrounding area.

And it was on one of these selling forays that Joseph finally came across a small coaching inn on the coast road eastward out of Lynmouth and in so doing he also came face to face at last with Jessie, his vision of an angel. After so much time of just seeing each other from a distance, they were there within touching distance and unable to utter a word. Although it was more than obvious to both that the attraction had not dwindled by a solitary jot.

But that situation did not remain for long. Each occasion that followed allowed a little more familiarity. At first it was a shy hello, but that soon extended into brief conversations and inevitably these meetings began to take on snatched moments of warm intimacies. Until the day that one was overheard by Jessie's mother and Joseph was banned from ever darkening their doorstep again.

But it was now too late to alter the path that destiny was dictating they should follow. With the boy bordering on manhood, and the girl teetering on the precipice of becoming a woman, they found that the only thing that mattered was each other, and that was a dangerous place to be.

Secret assignations that were coveted by both remained their only contact, until just after Jessie's sixteenth birthday, when the rumours that had reached Jessie's father were confirmed. Whereby he followed his daughter and confronted them together. An argument broke out, but Mr Gray was no match for the now powerful seventeen year old Joseph. The outcome was that the swearing parent received a split lip and the young couple ran away to the cottage Joseph shared with his brother.

The father only visited the cottage once and in the very short time that he spent there he only gave his daughter that one opportunity to return with him. She declined saying her life was with Joseph and whatever that fate should decide for them. So fearing scandal, humiliation and disgrace the father walked away never to see or speak to his daughter again. Such was the man, that he forbade his wife and son Clarence from ever speaking her name or making any reference to her whatsoever.

It is true to say that although Jessie lived with and for her love for Joseph, the older brother Jacob loved her equally, and their lives became as intertwined as they could possibly be, with Jessie dotting on Joseph as a husband and on Jacob as devotedly as a brother.

And so life changed dramatically for Jessie and Joseph, and for Jacob. But in a way it was a good life even though it was hard with no confirmation that the future would ever see it change for the better. Such was the common bond of survival within the small, tight knit community that Joseph and Jacob belonged to, that Jessie was soon accepted as one of their own. And with each day that passed she would share the hardships and dangers of living hand to mouth with a stoical philosophy of accepting each morning as a blessing for whatever it might bring.

So for the next three years Jessie never saw, or heard or had any contact with her family in any way. There were times when she would admit that she would have wished for a different outcome, but there was never any real regret.

The brothers continued to sell their herrings and lobsters directly to the local shops and hotels, even travelling to the markets in the surrounding villages. It all added pennies to the household coffers, but it meant more and more pressure to work. And all the time having to keep looking over their shoulders for the Revenue men, for they still maintained a foothold in the illegal trades.

That was until one fateful day when Jacob had gone to Lynmouth on some errand, leaving Joseph to take the boat out alone from the quay of Stepdown Cove.

Jessie as always watched him go as he set the small sail and rounded the opening to the cove from there he was soon out of sight.

So often she had watched and always she would admit how tiny and vulnerable the little craft looked amidst the tossing waves and the swell. And then later that day, as was her custom she made her way down the rough hewn steps to the quay to await her mans return.

And she waited and she waited. Until the day began to darken into the evening, and her heart began to sink in despair, along with the dipping wintry sun. The evening turned to a cold black night and she waited with her lantern lit and held high for her man to be guided homeward. And the long night turned to daybreak and still she waited until Jacob found her shivering, barefooted and bordering on unconscious. He managed to carry her up the rough steps of Stepdown Cove and back to the cottage but she was ill with the cold and exposure and in desperation he ran the distance to the far side of Lynmouth, to the coaching inn of Jessie's family. But even though the father listened to Jacob's pleas for help in getting a doctor the door was slammed in his face.

On his return to the cottage he found Jessie's bed empty and he, along with everyone from the other cottages searched all over the surrounding area, but deep down Jacob knew where he would eventually find her.

So it was that Jessie's body was washed up on the shifting sands of Stepdown Cove a few days later, though Joseph's body or his boat were never found. A little ceremony saw Jessie's body buried in the circular stonewalled grave yard that served that small community. At its entrance was the tiny stone tower that housed the warning bell and this was rung at five second intervals during the service which was taken by the rector from the neighbouring church of St Andrew's, who had befriended the small community. A roughly shaped stone cross with her name carved on it was then placed at the head of her grave.

And so the story ended, and the storyteller fell silent to sip at his tankard of cider in thoughtful reflection.

"What happened to Jacob?" I enquired aware that I was breaking the silence.

"He never went to sea again, or followed the runners trade," Mr Coates said gazing deeply into his tankard. "The rector from Saint Andrew's over yonder took him under his wing so to speak. Jacob became the Sexton of that church without pay, but for board and lodging. The rector's wife taught him to read and write. He took to it like a convert, a more religious man you'd not have found round these parts."

Mr Coates refreshed his tankard before continuing.

"When Jacob became too frail to work, my grandfather brought him here to finish his days. He had taken to him you see, him being devout about his faith as well and also being a member of the same congregation. The box of books and a few odd things was all Jacob left and they've been gathering dust in a cupboard ever since he died in November 1859. So clearing them out they was collected for some fete or other. As for Jessie's family, well I can't comment on that," he stated with a dismissive grunt. "All this was handed down to me in great detail by my father from his father, the story being told to me on many occasions as a guidance for my own journey through life. My father when he was a boy could remember Jacob Baunsall coming to live here and this story haunted him as it has haunted me since I first heard it."

"The ballad says that Jessie Gray is seen on the quay," Thomas questioned. "Is that true?"

"Some say it is!....Some say it isn't!" Mr Coates said still with dryness in his words. "You needs to believe what you wants to believe I say...I've never seen her. Then again I've never gone looking."

For a moment the stern features seemed to relax as he seemed to muse with an inner decision before speaking again.

"The ballad you refer to was written in this house by old Jacob Baunsall in the last weeks of his life. My father remembered Jacob writing it and he also said he remembered Jacob as being old but not in years and thought that he knew he had come to the point when he wanted a release from this life. I was told of the ballads existence but I never saw it until today because we believed it had been lost. We never thought to look between the pages of that old book that was with his other few belongings and stored away. Though I'm glad it survived and that I was able to read it."

He paused looking intensely from myself and then to Thomas as if considering his words before he would speak again.

"A fact that was known to no one at the time," he continued. "But was told to my grandfather by Jacob, was that Jessie was with child when she died. She told this to him when he had carried her from Stepdown Cove. It was the last thing she had said to him. Then, as you know Jacob went for help from Jessie's father. But alas, that was not forthcoming," Mr Coates concluded.

I searched hard at the sincerity on the features of the man who had just delivered this narrative and especially the last few words.

"Mr Coates," I said after a long pause. "I want you to know how grateful I am for what you have told us today. Mr Coates thank you......thank you!"

"I'm glad it has so much meaning for you Mr Kempe," he replied looking me directly in the eye and with the suspicion of a knowing but warm smile. For a moment I wondered what had been the context of the conversation that had passed between Thomas and Mr Coates before I had joined them.

However, there now seemed nothing more to be said as a silence seemed to pervade and settle through the dark oppressive shadows of the room and so, after again offering our thanks and expressing our gratitude, we took our leave.

The atmosphere that accompanied us on the drive back was subdued and thoughtful. In fact, I cannot remember a word being spoken until we pulled up outside the vicarage, were even then it was a few moments before the Reverend spoke.

"What a story Paul!" he exclaimed slowly shaking his head. "What a story! This whole adventure reads like a Conan Doyle."

I did not answer him for my mind was still full of the myriad images that the narrative had conjured up. It was like a tale from fiction, but the truth of it was never in doubt for me. I had followed every syllable that the strange Mr Coates had delivered. And in the darkened embrace of that dowdy room it seemed like the figures of the principle players had moved, inexorably around us as if they were staging their own silent, true life dumb show.

"You won't find that place you know," Thomas said turning to me. "Stepdown Cove I mean. I take it you will be going there tomorrow?"

"That I will Thomas....Most certainly I will," I answered.

But then after a deliberate pause designed to mischievously tease my friend, I added.

"But I won't be going unless you accompany me," I said with a smile.

"Oh!...I'm so very pleased you said that," came the reply that was tinged with a flare of boyish excitement. "What time?"

And so arrangements for the next day were made and I found myself driving back to the White Horse in a very sombre, thoughtful frame of mind.

What would tomorrow bring?

****

For the first time in a number of days I awoke refreshed after a night of untroubled, dreamless sleep. It was a little after seven and the sun was flooding in from a clear blue sky as I lay back on my pillow ruminating on the previous day. The intriguing saga that had been narrated to us and the pictures that had been evoked in my mind made me wonder why I had slept so peacefully, and then I decided that it was because I could now see an end to my quest.

I washed, shaved and dressed, and as I straightened my tie in the mirror I stopped to take a long look at myself. I stared at the face staring back at me, a face that was at the wrong side of forty with hair well groomed and parted to the right with just a hint of grey at the temples. There had been lines and shadows that had begun to show beneath my eyes that now had almost disappeared. And there was the eager glint in the eyes that I thought I would never see again. Even the mouth was adopting something of the young man's cheeky grin that my Jessie had found both annoying and attractive. All in all, I felt quite pleased with myself and I put it all down to the invigorating last few days.

Being first down to breakfast at eight o clock I was able to make a few arrangements with George. Then I was on my way motoring the short distance into Lynton, which sat overlooking the harbour of Lynmouth. I managed to park easily and spent an hour or so browsing round some shops, where I bought some presents for Catherine and Steven, and a small framed picture of old Lynmouth for Jessie's parents. I also purchased a torch and batteries, two films for my Kodak, two large Thermos flasks, two enamelled mugs and a canvas rucksack.

Then I took the funicular railway down the steep cliff into Lynmouth itself. It was now that a moment of nostalgia bit at my throat and brought a quickly wiped moistness from my eye. The last time I had ridden this spectacular ride had been with my Jessie.

And even though it had been over seven years before, I imagined the feel of her body pressed up against mine in tense apprehension after glimpsing the diminishing height through the cabin window. The moment had not lasted long before we had reached the bottom and I had succumbed to her mock anger at my ridicule and sniggers. But all had been forgiven when we had found a tearoom. Today that memory had been so strong that it left me with the feeling of just how much I missed her.

Because of my adventures over the last few days I could now view Lynmouth in a completely different light. I walked the full length of the quay area quite easily imagining the bustling, fishing industry that would have filled every inch in those early years of the nineteenth century. The baskets of the freshly landed catch, the handcarts and horse drawn drays, the curling tobacco smoke from the mingling fisher folk who sometimes would form into small secretive huddles.

I was even able to find the notorious Rising Sun Tavern and was tempted to go inside for a drink, but something prevented me from doing so. I had built such a definitive picture in my mind of the dark, other world of its interior, of the corruption and dirty dealings that would have been the norm within those dimly lit, smoky rooms. It would have been a very brave Revenue man indeed who would have ventured alone, across that threshold I thought. And somehow I had no desire to disturb that picture so firmly slotted into my mind.

Leaving Lynmouth and Lynton behind, I motored in a somewhat reflective mood to the vicarage and the Reverend Thomas Millican. He was eagerly waiting for me in his long brown coat over his clerical cassock and again sporting his frayed panama hat. He also carried round his neck a pair of powerful binoculars and the ample leather satchel over his shoulder.

"Right!" he said enthusiastically as he climbed into the passenger's seat. "Off we go!"

"Not quite yet," I answered. "First stop is back to the White Horse!"

And so, the first stop was a hearty lunch and the chance to fill the two recently purchased Thermos flasks with tea, and to collect a small hamper that had been prepared by the fair hand of Aggie.

It was while we were ploughing our way through our ample stew, potatoes and vegetables that Thomas quite openly admitted that he believed every word of the story related to us on the previous day, until it got to the point that the ballad described Jessie appearing on the quay as if waiting for her beloved Joseph.

I admitted that I was not sure about that and explained the feelings I had felt on the funicular railway. How I had so easily imagined my Jessie pressed up against me. Thomas calmly explained that he thought I felt that simply because I wanted to feel it. I said that it had been so real, and he had gently dismissed the idea by saying that all 'ghost' related experiences were merely figments of active imaginations.

"I'm not going to delve into theological theories as it would not be fair of me to do so," he concluded. "But to be honest, I accompany you as a friend, and in doing so I must also admit to being a confirmed sceptic on the matter."

And so with one confirmed sceptic and one not too sure but wanting to believe, we motored towards our destination on the northern coastline, and to Stepdown Cove. I came to realise quite early on in the journey that I would never have been able to have found the place through the maze of lanes, side roads and dirt tracks, but after less than forty minutes my navigator declared.

"This is as far as we can go. From here it's on foot for about three quarters of a mile."

So arming ourselves with our resources I locked the car and we began our hike towards the distant coast line. It was a pleasant walk that gradually became more rugged and even more remote. I could not help but muse on the difficulties that the inhabitants of such an isolated spot would have encountered over a hundred years ago. They would most certainly have been of a very sturdy stock I thought, and this feeling persisted when we started to pass signs of habitations.

Not much remained now, not even the shells of any kind of dwelling, simply the overgrown mounds of their foundations. Such a strong heaviness of heart seemed to overwhelm me as my eyes settled on the varied rectangular shapes with the odd pile of stones scattered about. Looking around I managed to identify about a dozen of what I can only imagine would have been meagre, almost primitive shelters.

Seeking out my companion I could now see a mirror of my own emotions encrypted in his fair but taut features. And so we walked on

The Ballad Of Jessie Gray

with no words being exchanged between us, merely an occasional side long glance for reassurance.

Our short trek took us to a low, stone wall enclosure some twenty five yards or so square with a small gap that would have been an entrance. As we approached, Thomas pointed to a two foot square of stones that looked as if they had been the base to some small structure.

"That would have been the bottom of the tower for the warning bell," he confirmed rather pensively. "Not much of it left now but I suspect it would have stood about four or five foot high. A kind of miniature belfry built of wood and stone to house the bell."

"So this is the graveyard," I questioned.

"Yes," came the reply. "The bell would've been rung at times of emergency or danger. It would also have been rung at five second intervals at burials. But it does show what a tight community existed here."

I walked over to join my friend and as I did I noticed something in the undergrowth. Bending down I picked up what I recognised as being a cast iron hinge.

"Well they must've had a gate here as well," I said holding it up to allow it to be seen by Thomas.

For a few seconds I looked at that badly rusted relic of another time, another life and I was tempted to push it into my coat pocket as a memento, a souvenir. But something seemed to hold me back, for I felt that I did not want to take anything from this place other than memories. And so with a sigh I placed it down onto the wall.

Now moving slowly towards the opening we both stood looking at the overgrown tangle of weeds and undergrowth. Here and there an occasional crooked headstone or cross peered out as if refusing to be swallowed up completely. What we were being confronted with was such a sad, desperate impression of neglect and desolation.

It was a very strange feeling that filtered through my body as I stood absorbing the scene before me. If I was to say that I felt something had drawn me to this place I would not feel as if I was exaggerating. But to try and explain it either in the written form or actual spoken words I do not think that I would be able to.

It was then that Thomas broke into my thoughts.

"The people who lived in these small isolated groups, wanted to keep themselves to themselves, for many reasons," he remarked with a wry smile. "However, this area would've been consecrated and the local Rector might've been paid by the people to travel over to administer services."

Turning he pointed towards the distant spire of Saint Andrew's Church.

"From over there!" he said as he continued to scan the distant landmark and the surrounding countryside.

I cupped my hand over my eyes to cut out the sun's glare as I squinted in the direction that was being indicated. But once more my whole attention was diverted inexorably towards the scattered memorials of the long forgotten inhabitants of this long forgotten community.

"I need to look," I said. "I need to see for myself."

I realised my words were spoken with a slight hoarse tremor that I hoped had not been noticed by my companion. But a hand appeared on my shoulder and the slight pressure of reassurance by the fingers helped to ease my apprehensions.

"You take that side and I'll take this" Thomas suggested.

We both stepped into the graveyard and began searching for the stone cross that would hopefully identify the final resting place of Jessie Gray.

After some minutes of our quite intense foraging Thomas called me over to the furthest corner of the graveyard and pointed to a rough hewn stone cross that seemed to be supported only by the entwining vegetation. Reaching it I slowly bent down and carefully scraped the bindweed, thorns and moss from the sad epitaph.

Even though I peered hard, at first I was not quite able to make out what the badly eroded inscription was trying to tell me. Taking the flask of tea from my haversack I poured a little onto my handkerchief and scrubbed hard at the almost illegible letters. A sudden realisation brought my hand to a trembling halt as I leant back heavily onto my haunches, with my eyes refusing to believe what they were now seeing.

Thomas must have seen the difficulties I was having and leaning forward he began to read the inscription.

"It simply reads," he said. "Jessie Gray died 23 January 1832."

Pushing myself to my feet I stepped back in sheer confusion, wiping my face as a few beads of cold sweat must have appeared on my face as those words of confirmation bit hard into my reeling senses.

"What's the matter?" Thomas asked in concerned tones as he placed a soothing hand on my shoulder. "What is it?"

"It's....it's...the...date!" I said in a stammering whisper as the full implications of what I was now able to discern in the inscription fully impacted on my sense of reasoning. For it felt as if they were humming at such a pitch of intensity within my head as my whole frame seemed to quiver in an icy chill, even in the warmth of this late afternoon sunlight. I could feel Thomas standing beside me, statue like and just staring hard at the obvious changes in my countenance, almost as if he was unable to move or to help.

It took me almost a minute before I could bring myself to speak again.

"The date!" I said huskily as I attempted to control how I spoke my words. "The date she died.....is the same day, month and exactly one hundred years earlier than my dear Jessie.........My Jessie died on the 23rd January 1932."

A stone cross marks the simple grave.
But time will soon erase the name.

No more words were spoken as I stood transfixed by the inscription on the cross. Something bordering on panic formed a strangle hold around my throat, leaving me to feverishly mop my face and neck of the sweat that was running freely, even though I could still feel the frosted fingers that had embraced my whole body just moments before. All I wanted to do was to run, to vacate the place as quickly as possible, but my legs felt as if they were rooted to the spot, for I could not move them even though I could feel them shaking.

A hand rested itself onto my arm and a quiet voice asked.

"Paul, are you all right, you've gone quite pale," Thomas enquired at last in a voice that implied that even he was having trouble coming to terms with the information he was being asked to accept.

However, the softness of his voice seemed to still the murmurings of disquiet within my inner self and I took a deep, deep breath and slowly exhaled.

"Yes.......I think so," I answered breathlessly. "I'm afraid this took me completely by surprise. I never expected those dates would coincide."

Slowly, I was able to collect my jangled thoughts, even though we remained looking down at that pitiful image for perhaps another five minutes. I was tempted to take out my Kodak for a picture but refrained, for I felt the image was so well implanted in my mind that I had no need of a photograph. It also occurred to me that the action seemed somewhat disrespectful to the dead woman's memory.

Twixt the constant rolling swell,
And the chiming warning bell,
Yet cold comfort for this sweet maid.

A little reluctantly, we turned towards the opening once more.

We left that place, both visibly moved by the impressions that our graveside experience had left us with. My thoughts were totally absorbed by the frightening coincidence of the same dates of the deaths of both my Jessie and the Jessie whose earthly remains lay beneath that crooked stone cross in that bleak and barren graveyard.

However, I could now see by the tense expression on my companion's face that even he was struggling to come to terms with what we had been confronted with. And it made me wonder how it might affect the strict reserves of his conscience and beliefs.

Without looking back and in a thoughtful silence we continued up a thin pathway that led to the cliff edge and the expanse of blue sea across the estuary towards the distant, misty coast of Wales.

****

The evening was now drawing in with the western sky taking on a golden glow that deepened by the minute. It seemed to draw up the warmth that the day had offered, to leave a chill that forced both of us to pull the collars up on the heavy coats that we were now glad we had brought with us. Apart from a brief stroll back to the sad, melancholy graveyard to take one last look at the stone cross, we had sat in a solemn silence eating without really tasting, the delicacies so meticulously prepared for us by Aggie.

Although, we did allow ourselves a few minutes to stand and peer down at the shifting sand and shale beach below the steep craggy cliffs of the sheltered cove that not only had provided a haven for the small fishing boats, but protection from prying Revenue eyes. Without any effort we had been able to pick out the descending rough hewn steps that ended at the narrow cobblestone and slab ledge. From there it seemed to sweep around to the right following the curvature of the cliff and acting as a quay when the tide was high.

It was such a puzzling combination of feelings that I felt as I gazed down on the sad, forlorn setting of those tragic events of a century ago. I could almost visualise the receding tide, creaming through the sand and shale of the empty beach to leave the lifeless, young body of Jessie Gray washed up like a bundle of discarded sodden rags. It was such an easy process for two lines from the ballad to once again resonate in my mind offering me a strange affinity with the writer.

She died by her own trembling hand,
Flotsam in the surf and shifting sand.

As a consequence, such a desolate feeling seemed to flow over me, like a sultry engulfing wave of emotion. It was a feeling that I had not experienced since my dear Jessie had died, and once again it was necessary for me to wipe a decided mistiness from my eyes.

I felt a consoling hand on my shoulder.

"It's a beautiful evening Paul," Thomas confided. "And it looks like it will be a clear sky to night as well."

It was obvious that Thomas was recognising how this whole experience was affecting me, and so his words had a comforting edge to them which made it easier for me to lift myself out of the doldrums that my mind was wallowing in.

"Yes!" I agreed. "Is there any tea left in the Thermos?"

We edged away from the cliff to continue our vigil, only this time with the warming tea a sporadic conversation ensued as we watched the light seep from the sky.

The plans we had made meant that we would wait till full darkness when I would descend the steps and wait, hopefully for an appearance of Jessie Gray. We had been encouraged in our quest by the words of the ballad.

Each night come fair weather or storm,
She keeps her silent vigil alone

But now the anxious waiting was over, even so many questions and apprehensions still laced my mind as the time came for me to make my move. We had agreed that Thomas would watch from the cliff top in support. In the back of my mind I wondered if he was worried about facing his own scepticism, but I left my thoughts unspoken.

The chill had deepened, as if to accompany the full moon that was now rising out of the north eastern horizon. And as it continued to climb high above us it brought into stark, silvery detail every crag and fissure of the cliff face with the uneven steps down to the quay. Rows of white, phosphorescent crested waves could also be seen in the light of the moon as they obediently began their relentless invasion of the shifting sands, to complete their timeless mission before their dutiful retreat, whereby the whole preordained process would begin all over again.

I looked at my watch in the torchlight, it showed me eleven twenty and I decided to make my move. Thomas had already taken up his chosen vantage point to watch, and so I began my descent.

With my Kodak round my neck, my torch and the moonlight were sufficient for me to descend the rough cut steps with confidence, although I kept my right shoulder hard against the solidness of the cliff face for support. Each step had a drop of about eighteen inches, and this did give me a few moments of concern regarding the stability of my right leg.

But I reached the bottom without incident and found I was standing on the four foot wide cobblestone quay and looking along its length I saw that it seemed to widen towards the far end. I leant my head back and peered up the eighty or so feet to the top of the cliff and could just make out the dark silhouette of my friend against the paler night sky.

And so, I began my vigil while making myself as comfortable and as inconspicuous as possible.

When it is necessary to remain silent and absolutely without movement a sense of the passage of time becomes distorted. You tend to sink into a frame of mind whereby you are totally focused and only aware of your own breathing.

Even so, after what seemed like an age the intensity of watching and the immobile position that I had adopted soon started to have an effect on my body as well as my judgment. So in easing my cramped limbs I also found that I had to readjust the focus of my observation along the quay. This came as something of relief for the effort of concentrated staring in the subdued moonlight was a strain on my eyes and I found it necessary to continually wipe the seeping wetness away with my handkerchief.

Now the chill had also begun to permeate through my clothing and into my bones and I became very mindful of my right leg and the stiffness and ache in it made it imperative for me to fidget and to move. Even so it became more and more difficult to do this until instead of crouching in the shadow of the cliff I found it much more acceptable to stand and to move my legs one at a time.

I slowly brought my left hand up for the luminous face of my watch to show me a quarter to two. And as I did I began to realise that I could not remain pressed up against the rock face for much longer as the discomfort I was feeling was now becoming an urgent factor. For a moment I forgot the discipline of my vigil and moved for the umpteenth time to ease the stiffness in my joints as my mind began to stray to the remnants of the warm tea still in the Thermos and the comfort and warmth offered by the bed in the White Horse. I was also beginning to think that my expectations of hopefully seeing something were somehow greater than what reality was going to allow me.

But then my eyes caught a glimpse of what can only be described as a feint, yellowish pin-prick of light at the far end of the quay. The strangeness of the moment made me frivolously compare it to that of glow worm. However, I continued to watch thinking that it must be some natural, nocturnal phenomenon. But it seemed to be moving with a slight swaying motion. Was it getting closer, I could not be sure, but each time I thought it to be closer it did seem to grow a little in brightness.

Then all at once it was closer, and then if I blinked my eyes from my staring, it seemed to be further away. Yet it did appear to maintain a kind of resolute approach towards me and I became more and more transfixed by what I was seeing and all discomfort and anxiety were forgotten. I felt nothing, either pain or fear, and as it got nearer to me a kind of frozen acceptance took over. I fumbled for the torch in my pocket, but then watched it spin from my fingers, first to the ledge of the quay and then into the sea. I lifted my camera to take a picture, but my trembling fingers could not hold it to point and I let it drop against my body.

The glowing light seemed to flicker and was now no more than four or five feet from me and as my eyes struggled to focus it took the shape of a slightly swaying lantern. The light seemed to brighten and expand to illuminate the form of a person in the yellowish glow. It was a figure clearly visible in a long ragged dress of sorts, where the toes of one foot peeked from beneath on the hard surface of cobblestones. Round the shoulders and the head was a heavy woollen shawl.

Pounding sharply in my head I could hear the words of the ballad so clearly being recited.

> *Tight wrapped in widows shawl,*
> *Tattered skirts to the floor,*
> *Bare feet on the cold cobblestone.*

The glow from the lantern brought the face of the apparition into stark prominence. It was a young woman's face that could easily be considered as being beautiful, but equally so very, very sad. The eyes seemed bright and inquisitive, and sparkled with a glimmer of anticipation as the light was lifted higher as if to examine the figure that stood before it. Then the expression seemed to waver in the glowing lanterns light and adopted a look of disappointment at what those eyes were seeing. A disappointment my befuddled mind was assuming was because I was not her beloved Joseph.

And as I continued to watch the features of the face began to change, and for a number of very precious seconds I stared, totally dumbfounded at the smiling face of my dear Jessie. So familiar was the smile, and the eyes that always seemed to increase its warmth, that it held my attention in a fascinated gaze. Now I looked on that face, as I had done on so many occasions since I first saw it, with every fibre of love that I could muster and more.

Without taking a step forward I held out my hand as a hand appeared to stretch forward from within the folds of the figures heavy shawl. My heart began to beat a vibrating tattoo, the beating being so hard that I felt it might burst through my rib cage as our hands stretched out to each other. But our fingers did not touch, they merely seemed to mingle and intertwine in the ethereal glow from the lamp that now appeared to engulf both myself and the apparition before me. Even though our fingers did not touch it was as if I could feel the gentle, sensitivity of my dear Jessie's hand in mine. The gentle, sensitivity that was so clearly ingrained in my memory.

Then suddenly a husky voice broke the moment.

"Jessie!!!!" it called.

It seemed to be all around me at once, and even if I could have moved my head from the mesmerised position it was locked in, I doubt I would have been able to discern from exactly where it had originated from. Instantly the features of my Jessie had gone and had reverted to the young woman's face from before. But this time the sadness had vanished and only a look of total surprise and sheer joy filled the eyes and the expression as the head turned slowly seeking out the voice.

I stared past the light of the lantern towards the end of the quay and there in the silvery light of the moon I could just make out a dark, shadowy figure. Peering hard I could just see the vague shape of a youngish man clad in a ragged coat, trousers and knee length boots, who just seemed to be standing and waiting. Below him I could clearly make out the lines of a small boat with a mast and furled sail, gently bobbing to the tidal swell.

The figure in front of me turned slowly away and towards the dark form at the end of the quay. With the lantern held high it seemed to drift effortlessly over the cobblestones and along the narrow quay. I watched completely unable to move as the two figures melted into a tender embrace, and in one single floating movement they slipped down into the boat. Then as if by some phantom hand the sail was unfurled and the boat with its two passengers slipped away from the quay. It appeared to glide, slowly and sedately out over the shimmering moonlit sea towards the opening to the cove.

A hazy vapour materialized and began to rise around the little vessel. Gradually it thickened into a kind of mystical mist as if the whole silvery surface was evaporating before my eyes. I continued to watch totally enthralled by what I was seeing as the mist condensed into a vast drifting cloud that swirled and billowed as the tiny craft moved steadily towards it, eventually to become totally engulfed by it until finally, it was gone from view. I strained my eyes into the swirling gloom and for a few cherished moments I could just discern the diminishing soft yellow glimmer of the lantern, until even that was no more.

Slowly, purposefully I walked towards the end of the quay, my stiffness and aches beginning to show signs that I should be reminded of their existence. My thoughts were in turmoil and I could feel my spirits draining away as an overwhelming surge of despondency seemed to grip my senses. I was fighting hard to understand the events of the last few minutes, trying to comprehend against all my logical reasoning what I had actually witnessed. And as I gazed out beyond the entrance of the cove the mist seemed to clear leaving the sea, once again just an empty expanse of water as it stretched northwards to the dark, distant coastline of Wales.

Stretching my neck I continued my study towards the night sky but there were no stars to be seen, for the rising mist had left a thin veil to obscure the heavenly bodies. Even the starkness of the moons features had become hazy and now wore a halo of golden light around its milky dial.

Strangely, this only seemed to add a deepening to the darkness around me and a quenching of my previously exalted spirits, thus leaving me with a growing feeling of anticlimax.

I inhaled a deep gulp of the night's crisp air and slowly wiped my hands across my eyes and face. Nothing seemed to make any sense in the churning confusion in my mind, with all the contradictory ingredients of information that it was being asked to ingest and decipher.

Suddenly, I sensed a presence behind me and turning I gazed into the astonished face of the Reverend Thomas Millican.

"Tell me," he said with a shiver in his voice. "Please.....Please.....Tell me that I did not see what I saw!!!" he exclaimed trying desperately to control his stuttering words.

"I can't do that my friend," I said collecting all my thoughts and emotions into one acceptable bundle. "I can't........because I saw it as well."

We both stood side by side, speechless in our astonishment and gazed into the darkness that was even now thickening by the minute as the misty moon dropped stealthily behind the cliff top above us. How long we stood there I cannot say, minutes it could have been an hour for all we knew. For both of us were in shock and disbelieving our own eyes. We remained in silent contemplation, desperately trying to come to terms with what we had witnessed and the enormous significance on our diverse, yet ardent held convictions.

However, it was now becoming clear to me that this was an event that had been waiting to happen. Almost you might say, a moment that fate had dictated. To me this was a time of both release and reunion for the trapped soul of Jessie Gray. And destiny had directed me to this spot, and in so doing I truly believe that my dear Jessie had been able to fulfil her own journey onwards, in good company with Joseph and his Jessie. And if for no other reason these thoughts gave me tremendous comfort.

It was with an increasing sense of ease and peace of mind, as these notions began to materialise within my troubled thoughts. Like the merest glimpses of reasoning through an all encompassing fog was how I was beginning to view it. I was still very bewildered at what truth really lay behind all that had happened, here on this remote cobblestone quay on the edge of Exmoor.

I looked towards the heavens and I gratefully marvelled at the abundance of stars that had now appeared in the clear, moonless, black velvet sky.

Turning I looked at my companion, and without a word being spoken we edged our way back along the quay to the steps. Then with stiffened joints and a keen awareness of the encroaching, biting cold and darkness we carefully followed the light from Thomas' torch up the rough hewn steps. From there down the narrow path where we passed the eerily silent graveyard and the remains of the dwellings and then finally onto the welcome comfort of my car.

> *So I tarry awhile to pray,*
> *For the wretched Jessie Gray,*
> *Will her restless soul ever be free.*

And for a few moments before starting back and with these lines and all the pervading images and contradictions still so sharply clear in my mind, I allowed a secret smile to formulate on my lips as I came to at least one firm conclusion.

"Yes," I thought to myself "Her soul is now free!"

It was close to five and the sky was beginning to brighten with the coming dawn before we found ourselves sitting opposite each other in the vicarage study. We each had a thick cheese sandwich and a mug of cocoa, and even after our night's adventure we were still wide awake. For something like the twentieth time Thomas let his head roll back onto the armchair and spoke in a voice full of exasperation.

"Please!......Paul my friend...Please tell me I did not see what I saw!"

I was beginning to question my own memory as well. Did I actually witness a ghostly visitation of such real and stunning clarity. Did I see my darling wife appear to me so vividly that I could almost stretch out and touch her face. Yes I did see it. We both saw it all. The animated conversation as we motored back was so accurate in every detail that it only confirmed to both of us, that what we had seen, what had been played out before our eyes, had actually happened, had actually taken place. In truth there really was no doubt whatsoever.

When Thomas had first seen the light approaching me along the quay he had made his way quickly down the stone steps in case I needed help. For at that moment he did not or could not understand what it was. His first thought was that I might be in some kind of danger.

However, he had managed to reach me just in time to witness the whole of the forming of the apparition, even to the changing of the facial features and the almost touching of hands. He also confirmed before I could mention it, that he had heard the voice calling "Jessie" and the figure of the man, the boat and the reunion, and also the boat sailing away into the mist. It was all too clear in every detail for it not to have happened. And when I told him that I truly believed I had seen my very own Jessie in the changing features of the apparitions face, albeit for only for a few treasured moments, all Thomas was able to say was.

"Please tell me I did not see what I saw!"

Even so, that cherished but momentary image will be my strength for the rest of my days.

We went over every aspect of our nights work in every searching detail, as the conversation flowed along with the consumption of more mugs of cocoa and cheese sandwiches to aid the revitalisation of our inner strength.

I explained that I was very disturbed at the coincidence surrounding the date on the gravestone and the date my dear Jessie had died. Thomas had remarked that if there was any doubt to over shadow our testimonies of the nights events, then the mere factual truth of those dates could never be denied.

Finally, the subject of the ballad crept into the discussion. I remarked at the fact of how much emotion seemed to lie within the tortured lines and how they had affected me.

"It strikes me," Thomas said leaning back in ruminative mood. "That now we know a little more about the history of the Baunsall boys and especially Jacob, that those verses could not be the result of spontaneous writing. I think he wanted each word or phrase to say exactly what he was feeling when he thought of them."

Thomas leant back in his chair and sipped thoughtfully at his mug of cocoa before continuing.

"So remembering what Mister Coates said, that until Jacob was adopted into the household of the good Rector of Saint Andrews he was totally illiterate and it was the good Rectors wife who taught him to read and write in part payment for his services as Sexton. I believe it would likely have been she who helped to correct any spelling and meaning until the sad Jacob was ready to commit the whole to paper. That's when he was taken in by Mr Coates' grandfather in the last days of his life. He must've stored all that he wanted to say and how it should be said, for that one last effort before he finally passed away."

"Yes," I said pondering over my friends thought provoking reasoning. "Which only adds such a mournful touch to this already so sorrowful story," I continued. "But I believe you could be right, although I have to admit the same thoughts had occurred to me."

However, it was with a measure of remorse when we realised that the clock on the mantle was indicating a quarter past seven. I needed to get back to the White Horse and Thomas had to prepare himself for his Sunday duties. So promising to see him before I left for home and my family, I shook his hand, the hand of a friend, a friend who I had shared such an enlightening experience with and someone in the few days that I had known him had become someone I had grown very fond of.

****

Reaching the White Horse just after eight I sat down to breakfast trying to ignore the quizzical looks from my hosts. It was obvious that they were aware I had not slept in my room, and equally I was not at all forthcoming with any reasons as to why either. I found myself smiling into my cup of tea at the thought of what they would say, let alone think if I was to tell them of all that had happened. Even though I had agreed with Thomas, that to avoid being called liars or thought of as being mad, it would be prudent to keep our own council and not to divulge anything to anyone.

After washing, shaving and packing my cases, I settled by bill and with genuine thanks to George and Aggie I motored over to St Michaels Church just in time for the eleven o clock service. Sitting in a rear pew I was able, with twenty or so other souls to witness my new friend at his work.

Normally, I would say that I am a Christmas and Easter churchgoer, albeit having been brought up with a certain amount of the fire and brimson delivered from the Methodist pulpit. To an extent this had hardened me against being a regular on a Sunday.

However, watching the Reverend Millican I was able to admire his strength of character and conviction. Also to respect the fact that during the whole of our short acquaintance not once had he tried to pressurise me with the dogma that is associated with his vocation. I watched him as he gave full vocal thrust while competing with the over exuberant organist and then with his eyes closed with passion through the prayer readings. But it was the ironical humour of his sermon that brought a smile to my face and I believe to his, although he managed to triumph over the impulse and disguise it.

He began by saying.

"I take for my text today from the gospel according to Saint John chapter 20 verses 24 to 31. It is the story of Thomas, doubting Thomas and a story that will be familiar to all of you. So I will only remind you by reading the relevant verse for my address to you today."

And he began to read.

> *"Verse 29. Jesus saith unto him,*
> *Thomas, because thou*
> *hast seen me, thou hast*
> *believed: blessed are*
> *they that have not seen,*
> *and yet have believed."*

And so, for the next twenty minutes or so I listened entranced, not only with his words but in the sincerity of their delivery. Without a single mention to our night's experiences he was able to use himself as a glowing example of a doubting Thomas. Saying that even in his chosen calling there were times when he had misgivings, as any truly honest person should admit to. He compared it to those who had gone "over the top" in the gory battles of the first word war. Only the foolish or the mad would say they were not afraid, and if they were to be honest they would admit to have sought some comfort in a silent prayer, even if they had never entered a church in their lives. In those moments did they believe, he suspected that they did, for with the fear of imminent death many have sought to seek the face of their saviour.

And he placed a question to the gathering in front of him, to search their memories and be truthful to themselves when they had doubted a truth only to be brought to task afterwards. So it had been with Thomas the disciple. He had witnessed Jesus being crucified. He had seen his body prepared in the sepulchre. He had seen the stone placed in front of it. All this Thomas had witnessed with all the others, and yet he had doubted all that Jesus had said and prophesied and also the confirmations of the other disciples. Thomas the disciple had needed proof, visible proof.

Finally, the Reverend had asked his congregation to search their souls and ask themselves the question.

"What is the real reason that you attend church every Sunday?"

He finished with a pointed finger at each of those who had sat so enthralled, by saying.

"Is it fear of the unknown, of going 'over the top', or is it true belief?"

It was a very sombre procession that filed out of the church and that included myself. Each one shook the hand of their vicar and thanked him, for I truly believe that he had managed to reach each one of them and their inner consciences. And I can also add myself to that number.

For an hour or so after the church had cleared, we sat on the stone seat inside the lych gate talking and musing over our experiences. Every detail coincided it seemed and was so profoundly set in our minds as to alleviate any possibility of doubt that what we saw did actually happen. For there was still an air of wonderment at our night's experiences, which left us in full agreement that we had both been severely moved and affected by those nocturnal sights and impressions.

It was in a brief moment of silent reflection that I posed a question to my friend that had been intriguing me.

"And what about your scepticism?" I said with a wry grin and a slight twinkle in my eye.

"Ah!" he replied as a broad, slightly embarrassed smile spread across his face at being caught out by my query. He shifted uncomfortably on his seat as he continued.

"Paul my good friend," he said rather sheepishly. "I fear that must remain a matter for my own conscience."

Just for a few more minutes we sat in an atmosphere of firm, amiable companionship before I very reluctantly announced that I felt it was time for me to take my leave. And so it was with a strong, resolute handshake and a true sense of sadness, though with promises that our friendship would not end here I clambered into my car.

However, as I sat with the engine running Thomas leant forward through the open window and pressed a sealed envelope into my hand. Then as he stepped back with a wave, I regretfully I drove away.

I did not open that envelope until I reached home and was sitting alone in my small study. The envelope contained the scrap of paper onto which in 1859, the aging Jacob Baunsall had written The Ballad Of Jessie Gray.

****

EPILOGUE
(added to my original manuscript on Wednesday 19th September 1962)

Today has to be one of the saddest days of my life. Today I received a telegram from Mrs Eileen Dickson the housekeeper of the Reverend Thomas Milican, who was also the daughter of the late Mrs Gibbs, the Reverends previous housekeeper to say that the vicar had passed quietly away the day before after suffering a heart attack over the previous weekend. She would inform me of the funeral arrangements.

If my writing looks disjointed, perhaps the reader will understand why.

In Thomas I had found the kind of friend that only happens once in a life time as this little epitaph I hope will confirm. Over the years we shared a number of little adventures that now, with his sad passing, I will commit to paper not only for any reader to find in the future, but also to remind myself of some truly wonderful times.

My real sadness comes from not being by his side at the end, as I know he would have been at mine if the circumstances had been reversed, and also the fact that I had not been made aware that my friend was even ill. The fact that I am now succumbing to the consequences of the wounds I had suffered in 1918, in what seems like a previous existence, would not have stopped me had I known.

But I will be at the funeral of the man who has taught me so much about myself through his own example. And that there is a meaning to everything even after losing such a major part of a person's life, as I had experienced when my dear Jessie had passed away in 1932. Thirty years seems such a long time ago now.

Also to the man who wanted to share his faith with those in conflict by giving up his cosy position in 1940 to become chaplain to a Somerset Regiment until 1946. Fortunately, he was thought enough of to be able to return to his beloved Saint Michaels. On a number of occasions he related to me many of the horrors that he had seen and was involved with and which I know had deeply affected him. Though this only strengthened my abiding respect for a truly honest and sincere man.

And so to you my friend, who I am already missing as I say goodbye with a toast from a glass of the cider you sent me for my birthday.

God Bless you Thomas, as I am sure he will.

As for the poem 'The Ballad Of Jessie Gray,' I still have it safe.

****

FOOTNOTE.

This is by way of a few final lines to follow on from my previous introduction.

The wooden chest left by my father also contained a collection of stories written by my grandfather and which may, sometime in the future see the light of day for the enjoyment of a wider reading public.

One last item was the envelope that contained the 'Ballad' that was given to my grandfather by the good Reverend Thomas Millican. The flimsy scrap of paper containing those sad but evocative verses has now, I am pleased to say, been preserved and framed and hangs with a pride of place in my small study.

This is the original scrap of paper that the Ballad Of Jessie Gray was written on and which has been attributed to Jacob Baunsall 1859.

My real sadness comes from not being by his side at the end, as I know he would have been at mine if the circumstances had been reversed, and also the fact that I had not been made aware that my friend was even ill. The fact that I am now succumbing to the consequences of the wounds I had suffered in 1918, in what seems like a previous existence, would not have stopped me had I known.

But I will be at the funeral of the man who has taught me so much about myself through his own example. And that there is a meaning to everything even after losing such a major part of a person's life, as I had experienced when my dear Jessie had passed away in 1932. Thirty years seems such a long time ago now.

Also to the man who wanted to share his faith with those in conflict by giving up his cosy position in 1940 to become chaplain to a Somerset Regiment until 1946. Fortunately, he was thought enough of to be able to return to his beloved Saint Michaels. On a number of occasions he related to me many of the horrors that he had seen and was involved with and which I know had deeply affected him. Though this only strengthened my abiding respect for a truly honest and sincere man.

And so to you my friend, who I am already missing as I say goodbye with a toast from a glass of the cider you sent me for my birthday.

God Bless you Thomas, as I am sure he will.

As for the poem 'The Ballad Of Jessie Gray,' I still have it safe.

****

FOOTNOTE.

This is by way of a few final lines to follow on from my previous introduction.

The wooden chest left by my father also contained a collection of stories written by my grandfather and which may, sometime in the future see the light of day for the enjoyment of a wider reading public.

One last item was the envelope that contained the 'Ballad' that was given to my grandfather by the good Reverend Thomas Millican. The flimsy scrap of paper containing those sad but evocative verses has now, I am pleased to say, been preserved and framed and hangs with a pride of place in my small study.

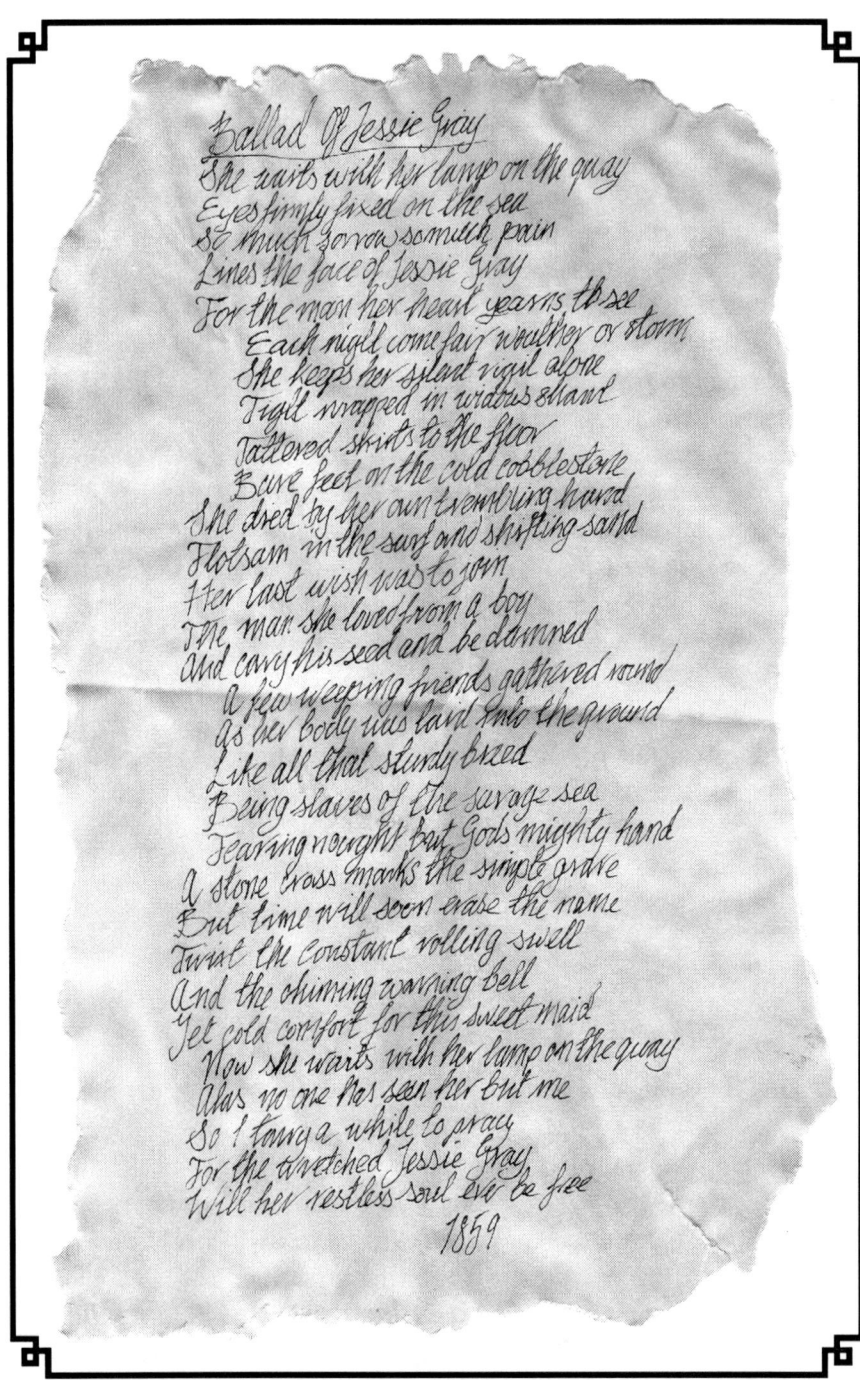

This is the original scrap of paper that the Ballad Of Jessie Gray was written on and which has been attributed to Jacob Baunsall 1859.

By the author

Beneath The Fickle Moon
Xlibris
www.xlibrispublishing.co.uk

By the author as a songwriter.

Scenery (Paper Bubble) - vinyl album, CD (Retro 831), and itunes and Amazon download.

Coming Home - vinyl album, CD (DPL0116), and itunes and Amazon download.

Some Things Seem So Right - vinyl album, CD (DPL0154), and itunes and Amazon download.

Nothing Comes Easy - vinyl album, CD (AS7/445), and itunes and Amazon download.

Old Town - CD (CD1011SBS), and itunes and Amazon download.

Brian has six other albums currently in the process of re-release.
For more information please visit www.stillbreezemusic.co.uk and www.cherryred.co.uk.
Also www.briancranesongs.com or Brian Crane Homesite.

****

I have always admired Brian as a talented singer songwriter, and have been proud to be associated with him over the years through his recordings, his albums, his CDs and more recently his download releases.

When Brian's first book "Beneath The Fickle Moon" was published in 2014 I came to appreciate even more the extent of his talents. And again and again I find myself picking up my copy of his book and indulging in a few hours with the characters Brian has created with his writing.

But now with his second book "The Ballad Of Jessie Gray," I have not only an increased respect for his talents but I also feel very humbled by his gift for such inspired and incisive writing. The seven stories that make up this collection literally draw the reader in to such an extent that you feel you are an active participant in the action, something that very few authors are able to achieve.

I feel certain that anyone reading the stories in this volume, cannot fail to come to appreciate the very real gift that Brian has.

And I am already looking forward with great anticipation to the follow up to his first book 'Still Beneath The Fickle Moon' and his second collection of short stories.

Marianne Forbes.
Stillbreezemusic.
January 2017

Lightning Source UK Ltd.
Milton Keynes UK
UKOW01f2319150217
294529UK00001B/86/P

9 781524 597375